BOLEYN TIME

DEBORAH COHEN

BOLEYN TIME

DEBORAH COHEN

CITY OWL
PRESS

BOLEYN TIME
The Boleyn Bloodline, Book 2

CITY OWL PRESS
www.cityowlpress.com

Cover Design by MiblArt. All stock photos licensed appropriately.

Edited by Yelena Casale.

For information on subsidiary rights, please contact the publisher at info@cityowlpress.com.

Print Edition ISBN: 978-1-64898-302-3

Digital Edition ISBN: 978-1-64898-303-0

Printed in the United States of America

For Michael

AUTHOR'S NOTE

When I began writing the Boleyn Bloodline series, I was fascinated by the legends surrounding the infamous English queen, Anne Boleyn. A profound historical figure in her own right, Anne Boleyn has captured the hearts and minds of people around the world, and many truths and mistruths still circulate about her today. Anne Boleyn was the second wife of King Henry VIII, put to death on May 19, 1536, on charges of treason against the king, adultery, incest, and some say, even witchcraft. My goal was to write a book series that blended the facts of Anne Boleyn's young life in France with the alluring fiction that still surrounds this captivating woman.

Anne Boleyn lived her teenage years at the French court between 1514 and 1521, during the same period the celebrated Leonardo da Vinci was also in residence. It was this concrete fact that became the premise for my second book, *Boleyn Time*. In my story, Anne Boleyn is Leonardo da Vinci's loyal apprentice who serves her master at the Château du Clos Lucé. In actual fact, Leonardo's true apprentice was named Gian Giacomo Caprotti da Oreno—better known as Salaì. It should be noted there is no formal historical record verifying that Anne Boleyn knew Leonardo da Vinci, but in her service as translator to Queen Claude, who lived in the same small city of Amboise, in my opinion it would have been almost impossible for Leonardo and Anne not to have at least been acquainted.

Da Vinci, the Italian painter, engineer, and architect, was the "Light of the Renaissance" and a fascinating subject in his own right. He is most famous for paintings such as the *Mona Lisa*, the *Last Supper*, and the *Lady with an Ermine*. But Leonardo da Vinci also produced the *Vitruvian Man* drawing as well as hundreds of notebooks with designs for modern-day inventions such as the bicycle, an armored military tank, scuba-diving gear, a helicopter, several flying machines, as well as a mechanical robotic lion. These items are scattered throughout the scenes in my novel, paying homage to his genius. Many of these inventions are on display in the gardens of the Château du Clos Lucé today.

In 1515, King Francis invited Leonardo to France to serve as the king's first painter, engineer, and architect. Da Vinci, who would have been in his sixties, traveled to central France on a mule, carrying with him sketchbooks and unfinished artwork, including the *Mona Lisa*. Leonardo lived out his final days at the Château du Clos Lucé in Amboise, serving as the king's favorite advisor until his death on May 2, 1519.

Francis and Leonardo's deep friendship is well documented. So much so, that King Francis installed a secret tunnel between the Château du Clos Lucé and the Château d'Amboise so the two men could meet in secret—away from the prying eyes of the court. What they discussed during these meetings, however, will forever remain a mystery.

Before his death, Leonardo designed the double helix staircase at the Château de Chambord, one of the most beautiful and well-visited castles in all of Europe. Having visited it myself, I can attest to the fact that da Vinci's staircase is still as breathtaking today as it was five hundred years ago. The primary architect of the Château de Chambord was Domenico da Cortona. He designed the building and surrounding grounds initially as a hunting lodge for King Francis. Domenico da Cortona, who is the villain in this story, most certainly was not responsible for the evildoings I attributed to him in *Boleyn Time*.

I would also like to mention some of the historical accuracies related to witchcraft trials in this novel. In the early 1500s, Europe saw an increase in witchcraft trials, a horror that reached its terrible climax the following century. The Hammer of Witches was the go-to guide for court inquisitors, and it provided guidance on the forms of torture that would be effective in obtaining confessions. It is this book, the *Maleus Malifecarum*, that graces the edges of Anne's storyline throughout the Boleyn Bloodline series.

Medieval torture methods of the 16th and 17th centuries were barbaric and included heinous devices such as thumb screws, the Judas Chair, the choke pear, and the Strappado—otherwise known as the rack.

The rack, the torture device that takes prominence in this novel, was a device so horrific it almost always drew a confession from the accused. People who survived it were usually paralyzed for life.

In 16th-century France, unlike other countries in Europe, no national Witchcraft Act had been enacted. As a result, people accused of this crime (almost entirely all women) fell under the jurisdiction of local courts and the witch hunt differed between regions. The witch trials of northern France fell under the jurisdiction of the Parlement de Paris, largely guided by the recommendations of the *Maleus Malificarum*. It was this parliamentary system that assessed and determined justice in my novel.

I wanted to provide an accurate depiction of the French court system of the time, so that the events that played out around Anne could have unfolded the way they did in my story. According to the judicial court structure in 16th-century France, the king and his personal judicial court, the Grand Conseil, was the highest in the land. Witchcraft and heresy trials, crimes that fell under the Cas Enorme, usually proceeded without the king's interference. However, on occasion, and when it suited the king's personal interests, he could enact the Lit de Justice (the Chair of Justice). This act permitted the king to intercede in court decisions by entering the judicial process while in session.

King Francis I, at the bequest of his sister, Marguerite de Navarre, enacted the Lit de Justice at least once during his reign, at the trial of Louis Berquin, an academic accused of heresy. In this trial, King Francis intervened by invoking the Grand Conseil, and the accused was set free three days later. It is this historical fact that became the underpinning for the climax of my novel.

VOLUME I

"And so in this twilight and evening of the world, when sin is flourishing on every side and in every place, when charity is growing cold, the evil of witches and their iniquities superabound."

— Montague Summers, The Malleus Maleficarum of Heinrich Kramer and James Sprenger

JANUARY 1519
CHÂTEAU DU CLOS LUCÉ, FRANCE

The tiny gear trembled in the old man's fingers, unwilling to comply. His other hand lay lifeless on the table beside him. It had grown so wasted over the last few months, it was no longer much good for anything.

It pained Anne to watch Leonardo when he worked now. He had become so frustrated, so angry, she almost didn't recognize the man he once was. His patience stretched like a thread pulled too tight. His moods swung between thunder and lightning. Most days, he was a tyrant to be near. But she stayed by his side, no matter how unpleasant he became. No matter the outraged hysterics, the sulking silence, the general malaise. It wasn't his fault. It was his sickness.

"Why don't you let me try?" she asked.

He swiped her away with his bad hand, a sure sign he would have none of her coddling today. The gold wheel fell to the table and rolled into Leonardo's lap.

"For all that is holy!" he seethed.

Anne crossed her arms, unwilling to be cowed by his fury.

Teeth gritted, he picked up the gear and tried again, the piece rattling between his thumb and index finger.

She sighed. The length of his nails was a problem too, but Anne was not permitted to trim those either. He had refused any care, except for allowing her to occasionally clear away his dishes and to study the books he ordered her to read. It had been that way for months, and a mess of papers and notebooks littered the floor among dirty nightshirts, spilled inkpots, and half-eaten loaves of bread.

Leo's tongue curled around the dimple in his upper lip as he extended the cog into the clock's central mechanism, more determined than ever. The golden piece glinted with cheeky disdain in the candlelight before falling to the table again.

He pounded the desk and howled.

A goblet of half-finished ale toppled beside him, and Anne had to catch it before it spilled on the blueprints.

"Leonardo," she snapped. "I'm getting tired of this. You must let me help."

She set an angry gaze upon his and found an equally stubborn one staring back. The exchange sparked between them, igniting into flame. They stayed in that impossible standoff for a time, her brown eyes boring into his blue ones.

But Anne's temper fizzled as quickly as it flared. This was not her Leonardo. Not the man she knew.

His frustration was understandable, of course. When Leo first collapsed in January, Anne had worried he would die. He could barely move. The left side of his face sagged. Even his words were jumbled. It had been months of work, lifting his arms to strengthen them, helping him shuffle across the floor on legs that no longer seemed his own. In time, he had regained most of his functioning. His speech and his sharp mind had returned too. But his left arm still hung like a piece of meat, and the right one retained a slight tremor. He was getting better, but the illness had left behind a residue, and it followed him like a shadow.

Anne's resolve was melting, as it had done so many times before, but she held her ground. If she looked away, she would lose her advantage and he would go back to trying to install that impossible gear.

"I don't want your help."

"You *need* it," she said evenly. "You are an old man. Not a two-year-old. Enough with the tantrums."

His eyes grew round at the insult, and she braced herself for his ire.

For a moment, she thought he might order her from his chamber. Perhaps he would tell her to go away forever.

Instead, the corners of his eyes creased, and his lips parted into a resentful smile. He chuffed out a breath.

"Sometimes I wish I *was* a two-year-old," he said dryly. "At least I would have use of my hands again."

That was it, a glimmer of the man she remembered. The man she loved as an ally, a mentor, a friend. She couldn't waste the moment. Anne had stumbled onto something with this last exchange. For months she had tried to be helpful, to be caring. But she now realized her mistake. Leonardo didn't want sympathy. He wanted a partner, not a nursemaid.

"If you were a two-year-old, you would still be wetting your tunic," she chided. "Or do you wish to be swaddled in a diaper cloth? Because I can have that arranged."

Da Vinci snorted. At first it sounded like a hiccup, but soon a gushing laughter bubbled from his chest, full and low and hacking. It was the sound of old times, when Leonardo laughed like this every day. When they all did. When Marguerite was still free to write her stories, and Claude and Anne were two girls running through the poppy fields. A time when things had been simple. Before Francis had taken the throne and everything had changed.

Leo's laughter didn't last long, but when it ended, their argument was done. A silent exchange for their collective loss. Life was different now. They only had each other, and they both knew it.

"I'm sorry," Leonardo said softly. "I have been an odious lubberwort these last few months."

She snatched the gear from his palm.

"That you have," she said, raising an eyebrow. "And a horse's arse."

His nostrils flared at the jab, but he didn't retort.

"Let me help, Leo. Please. Or I shall go mad watching you."

Anne let the request swing between them, long and creaking, like a hangman's noose. He would probably refuse, like he had all the other times. It had felt like forever since she had studied the blueprints, fetching fresh ink for her master, preparing calculations and measurements, or sketching out design ideas under Leo's direction. But she had never been allowed to touch it. The role of clockmaker was Leonardo da Vinci's job, and his alone.

The old man's mouth formed a thin line, moustache twitching, his eyes still fixed on the little wheel in her palm. But something in his gaze was softer. It came across as a flicker, a dampening, so subtle it was almost undetectable.

Anne dared not to look too enthusiastic.

When he finally spoke, Leo's words came out in a low growl. "You are more stubborn than a mule, Mistress Boleyn."

"I learned from the best, Master da Vinci," she growled back.

Leonardo's slippers poked from beneath his nightdress, and with a little grunt, he braced himself for his weight. Pushing against the desk, he eased himself from the chair, his ancient body teetering.

"Take my seat," he said with a mild edge. "You will need to be steady if you are to act as clockmaker. You must guide the center gear into the mechanism. The rivets connect with the lattice hammer."

She sank into the chair, nodding at his acquiescence like it was the only logical conclusion. But her whole body was tingling. She couldn't believe it had worked. Leo was going to let her touch his precious clock.

He breathed over her shoulder as she leaned forward, eyes focused. She pinched the gear tight, lowering it into the complex layers of silver and gold.

"Easy now," he advised. "Don't drop it."

Anne took a breath, thankful that her hands did not shake. Hers was a steadfast dexterity, something that came with the sixth finger on her right hand. Besides, Anne reminded herself, after all these months, she was sure of its placement.

"Not quite there, over to the left a little," he commanded.

Slowly, Anne looked up at her mentor. "Leonardo, I know where it goes."

Da Vinci's face fell, but he closed his mouth.

Anne returned to her work, biting back a smile. Now that her master wasn't barking orders over her shoulder, she could concentrate. She knew she had to be careful. This particular gear had been difficult to produce. It had multiple tracts and rivets that spun left and right. Leonardo had sent complex drawings to the royal goldsmith and for months had always returned the piece for revision because of some insignificant flaw or another. When this version had arrived, he had seemed pleased, until his trembling fingers refused to comply with its delicate placement.

Her confidence grew as she worked, holding the piece as constant as a ship on calm seas. "Why is it so important we have the clock finished?" she asked in a faraway voice.

"Concentrate, Anne."

"I am," she insisted.

Leonardo squinted through his wireframe glasses, his voice hitching with enthusiasm. "You've almost got it. The teeth of the top rotating spindle must catch with the lattice hammer. Pull it back slightly and then turn the central cog."

Anne eased the hammer back, using her fingernail to nudge the gear train. And just like that, the mechanism snapped into place with a tight click.

The old man blinked with surprise.

She couldn't help flashing him a grin. After weeks of Leonardo's work, Anne had completed the task in a matter of minutes.

"I told you to let me help you," she said, allowing just a hint of smugness to come through.

But Leonardo did not take the bait. He did not lecture her on modesty or humility. Nor jest about her likeness to a mule. He simply walked to the window overlooking the gardens and sank into an armchair.

Anne's smile slipped away.

"I should have asked you to do this weeks ago," he said with a hollow tone.

A familiar worry now bloomed in her chest like a poisonous flower. The jest was over, as quickly as it had begun. Her sparring companion had retreated, and the haunted look had returned to the old man's eyes. The weight of the world, it seemed, sat heavy on his shoulders.

"Do you need to lie down?"

He glanced back at her, his blue eyes refocusing through his lenses, dragging himself back from the dark place he went to so often. "There is more work to do. The clock is not finished. And we are running out of time."

Anne frowned. She'd heard this before, and he'd been impossible to sway. But today, something about his resolve had weakened. He looked so very tired, so very old.

"The clock can wait. You need to rest."

Leonardo shook his head. "No. The clock must be finished. It's crucial."

Anne knelt at his side, gathering his hands in hers. He was doing it again, pushing her away, just when she was so close to understanding.

"Could you just tell me why, Leo?" she pleaded. "You can trust me."

He returned his gaze to the winter-swept trees in the gardens beyond. A fresh dusting of snow covered the horse barn in the distance. "I have little time left, Anne."

She'd heard this before too. "Nonsense. You grow stronger every day."

His eyes were shadowy and serious now. "But it is not my death I worry about," he said wearily. "It is yours. And the death of the girl from the future."

Anne's eyes grew wide. She had waited months for this moment, when he would finally explain what haunted him so. But she certainly had never expected to hear of her own demise.

"She is your kin, Anne. The girl from the future. A lovely young woman with long auburn hair and black eyes. She could be your twin if she were not born of another time."

Heat inched up Anne's cheeks, and she could feel the red spots forming on her china-doll skin.

"What do you mean, born of another time?"

"The girl will be born of your bloodline, many generations from now. And she shall be the last, if we do not get this clock working. There will be no others of your kin to follow. And that shall be most disastrous."

The petals of the poisonous flower in her chest fell from the stem, leaving behind only bitter seeds of dread. Clearly, this was the information Leonardo had been harboring all these months, but now that she had it, she didn't know what to do with it.

"Last of my bloodline?"

Leo nodded. "Something terrible shall befall the girl from the future.

And it will happen at this very castle, some five hundred years from now."

Anne waited for more, holding back the questions that wanted to come. She had to be careful. If she pressed him now, he might stop talking.

Worry sewed through Leonardo's words like tattered French lace. "Her fate is tangled with your own in the cosmos. Twisted in a way I don't understand. But your curse connects you. And unless we can find a way to help her, the girl's suffering will become yours."

She rubbed her forehead. None of this was making any sense. "But how can we help someone hundreds of years from now?"

"With this clock," he said, eyeing the blueprints. "When it is finished, it will not only keep time. It will also bend it."

"Bend time?"

Leonardo put his good hand on her shoulder, its light tremor apparent under his touch. "That is right. It is the only way we shall save you both from the Goddess."

PRESENT DAY
ALGONQUIN PARK, CANADA

The blackflies were a swarm of little devils. It was always this way in early May in Algonquin, but this year the insects came in droves, descending upon us like an army of bloodthirsty soldiers.

Grapes was making her anti-itch salve from a greenish mushroom growing on a decayed log on the beach, as the rest of us set up camp on an island off the mainland of Stratton Lake. Already, Lily had three angry welts behind her right ear that were turning a torturous shade of purple. I felt bad for her, given it was her first camping experience, but she was being a good sport about it.

"The ointment is almost ready, Lily dear," Grapes, my great-grand-mother, singsonged. "It's gonna fix you right up."

Lily gave Grapes a grim smile. She had been dutifully searching for kindling for over an hour, carrying armfuls back to the bonfire site. I had to give her credit. She worked hard whether she was acting as my research partner in the library or playing the role of a pioneer woman out here in the wilderness.

The park was ancient and vast, never touched by urban development and city sprawl, and it echoed with memories of my childhood. It was a place I hadn't visited for over a decade, but it was as beautiful as I remembered. There was no one else on the lake because it was too early in the season, so we had the place to ourselves. Except for the wildlife, and they didn't seem to mind that we had crashed their party. A bale of turtles sunning on a log plopped into the water, forming rippling circles as we arrived by canoe. A great blue heron watched like a gawky scarecrow as we unloaded our gear, plunging his beak into the lake to catch tadpoles when he got bored of our antics.

But camping was work, at least upon arrival, and Dez and I were so busy bickering over the tent, we barely noticed Lily's bug-bite misery. When we argued like this, it was hard to remember we were best friends. We had fought about every aspect of this bloody big canvas and had made little progress. At the moment, we couldn't agree on which rod slipped into which flap. To be honest, the thing resembled a parachute that had blown open in the sky, having killed its parachutist, and fallen through the woods to our campsite.

"Can't you just use magic to put up this freakin' tent, El?" Dez snapped. "What good is it if you can't use your talents for something practical."

I stepped from beneath what should have been the back porch and glared.

"It is not magic. It's witchcraft. And if you want me to use *my* talents, I'll light the tent on fire. And then we can all sleep under the stars. With these bugs, Lily's ears might fall right off."

"What?" asked Lily from the trees.

Dez smacked a mosquito and cursed under his breath. "Don't be so dramatic. Just start putting the pegs in the ground."

I threw a spare peg at him with a begrudging huff and got back to work.

"I love camping," crooned Bernice from the shoreline, her oversized blue jeans patched with pink hearts were cinched at her waist, just under her generous bosom. "It's been years, hasn't it, girls?"

Grapes looked up from her mushroom paste on the beach. "It sure has," she called.

Gerty sank into a portable camp chair and looked over the water with satisfaction, her birdlike body swallowed by the sag in the seat. She took a swig of gin from a tin cup. "Attagirl, Lily. There're some real nice firewood to your left."

"Come on, El," said Dez, wiping his brow. "Let's just get this impossible tent up so we don't get eaten alive."

I huffed again. This time it came between clenched teeth, but I couldn't disagree with the sentiment.

Working together now with some level of solidarity against the almighty tent-beast, Dez and I determined the basic footprint that would house our cacophonous crew. It was the same tent my family used when I was a kid, when Mom and Dad were still alive. My parents used to bicker when they put up the mutant canvas too. Dad called it the divorce-maker. It was the worst part of camping. But once it was up, we always settled into our happy backwoods routine, and I was counting on it for this weekend.

When Dez and I finished, we were a sweaty, sticky mess and the tent wasn't in much better shape. The entrance flap sagged, and the zipper stuck in the screen's mesh fabric. The second bedroom was a triangle rather than a square. But the damn thing was up.

We raised our water bottles in victory as the sun became a red fireball and sank into the lake. Dez put his arm around me and chuckled. "God, that sucked."

I found myself laughing, until another mosquito got me square between the eyes. I unzipped the door, fighting with a bit of screen jammed in the zipper. With a heave, I picked up Dez's backpack too and glanced over my shoulder.

Dez hustled behind me and stumbled into the first bedroom. He zipped us in frantically, waving a small crew of insects out so they didn't find us in the night.

But now that I was inside, I found I couldn't move. The blue fabric glowed with the setting sun, dappling shadows dancing across the surface with ghosts from long ago. A coffee stain adorned the side wall where Dad had dropped a mug one early morning years ago. There was a small hole in the floor thanks to the car's cigarette lighter. That was Mom's doing. She had tried to set up a mini-heater one unusually cold spring.

I took a long, slow breath as the memories filled my mind. A strange warmth washed over me in an angel's breath, of all the good times we had as a family. Along with the cold slap of horror of the day I lost Mom and Dad.

"You okay?" asked Dez.

I smiled. "It still smells like them. After all these years."

He unrolled his sleeping bag. "I'll bet it does."

I looked around the blue nylon, the little girl awakening inside me.

"I used to watch the campfire dance across that wall before I went to sleep," I said dreamily. "And right there, Dad got stuck in that back-door zipper. He was chasing a raccoon away from the cooler."

Dez unrolled my sleeping bag and laid it beside his. "Is that why you picked a camping weekend for your birthday? So you could be with your parents, at least in memory?"

"I guess so."

He smiled. "Well, it was a great idea. We're gonna have an awesome weekend. It's amazing we got the whole Titanium Trio out here. I thought we were going to tip the red canoe when Grapes started waving that family flag around."

The Titanium Trio was the name of my great-grandmother's group of friends. These were the three old ladies who raised me after my parents died, with as much love and affection as any kid could hope for. I could hear them outside telling stories by the shoreline, still bossing poor Lily. Something about their voices eased the tension from my body. I wrapped my arms around myself, cocooned in the glow of the past as it shimmered in the here and now. This was my family, for better or worse.

Dez sat on his heels and studied me, the freckles on his cheeks twitching. "Ellie? Are you okay?" he asked. "You've been...funny lately. It's like...you're only sort of here."

I waved his concern away. "It's just the memories. I'm a bit distracted."

"But you've been like this for months. It's like you've forgotten about everyone else."

"It's fine," I insisted. "*I'm* fine."

Dez wrinkled his nose. "Ever since John went away, you've been in your head all the time. I mean, are you guys even a couple anymore or what?"

The warmth in my belly turned cold. I didn't want another lecture about John right now. Dez just couldn't get used to the fact that we had paused our relationship. We had been hot and heavy at the beginning, but John's term abroad in New Zealand had left things to fizzle. We hadn't broken up exactly. But it was hard to have a relationship with someone on the other side of the planet.

"Listen," I said flatly, "John and I are fine."

"Oh really? When was the last time you spoke to him?"

"A couple of weeks ago, maybe?" I muttered, punching my camping pillow into shape.

He put his hands on his hips. "Ellie, you haven't spoken to John for over a month. He told me so himself."

I ignored him, not willing to continue with this line of questioning. Not on my birthday weekend. Dez had been after me for weeks about it, and I was getting tired of his lectures. I was determined to forget about John this weekend and just enjoy my family. And now that the tent was up, we were going to have fun, damn it. Whether we liked it or not.

Dez was still staring, his eyes demanding an answer.

"You haven't exactly been available either," I snapped. "You've spent every waking minute with Lucien. Even now that he's back in France, it's still all about him. All you ever do is text and FaceTime. Lucien this... Lucien that...I mean, I get it. You're in love. But come on. It's kind of nauseating."

I hadn't been planning on saying it, and I knew I was being harsh the moment the words left my mouth. But I couldn't help myself. Guilt gnawed at my gut with ratlike teeth.

Still, there was truth in my words. There was something about Lucien that bugged me. Come to think of it, there was something about Dez, when he was with Lucien, that bugged me too. At least I could say I was being honest.

Dez met his boyfriend around the same time John left. The university had offered a series of international exchange opportunities, and just as John jetted off to New Zealand, Lucien had arrived from France. As a result, I had no choice but to watch their romance blossom as my own relationship was falling apart. Every day I had to put on a fake smile and act like I was happy about it.

Dez's smile smeared, as if I had scrubbed it away with a sandpaper washcloth. He stood looking at me for a long time.

In silence, I pulled a mini-coffeemaker from my pack and laid it beside the java beans. Then, ever so carefully, I lined up six camping-style coffee mugs.

Dez watched me complete my chores with unnecessary fastidiousness with a look of exasperation. I could only manage a few side glances, but I knew he was mad.

Finally, he made his way to the entrance, half-bent by the height of the tent. He turned to look at me before leaving.

"Just because *you* suck at love doesn't mean you have to be a total cow about my happiness."

I flinched, but I kept my eyes on the coffee grounds. I had been harsh, it was true, but I did have Dez's best interests at heart. Lucien wasn't right for Dez, that much I knew for sure, but I had never had the guts to tell him. Now that the discussion was out in the open, I knew I needed to be honest with him. Best friend to best friend.

"Look, Dez, I'm sorry if that came out the wrong way," I tried with a new conciliatory note. "It's just that Lucien is..." I searched for the right words. "It's just that he's so different from you. He's polished and slick, and he wears that musky man-scent cologne."

"Really, El? You don't like him because of the way he smells?"

"I didn't say I don't like him," I replied too quickly. "I just...I don't get him."

His eyes rolled heavenward. "Well, I *do* get him. And he gets me. And I can't believe you are being so horrible about all of this. Are you really so jealous that you can't be happy for me?"

Now it was my turn to be stunned. This was simply not true. I wasn't the problem. It was Lucien. He was arrogant and obnoxious, and his cologne was strong enough to gag a pig.

"I'm not jealous!" I said with a level of shrill that might have woken the dead. "And *I'm* not the one being horrible."

Dez's hands flew to his hips again.

"Um, yes, you are, on both counts—jealous and horrible," he sneered. "In fact, you're being such an ass, I almost don't even want to tell you my news..."

I stopped. Something cold slithered across my skin and I was left with a snaky vibe that made my hairs stand on end.

"What news?" I asked levelly.

Dez's mouth twisted into a smile.. He stood a little taller, his head squishing into the top of the tent. Despite his proud stance, his words came out as wobbly as a newborn doe's.

"We're getting married. Lucien asked me a couple of weeks ago, and I said yes."

My hand flew to my mouth. "What?"

His eyes were glued to mine now. I thought I saw a hint of dew behind his lids. There was a vulnerability there I hadn't seen in years. It reminded me of his broken expression after he'd come out of the closet in first year. He had been rejected by his parents. They hadn't spoken to him since. That was the year we had become best friends. The year that Grapes and I became his family.

I got to my feet, knocking over the carefully arranged coffee mugs.

"You're getting married?"

Dez dropped his eyes. "I never thought I would fall in love, El. And it finally happened for me."

I closed my mouth, not sure what to say next. I had just been about to tell him why Lucien was exactly wrong for him. Why they didn't make sense together. Why it wasn't worth investing anymore in the relationship now that he'd gone back to France. But my tongue was stuck in the back of my throat.

Dez shrugged. "I came on your birthday weekend hoping to ask if you would be my best man."

"Oh," I said like an idiot, still fumbling with arranging nouns and verbs into a sentence. "I...uh...well...uh..."

Dez winced. "It would mean a lot to me, El. My own family, well, you know how they feel. I was also planning to ask Grapes to walk me down the aisle, if that's okay with you?"

A five-alarm fire had broken out across the back of my brain, and I had to drag out the hydrants to put it out before I responded. I swallowed hard and unstuck my tongue. Something told me I needed to change tactics. My best friend put up a good show with his sarcastic attitude most days, but I knew him better than anyone. Inside this red-haired giant's heart was a trembling bowl of Jell-o, so jiggly and soft that it could be damaged with the slightest stab of a fork. And I couldn't be the one to slice through his squishy, quivering happiness.

"Of course, that's okay. My family is your family. Grapes would be honored. I...would be honored."

Dez let out a long sigh that seemed to go on forever. "Ohhhhhh, thank God. I thought you were going to tell me to go to hell." He gave me an enormous grin as he threaded his fingers through his bushy hair. "I was hoping you were just being grumpy. It would have killed me if you told me you really don't like Lucien."

I forced down a bubble of nausea. "No, I was just being a cow. Like you said. Lucien is great. You guys are perfect together. I'm really happy for you."

Dez let out a squeal and grabbed me up in his arms, spinning me around until the tent almost collapsed.

"The whole gang will be invited. It's all arranged. The Titanium Trio and Lily..." he breathed into my hair. "We will celebrate the wedding next month."

He put me down, and I almost fell over.

"Next month?"

Dez gave me one of his most charming Cheshire Cat grins. "This is the part I've been waiting to tell you, El. It's the craziest news ever. Lucien's family owns the Château du Clos Lucé in France. Like, you know—the *infamous* Clos Lucé? It's normally a museum, but the building is closed for renovations. So, they've invited us to have the wedding there. We're going to use it like a private hotel."

My eyes bulged. "The Clos Lucé?"

I put my hands to my temples to contain the fireworks in my head. Thousands of words, hundreds of journals, dozens of my own academic research papers spun through my mind. The Château du Clos Lucé? The place where Anne Boleyn lived out her days in France? The very place where I discovered the connection between our Boleyn and Bowlan families?

Dez stood there, grinning ear to ear.

"Holy shit," I whispered.

Dez leaned down and pinched my chin gently.

"Can you be happy for me now? We are going to spend a week for the wedding, the whole lot of us, living at a French castle. Your favorite one, in fact."

I grinned back at him, my chin still lodged between his thumb and forefinger. "For the Clos Lucé, I can be happy for anything."

As soon as the words left my lips, I felt their weight. This was Dez's life, after all. It wasn't just about a fun vacation to a place I'd always wanted to visit. Getting married was a permanent commitment. I had to know this was what he really wanted.

"As long as you tell me you're sure," I said. "As long as you know, in your heart, that you love Lucien. That's all I want for you. You know that, right?"

He pulled me back into a bear hug. "I know it in my heart, in my lungs, and all the cells in my body. Hell, I know it in my DNA. He's right for me."

I blinked over his shoulder, trying to shed that slippery snake feeling again. But what else was there to say?

"Then I will stand by your side, Dez. And I will be the bestest best man France has ever seen."

FEBRUARY 1519

CHÂTEAU D'AMBOISE, FRANCE

Anne pulled at her corset, the boning digging into her armpits. She hated the discomforts of ladies' courtier dress, but today she would endure it. She had to keep up appearances, for Leonardo's sake. She didn't want him looking any less than he was, the king's advisor accompanied by his master apprentice.

Today they were taking the tunnel that connected the grand château with the simpler country castle of the Clos Lucé. Although Leonardo would not explain why. The passage snaked through the earth like a viper in its nest. The tunnel was a solid piece of engineering, but Anne had always avoided it. Despite the sconces lit with torchlight, it was dark and damp, and it made her claustrophobic.

"What are we doing down here?" she asked, wrapping a fur around her neck.

Leonardo had slipped back into his cantankerous ways over the last few weeks, and he had refused to tell her anything further of the girl from the future. It was the clock that plagued him so. Some days, it turned him into a monster. The clock ran, yes. In their early trials, it kept time perfectly, but Leonardo still insisted it did not work to his satisfaction.

"You ask too many questions," he barked.

Anne stopped walking. "Leonardo, you were the one who told me to ask questions. Do you remember that?"

The old man continued his pace, unwilling to slow. His black cat trailed after him, its tail twitching in the darkness. Somehow the feline's loyalty irritated Anne further.

Salaì, she commanded in her mind's eye. *Stop following him.*

But the cat ignored her, padding after Leonardo like he was the only thing worth living for.

Leonardo kept his head down, advancing through the passageway. Soon Anne was standing in the dark with only the light of his lantern ahead. But she did not care. She would not run to catch up with him.

"If you don't want my company, just say so!"

Da Vinci turned toward her, a scowl fixed on his face, the lantern swinging in his fist. His long, white beard caught the light of the flame, his eyes blackened pits against pale flesh.

"I do want your company," he snarled. "Now hurry on."

"I will step no farther until you explain."

Leo set the lantern beside a puddle on the floor. "Child, you are as stubborn as they come." He picked up the cat that was now winding its way through his legs. "If you must know, we are going to meet the king."

She narrowed her eyes. "I gathered as much."

Anne was no idiot. Leonardo was the king's favorite advisor. If they were going to the Château d'Amboise, they were most certainly going to meet Francis. Still, Leo hadn't answered her question.

"But why do we not meet him in public. It is our usual custom?"

Finally, the old man relented. "We are going to meet King Francis and a man named Domenico da Cortona. He is an Italian architect I knew many years ago. Francis has invited him to develop a blueprint for the king's new hunting lodge."

Anne frowned. That hardly sounded like a big secret.

Leo put the cat down and began his hasty shuffle toward Amboise again, waving for her to catch up. "I have asked that we meet in the tunnels because there are other matters to keep from the prying eyes of the court."

"What matters are those exactly?"

But it was no use. He was on his way again.

Anne picked up her skirts and jogged after him, no longer able to contain her curiosity. He was mumbling to himself, something more about Domenico, but she couldn't make out his words. The cat's tail twitched mockingly at Leonardo's side.

Traitor, she called to the animal.

As her master surged on, she was plunged into darkness once again. A drop of fetid water splashed her cheek, and she wiped it away with disgust.

"Leonardo, you really are impossible."

A noise ahead pricked her ears, and she strained to make out the sound. It started like a set of hushed whispers, a shuffling of feet. Soon the clip of men's heels echoed down the chamber. She squinted in the blackness just in time to see Leo disappearing behind the bend in the tunnel.

Anne quickened her pace, unwilling to be left alone in the dark. When she reached the bend in the passageway, she found Leonardo sweeping a bow to two well-dressed men.

She studied them as she approached. It was easy to recognize the king, even at a distance. His slightly oversized nose, the careful trim of his beard, the way he thrust his shoulders back with all the confidence in the world.

King Francis hadn't always conducted himself with such poise. Anne remembered a time when he was boyish, before he had taken the throne. When he was pliable and soft, easily influenced by his sister Marguerite's ideas. But the power of the kingdom had changed him. His Groom of the Stool had ensured he wore only the finest furs; his jeweler decorated his fingers with the best royal gems. The ways of the court had buffed away his sensitive nature and polished it into a hardened diamond, and Anne no longer recognized the man she had once considered a friend.

King Francis and Leonardo were exchanging courtly pleasantries as she approached.

"I am sorry, my king," said Anne, dropping a curtsey. "Leonardo has gained his strength back as you can see, and he outpaces me once again."

But the king paid her no notice. Not even an acknowledging glance.

Anne bit her lip. Francis's disinterest stung. She had never quite gotten used to it. She had to constantly remind herself she was Leonardo's apprentice now, nothing more.

"You look in fine form, da Vinci," said Francis, slapping the old man on the back. "It is difficult to tell you have even been ill."

Leo wagged a finger. "It is all Anne's doing. She has been my only source of comfort these last months."

The king's eyes finally slid to hers, but his gaze barely landed before it bounced back to da Vinci.

"Anne is the finest apprentice I have ever known," Leonardo continued. "I dare say, she has a startling intellect that may one day surpass my own."

She blushed at her master's compliment, but the king seemed unimpressed.

"A woman apprentice, Leonardo?" asked the well-dressed man behind the king. "You were always one for strange ideas. Although I will say she is very pretty, so I suppose that is something."

Anne found herself glaring at this new man. He was tall and spindly, his gold-trimmed overcoat glinting in the torchlight. He wore garish silk hosiery and a pair of men's heeled shoes embellished with an enormous silver buckle. His large mustache curled up into sharp points like bull horns. In spite of his flamboyant dress, his salt and pepper hair was greasy, and he moved with an arrogant, twitchy energy.

Da Vinci nodded to this new man, but otherwise paid him no mind. Leonardo and the king continued with their pleasantries, almost as though he wasn't standing there at all.

Anne suppressed a grin. She knew it was small of her to enjoy this little snub. But she relished in it anyway. If the king could show her such disinterest, such apathy, she would content herself to know that Leonardo would put this man in the same place.

"And what of the dauphin?" asked Leonardo. "Is he quite well?"

The king's smile faded at the mention of his son. "I'm afraid little Francis has been ill. Claude and Marguerite are at his side. We continue to pray, of course. And they have administered their tonics. His fever has broken, but he remains lethargic."

Leonardo frowned with concern. "Claude must be tired. I hear a new child is to be born soon. Another son, I hope?"

A shard of glass sliced through Anne's heart. It was one thing to be discarded by the king, but Claude and Marguerite had been like family. The truth was Anne understood little of why they had drifted apart. Yes, it was more difficult now that Claude was queen. Marguerite, too, was in a public profile as the king's sister. But it almost seemed like her women friends had been avoiding her. She hadn't seen either of them for over a year.

Anne had tried to console herself by remembering they all had their roles to play. That life was different now, and that wasn't anybody's fault. She didn't regret taking on the role of apprentice to Leonardo. Not for a moment. Still, it hurt that her friends had forgotten her.

The man standing behind Francis cleared his throat now, like a small dog nipping at its master's heels for attention.

The king raised an unamused eyebrow and turned slowly to acknowledge him. "Da Cortona. I take it you and Leonardo da Vinci are acquainted."

Leo shook the man's hand, and Anne noticed a small card transferring between them. She couldn't be sure what it was, but the smile Leonardo produced for Domenico did not reach his eyes.

"Indeed, it has been many years."

Domenico jostled a set of blueprints in his other arm. "I am looking forward to showing you my designs of the new hunting lodge in Chambord. The king has approved every specification," he said boastfully, "and it shall be most magnificent."

Leonardo raised an eyebrow.

"The basic foundation of the hunting lodge is just the beginning," Domenico continued. "Once it has been laid, and we can buy the surrounding properties for royal land, the lodge shall be extended to a full-scale château. She shall be the jewel of the Loire."

"To be clear, da Cortona," the king said, raising an authoritative finger, "I have approved the designs, pending Leonardo's final word. He shall oversee your work."

Domenico's jaw stiffened, but he conceded the point.

"I shall be only too happy to review the blueprints," said Leo smoothly. "I shall ensure it meets the king's high standards."

"Then it is agreed," Francis announced. "Two Italian masters shall work side by side. Today is a good day for France."

Leonardo bowed, tucking his shaking hand beneath the long sleeve of his shirt.

"Da Vinci?" asked Domenico da Cortona, his upper lip hitched into a sneer. "Will your tremor not make it difficult for you to participate in the design of Chambord?"

A tension fell between the men now, one that Anne expected. It had happened on many occasions before. Artists could be fickle, and those who held Leonardo in high esteem could harbor plenty of jealousy. This was the time when the fracture would set in. A resentment that would grow between the two artists until it would become unbearable.

Her master eyed the man dangerously. "You needn't worry about me, da Cortona. I assure you, I am still quite capable. If the king asks it, then it shall be so." Leonardo reached for Anne's arm, and they turned back toward the Clos Lucé.

"I am sure your oversight will be brilliant, and I look forward to your input," called Domenico behind them. "Perhaps, I dare say, you will draw upon the talents of your apprentice. The one with the startling intellect."

* * *

A winter wind swept through the trees at the build site for the new Château de Chambord, biting into Anne's cheeks. She could no longer feel her toes, and her fingers were turning to icicles bigger than the ones hanging from the branches.

Despite the cold, scores of men dressed in heavy furs had begun digging, but it was hopeless work. They were making little progress against the still frozen ground. A makeshift cabin stood on the cleared land amid the tree stumps that jutted up like the wiry whiskers of a day-old beard. The property was unattractive now, but Anne had seen the plans. In the future, these grounds would become a manicured lawn surrounded by an acreage of lush, rich forest.

Smoke curled from the chimney of the cabin, a sure sign Leo and Domenico were at work inside. Anne had gone for a walk when they had begun arguing about the blueprints again. It was rather tiresome to hear them bicker. But now her toes were frozen, and her feet demanded she head back inside. The wooden door banged shut with a clack that could have been the twelve-bell choir at the Notre-Dame Cathedral, but it didn't stop the altercation between the two.

"Only the most brilliant Italian sculptor must develop the turrets. I shall send word to Michelangelo," said Domenico with a decisive snap. "I believe he is still in Rome."

Leonardo bristled. "We shall not invite that self-absorbed peacock to France."

"But his work on the Sistine Chapel is finished. My sources tell me he is open for a new commission."

Leonardo's eyes hardened. "Absolutely not."

Domenico looked aghast. "But Michelangelo is the best."

"No, I am the best!" Leo slammed his bad hand on the worktable. "And you shall not forget it. I am the overseer on this project. And I make the final decisions."

Anne hung her cloak on a hook by the door. Now that they were in private, there was no need for her to mind her position, and she often found herself playing the role of peacekeeper.

"Perhaps you gentlemen have had enough for today," she said coolly.

The men sat glaring at each other, neither willing to back down. She tried again, hopeful there might still be room for negotiation. It would certainly be a more pleasant way to spend their last day in Chambord.

"There are plenty of architectural details both of you agree on. Domenico, has Leonardo shown you his designs for the double helix staircase? It is a masterpiece to behold, even on paper. I can only imagine its magnificence when it is built."

"I shall take my leave," spat Domenico. "Da Vinci's ego is too big for this small cabin."

Anne bit her lip. She had never seen someone draw Leonardo's ire the way da Cortona did. Loyalty stirred her tongue into action, peace-keeper be damned.

"I assure you," she said, "if Leonardo says no to Michelangelo, then the answer is no. King Francis will not dispute it."

Domenico pulled at his moustache, his lip curling. "Your beloved master will not live to see the foundation of this castle dug. He can design his double helix staircase if he wishes, but in the end, it is I who will oversee its building." He gestured to Leonardo sulking in the corner. "That old man's time has passed."

"And what makes you so sure of that?" she growled.

Domenico pulled on his cloak and drew the fur-lined hood around his head. "Why don't you ask him yourself?"

The door slammed behind him, leaving an empty fury in his wake. The cabin was silent now, save for the crackling fire and the clanging of the men's half-hearted digging outside. Still, Leo did not take his eyes from the flames.

"Well?" said Anne with hands on hips. "Are you going to tell me what Domenico knows of your fate?"

Leonardo raised his eyes to meet hers. Great, bushy eyebrows drooped across his heavy lids. "Da Cortona made it clear to me. I shall not last the year."

"And why should you believe him?"

Anne put another log on the grate. She didn't see why Leonardo would put so much faith in anything Domenico said.

Her master tented his long fingers, flexing them slowly as he processed his thoughts. "Because Domenico da Cortona has connections to those with great magical power. He is a member of the Garridan's Trifecta."

"What is that?"

"A Garridan is a keeper of secrets. A scoundrel. A spy," Leo said darkly.

Anne studied him. She still wasn't buying Domenico's story. But there was something about Leonardo's gaze. It wasn't quite fear, but there was a certain resignation there that worried her.

"But he is not your friend. You don't even like each other," she said. "Why would he tell you this...secret?"

Leonardo shook his head. "I do not understand his motivation, but he provided me with proof. It was last month, in the castle's tunnel."

Da Vinci reached beneath a fold in his robes and pulled out a tattered card, handing it to Anne.

As soon as she touched it, the flesh on her hands wriggled, as if they were crawling with maggots. The sensation was so vile, she almost dropped it.

The playing card was yellowed with oil and very old. It looked to be made of thick Italian vellum, and it seemed to contain an energy of its own, as if it was pushing back against her fingers. Instead of putting it down, she grabbed it a little harder, but it didn't bend the way it should. It just sat in her hands, evil and threatening, resisting her touch. A robed figure holding a sickle stood at its center. Black ravens arched their wings in the background. A skull rested on the ground amid a pile of bones.

Leo closed his eyes. "It is a seer's card. The card of death."

Anne had not heard of those who could divine the future from a stack of cards. It was not something Marguerite had ever shown her. It was wrong. She wasn't sure how, but she knew it for certain. This thing was dirty and dangerous.

"Where did Domenico get this horrible thing?"

Leo looked out the window. "I do not know."

Something icy inched up Anne's spine, a sense of foreboding that she could not deny. "We should throw it in the fire. It feels like dark magic."

Leonardo took the card and held it in his lap. She was glad to let it go, but she noticed how heavily it weighed in his trembling hands. It had somehow attached itself to him, like a leech that grew fatter with every suck of his blood.

"No, Anne. We cannot. But whether he intended to or not, Domenico has given me useful information. It is his gift to me. Much like my gift to you. I can foresee your death. And he can foresee mine. Only with this knowledge may we change the direction of things."

"You need to throw it away," she insisted.

"Sadly, I cannot," he said wearily. "It is fated to me. I am at its mercy."

Leo slid the card into a hidden pocket in his cloak and looked at her with hollow eyes. A strange heat in Anne's cheeks ran down her neck and spilled like refuse into the pit of her stomach. It sat there in a blackened clot of dread.

"Come, child," he said, reaching out a hand for her assistance. "It is time to summon the carriage. I am in need of a warm bed for the night."

PRESENT DAY
QUEEN'S UNIVERSITY, CANADA

Thick ivy climbed the walls of our red brick home, leaving only the windows and doors exposed. Carpets of lily of the valley grew under the big old trees in our side yard, the scent sticky sweet in the June afternoon heat. The garden, as usual, had exploded with color as soon as the weather turned warm. Soft purple forget-me-nots, buttery-yellow daffodils, and bright pink phlox decorated the sloping rock garden. It was all Grapes's doing, of course. Each year, she spent hours coaxing every new shoot from the ground, every bud on the trees. And now her garden was a masterpiece.

The only part not yet finished was the tomato patch. That had always been my mother's specialty, and I had inherited the responsibility. As a result, they were the only plants that didn't thrive. Despite perfect growing conditions, little green worms grew fat and happy on them every year.

Trowel in hand, I stared at the tomato box. I neglected my gardening duties at the best of times, but today my fingers were so twitchy, I was having trouble making any progress whatsoever.

I was light-headed, my guts twisted. My world seemed upside down. Today, John was coming home from New Zealand.

Dez had gone to the airport to pick him up. We had made plans for a welcome back family dinner. Actually, Dez and Grapes made the plans. I had been informed. I think they assumed I would screw it up somehow if I was part of the planning committee.

I had spent the early afternoon in the kitchen with the Titanium Trio waiting for his arrival. But after a while, I decided it would be better to wait for John in the garden. I still wasn't sure what I was going to say. And I certainly didn't know what I wanted him to say in return.

I knelt by the tomato box and made a few tentative holes for the seedlings. Grapes had hand-grown the plants over the winter, and they were robust and healthy. Their lusty leaves rustled as I plopped the first few into the little troughs of soil.

"Grow nice and strong for me," I said, tamping them down a little harder than necessary.

"Hi," said John from above, catching me off guard.

To my surprise, his familiar baritone sent shivers up my spine. I'd forgotten how much I loved the sound of his voice, and I pinched my leg to get myself under control.

I squinted up at him, wiping a dirt streak across my cheek. The sun was so bright I had to shade my eyes. He stood like a Greek god in shadow, as muscular and beautiful as the day we met. He wore a simple white T-shirt and jeans, but he bulged in all the right places. Squared biceps and pecs, tanned forearms. From somewhere deep inside, I yearned to throw myself into his arms. But I didn't. I couldn't. The now familiar walls I always built around myself when things were too intense were going up faster than houses in a new subdivision.

"Hello," I said stiffly.

We stayed like that for a beat, staring awkwardly at each other.

"It's good to see you," he said.

I swallowed, my tongue thick and slow. "It's good to see you too."

John knelt beside me, his muscular shoulder brushing mine, and ran his fingers over the next few tomatoes in the line. My skin seared where our arms touched, a prickling that scuttled up my shoulder and tickled the hairs on the back of my neck.

"Can I help?" he asked.

I couldn't help but laugh. It was so like John to smooth things over in difficult situations. He had a knack for making me comfortable, even at the toughest of times. A few bricks in my wall came down in spite of my jitters.

"Sure," I said softly. "I'll likely kill these things if I'm left to my own devices."

He laughed too, a perfect chiseled smile showing off the dimple in his chin. The dimple I used to trace with my finger as we lay together after making love. I pinched my leg again.

"I'm sure they'll be fine," he said.

I continued digging, pretending it was perfectly natural to do gardening chores with the boyfriend I hadn't spoken to in months.

"Which one goes next?" he asked.

"How about that big fat one, right there?"

Somehow, in this queasy flustered moment, it was more comfortable acting like nothing had changed between us. Like John had never gone away, and we'd never grown apart. It was easier to pretend this was a regular day, with John helping around the house. And so, odd as it seemed, we set about planting the tomatoes. No muss, no fuss.

When John plopped the last of the seedlings into the hole, he wiped a bit of sweat off his brow. "Should we add fertilizer? My mom always said it turns out the best tomatoes."

"Nope." I shook my head. "That's cheating, according to Grapes. She's a real stickler for these kinds of things."

He placed the cages around the baby plants and stood back to admire our work. "Well, hopefully, you'll get lots this year."

"I doubt it," I smirked. "But at least when they die, you'll be as much to blame as me."

John raised a mock eyebrow. "So you were looking for a scapegoat. Were you?"

He extended his hand to help me to my feet, and I reached up and let him. We stood like that, close but not touching, electricity prickling between us. My careful brick wall had almost fallen away. Gardening with him felt so normal, so right. I could almost forget the painful distance that had grown between us. And in that very moment, I really wanted to forget it, more than anything in the world.

He looked at me now, his amber eyes fixed on mine. My small hand was still wrapped in his larger one, and neither of us were willing to let go. Somehow, we'd swung back into a familiar space that was tender and warm, and lingered with passion. I wasn't sure what to think. To be honest, I didn't want to think at all.

John kissed my cheek, right above the dirt streak. "Well, I will happily come back next year to plant more dead tomatoes with you."

My knees went weak at the quip. I think it was the suggestion that he would be around next year. The idea that we weren't completely over. That maybe everything would be okay. Contentment bloomed inside me like one of Grapes's prize-winning roses, something that hadn't been there for months. I couldn't stop myself from wrapping my arms around his neck, inhaling his familiar scent. That musk. That hint of aftershave. It took me back to a time when we were happy.

He put his arms around me now too. I couldn't help but register the firmness of his shoulders, his biceps, his forearms. The simple hug set my flesh on fire with his torso against my breasts.

"Welcome home," I said softly.

We stood in the garden holding each other for what felt like an eternity. Safe. Passionate. Together. The happily ever after that had never happened for us.

"I missed you," he whispered in my ear.

Somehow, my analytical brain fired into gear. I couldn't help it. Had John really missed me? His Facebook posts suggested otherwise. Every picture looked like he'd been having a blast with his research team and his pretty academic supervisor. Photos of John with a slightly older blonde woman with wireframe glasses. More photos of him at the Māori welcoming ceremony as he pressed his face up against the chief's. And yet more of John drinking beer at the end of a long day, a broad smile on his handsome face, his youthful, full-of-life team raising their bottles in a toast.

How could I ever keep up with that? How could John ever see me as anything other than boring old Ellie, covered in dirt in her great-grandmother's tomato garden?

My spine flexed so tight I might as well have been wearing a metal girdle. The fact was, John was the one who left. He left me and went off to New Zealand on some grand adventure. While I stayed behind to work in the darkened library stacks with Lily, churning out journal articles like discarded basement cyborgs.

He. Left. Me.

Boring old covered in dirt Ellie.

I pulled away and gave him my best hard-to-read smile. Suddenly, I didn't want to hug him anymore.

I led him to the bench under the maple tree. "How was your flight?" A stiff formality had crept into my tone. "You must be tired."

John sat beside me, his leg brushing against mine. But he had read me. I was shutting him out again, and he knew it.

His jawline flexed. "It was good," he said, defeated. "Thanks for asking."

We were heading back into polite conversation now. Aloof and distant, like a couple of strangers with no baggage between us. I reminded myself it was better this way. I was back in control. The emotional storm that brewed beneath was safely locked away behind the brick wall once again.

"And your final paper?" I asked, my words as clipped as a manicured shrub. "Did you get it done before you left? I saw you were working hard on it."

I bit my lip, knowing I had asked the wrong question. I had just admitted I had been following his social media posts, even though we hadn't spoken for weeks. Acknowledging that I knew about his research somehow twisted the invisible knife between us.

He rubbed his forehead, eyes squeezed shut. "Yes, Ellie, I got it done."

"And what was your final hypothesis?"

He shook his head slowly. "Do you really want to talk about this right now?"

I blinked, not sure where to go from here. And so we sat quietly, the distance restored between us as dark and vast as the Atlantic Ocean. John leaned back on the bench, looking suddenly exhausted. He stared up into the heavy canopy of the maple tree.

"Look, I've just come home from eight months away. We've barely spoken. We've barely texted. And now we're acting like it's a regular day at the Bowlans'. Like nothing is wrong. But everything is. Don't you think we should talk about it?"

I realized I was holding my breath, and in that moment, I couldn't take another. And yet, Dez's words echoed through my mind.

"Give John a chance...promise me..."

John gave me a sad smile. "Don't get me wrong. I'm happy to be here. It's great you guys invited me for dinner. I just wonder what this..." He gestured at the invisible thing between us. "...means."

Silence fired like a poison dart.

I stared into the rainbow array of flowers along the south wall, trying to find the right words. This was an unusual conversation for John and me. Even in the first few months of his exchange, when we talked every day, we kept it light. Never admitting how much we missed each other. Never admitting the empty space that was growing there.

"I'm not sure what this..." I gestured too. "...means either."

I wanted to continue, but tears were threatening, and I didn't want him to see the hurt there.

"Ellie, can I ask you a question?"

I gave him a phony smile. "Of course."

"Do you love me?" He sounded so vulnerable just then, it made me ache all over.

I winced. John had finally put the question on the table. The thing that stuck between us like a barbwire fence. Threatening to hurt. Threatening to maim. It was a topic of conversation we'd been avoiding even before New Zealand.

After our first few months together, in our hot and heavy phase, John had used the dreaded L-word. He said it was okay I wasn't ready to say it back. It went on like that for weeks. John would say "I love you," and I would always find something to deflect it.

I remember the day I dropped him off at the airport. He was at the security gate, a big bag loaded on his back. He fiddled with his passport, looking nervous. He drew me into his arms for our last goodbye and kissed me so tenderly I thought my heart would melt.

When we pulled away, he whispered, "I love you, Ellie. More than anything in the world."

That was the opportunity John was offering me to tell him I loved him too. Once and for all. I knew it would mean a lot. To be reassured that I would wait for him on his academic adventure. That he meant as much to me as I did to him. But my heart was in my throat, and tears were lurking there. To my horror, I found I couldn't say anything. And so I coughed, and checked my watch, and told him he'd better hurry or he might miss his plane.

The pain that registered in his eyes was so clear, it almost killed me. I watched him turn and go. My whole world was getting on a plane and leaving me behind. And there was nothing I could do about it.

John didn't look back as he passed through security. Not even a wave. I remember seeing his face in profile as he loaded his backpack onto the conveyor belt, the muscle in his jaw twitching.

As he disappeared into the lineup of people, my lip quivered. Tears finally filled my eyes, and my knees turned to jelly. It was the same sense of abandonment I'd felt when I stood on the porch all those years ago and the policeman told me my parents were dead. The day I resolved never to let anyone hurt me like that again.

"Do you still love *me?*" I asked him now, my usual deflection strategy back in action.

He shook his head wearily as if he'd prepared himself for this. As if he already knew what my reaction would be. He'd seen it enough times.

John took my hands in his. His voice was more serious than ever. "Of course, I love you. I have loved you since the day we met."

His amber eyes melted into mine, a soft warmth spreading through my belly. I didn't realize how badly I had wanted to hear that. That he hadn't forgotten about me. Every muscle in my body wanted to lean into him, to throw my arms around him and kiss him, hard. But I couldn't. The poison dart had paralyzed me.

This time, John didn't accept the deflection with a good-hearted smile like usual.

"You didn't answer the question, Ellie," he pressed. "I need to know. Do you love me?"

He waited for my reply, an ache registering in his eyes. A pain that was so vast and sprawling that it held me there too. And I couldn't look away.

My pulse twitched through my veins. John had me backed into a corner. After eight months of being alone, I was being forced to answer the ultimate question. I didn't know what to say. There was too much space between us. But he was waiting, and I had to play the next card.

"Honestly, I don't know if I love you," I heard myself saying. "I'm not sure how love is supposed to feel."

John's face fell. Clearly, he had been hoping for a different answer.

The minute the words left my lips, I regretted them. Dez had been right. I really did suck at this love thing. I tried to continue, to find the best way to help him understand. But resentment, loss, and fear were all fighting for space on my tongue.

"It's not that I don't love you. It's just that I don't know if I do," I finally managed. It sounded stupid, but it was the best I could do. "How do you know if you're in love anyway?"

He dropped my hands from his. "Love is love, Ellie. You just know it."

We sat in silence again, neither of us sure where to go next. A couple of starlings darted through the branches in a flirtatious dance. Two squirrels chased each other across the tree line. It was springtime in Grapes's garden and love was in the air, and yet, it was all so uncomfortable, so unpleasant.

"I'm sorry," I said pathetically.

John stared up into the maple tree again. "Maybe I should leave."

Suddenly a rock plunged through my stomach. The weight of his suggestion pulled me down, drowning me.

"Please don't go," I blurted.

Somehow, I couldn't stand the thought of watching him walk away again. This was all going so horribly wrong. Now that he was back, I wanted him to stay. At least I thought I did. But it just wasn't coming out right.

He looked down at me, confusion lifting one of his eyebrows.

I hooked my finger through his belt loop and gave it a tug. It was an old gesture that meant something to both of us. John used to do it to me when he wanted me to stay a bit longer, when he didn't want me disappearing back into the library.

"I want you here, with me. I want this..." I gestured again. "But you've been gone a long time. And I just need...I...well...I don't know."

My words were coming out in an incomprehensible string. "I just need some time to process," I finally managed. "Is that okay?"

He nodded, his expression hard to read. "I guess that's fair."

A grand commotion in the house was a welcome relief for us both. For months, the Titanium Trio had found the most awkward times to barge in on our romantic encounters. But today, the resounding bang from the kitchen provided just the distraction we needed.

He gave me a resigned smile. "So where do we go from here?"

My eyes darted to the house, suddenly desperate to find a way out of this conversation. "We could go inside and see what the Trio is up to. Grapes has been talking about you all week, and if you don't go eat some of her cooking, she'll be devastated."

John sighed half-heartedly. "Sure. Lead the way."

MARCH 1519
CHAMBORD, FRANCE

The return trip to Amboise had been a long and loathsome one. For two full days, Anne tended to Leonardo as he dozed on her shoulder in the carriage. She piled Leo with furs and wrapped her own cloak around his feet, but still she worried he would catch a fever.

Her master was exhausted from the journey. It was too far to make the trip in a single day, and the ale houses they had frequented provided only modest comfort to an old man. She knew she shouldn't have let him go to Chambord in the first place, but there was little she could have done to stop him. Especially after the king had asked for his help.

The guilt weighed like an iron yoke on her shoulders as they sat, toes frozen, in the cab. She should have tried harder to dissuade him, she told herself. Or at least, convince him to rest more along the way.

Anne's gaze swept over his bent form, his breath making vapor in the winter air. Something sharp pinched at her heart. This man was like a father to her. She was closer to him than anyone in her own family. And now, as she watched him, an ache traveled through her bones. What would she do if she lost him?

She pulled the blankets back over his shoulder where they had fallen away, letting her mind wander back to the little cabin on the build site.

She had been playing and replaying the memory in her mind. Was it possible Domenico was telling the truth about Leonardo's impending death? Or might he have been lying?

Anne wasn't sure of much, but she was certain of one thing. She couldn't stand to be near Domenico. There was something about him that made her skin crawl. And yet, he had foretold of Leonardo's death. And Leo had foretold of hers. And it all came down to making that strange clock work to save someone's life in the future.

The carriage halted, startling Anne from her thoughts. The door swung open, and the driver popped his head in, icicles hanging from his beard.

"We've had to stop, Mistress Boleyn," he said. "The snow has made the route too difficult to pass. But there is an ale house ahead where we can find lodgings."

Anne frowned. She had hoped to get Leonardo home this evening. "Are you quite certain? Monsieur da Vinci is in dire need of a comfortable bed and a warm fire."

A gust of snow blew through the carriage and settled on Leo's white beard, but he did not wake.

"There is little other choice, lady," said the driver. "If we press on, we risk getting stuck in the storm." His gaze slid to the old man's sleeping form. "And we do not wish to meet bandits on the road tonight."

* * *

The attic room was warm and comfortable enough. Two narrow beds lined the walls, piled high with quilts and furs. There were no bed curtains, Anne noted, and she wondered what kind of creature might drop through the thatch as they slept.

Leonardo lay sleeping, his cheeks chapped from the cold. She knelt at his bedside, studying his breathing. The whiskers of his moustache fluttered under his nose, and she was grateful she didn't detect laboring in his chest. Anne knew little of healing spells, but she'd had plenty of practice playing his nursemaid over the last few months. She felt Leonardo's forehead for any signs of burning, but he was cool to the touch.

Raising the candle, she assessed his coloring too. His lips were bluish, but his cheeks were a lusty pink.

"You're going to be fine, Leonardo," she whispered, more to herself than to her master. "You'd better be."

Anne returned to the desk by the window and pulled a quill from the inkpot. Her thoughts of home weighed heavy tonight, a gloomy echo of all the people she had lost. She had broken with her friends in France—those losses hurt most acutely—but she had also lost touch with her family back in England. If she lost Leonardo too, she didn't know what she would do, and she found herself gripping the quill, trying not to cry.

She stirred the ink, attempting to calm the storm brewing inside her.

There was one man in England, she consoled herself, whom she still had left. Her beloved Henry Tudor. He was a man she thought of everyday, and she yearned for him now more than ever. Despite the tears that wanted to flow, she allowed herself one happy memory of the night she and Henry sat talking over a bonfire back home. That was the night she fell in love with him. And that love had not faltered a day since, despite the distance between them.

Anne would never forget how he kissed that night, and how it had sent rippling tingles up her spine. Now, she only longed for the simple reassurance of Henry's arms around her waist. She could be content with only his friendship, his kindness, his laughter.

Setting pen to parchment, she continued the letter she had been composing.

Dearest Henry,

It has been so many months, my love, since we were united. I am having trouble remembering the blue of your eyes, the twinkle in them as we jest. It is difficult to recall the sweetness of your breath when you kiss me. Though I've never forgotten our love. That burns as bright and true as the day we met...

A knock at the door interrupted Anne from her writing, but she was grateful for it. An hour ago she had asked that supper be brought up, and she'd begun to worry the tavern's owner had forgotten. Her stomach growled as she cleared a small table of their traveling cases so the servant could lay the meal.

"Come in," she said, busying herself with one of their bags.

A tall young woman, her head wrapped in a silk scarf, brought the dinner tray. Anne's mouth watered at the savory scent of the stew in the crockery. They hadn't eaten since the morning, and Anne's hunger was a force of its own.

The servant hummed a strange tune as she glided through the room. She placed the tray on the table in the corner, watching Anne with brazen curiosity from behind her scarf.

Anne scowled. This girl was not the serving wench she was expecting. Her gown was a deep scarlet silk, tapered at a slim waist, with heavy skirts and a beaded bodice. She carried a confidence that did not befit someone of her station, and there was something about her bawdy staring that made Anne uncomfortable.

"Thank you. That will be all," said Anne, dropping some coins into the girl's hand. She wasn't interested in this harlot who was obviously servicing the men downstairs.

Anne picked up the tray and made ready to carry it to Leonardo. A thin vapor swirled above the supper bowls. Two thick, hearty pieces of still-warm bread sat beside a dollop of butter, so luscious she longed to wolf it down with abandon. But the young woman didn't leave. Instead, the girl plopped herself down on Anne's narrow bed and lay back against the pillow.

Anne's eyes grew wide. "What do you think you are doing?"

The servant removed her shoes, kicking the soft leather slippers across the room.

"Why must people wear such painful footwear?" the wench asked.

"I'm sorry?"

"And this bodice. I can barely breathe inside it." The girl struggled with her stomacher, unlacing the ribbon at the back that held the bodice tight. She tossed the garment on the bed and began working on the laced sleeves.

"What exactly do you think you are doing?" asked Anne.

The girl looked up at her, amusement on her pretty lips. "Do you not know me, Mistress Boleyn?"

Something cold slithered up the back of Anne's neck as the young lady doffed the scarf with a careless flick, exposing ravishing fiery red hair. Her skin was flawless. Her eyes, impossibly green, glinted like emeralds in the candlelight.

Anne sucked in a breath. "Get out!" she snapped.

She had not seen the Goddess in years, but she knew her in an instant. The Deity was disguised perhaps in human form, but undoubtedly, she was the same creature. The hair, the eyes, the skin, they were all the same. But Anne knew her most by her scent, ancient and earthy. It was an otherworldly odor that scratched at Anne's nose and made her eyes water.

The woman's lips formed a delicious pucker. "Oh, come now," she said coyly. "I should think you would be grateful for the food I brought you. It is rare that I play the role of serving wench."

For a moment, Anne did not dare speak. The noxious churn in her guts made it difficult to contain her panic. The young woman's presence was suddenly suffocating, pushing out all the air in the room. Every instinct told Anne to run, but she knew she couldn't. Leonardo was sleeping in the corner, and he would be helpless against this thing.

"I said, get out," Anne said weakly. "I did not ask for you."

The young woman chuckled, low and wispy. She stared at Anne as she rose from the bed, only a thin nightdress concealing her perfect naked form. The creature dragged a flirtatious finger across Anne's cheek, burning her flesh with a strange carnal energy.

"You have been avoiding me, my Fire Child," whispered the Goddess.

The Deity's plump breasts spilled from her dress. Graceful fingers caressed tendrils of long, red hair. Even her voice held a hypnotic quality. Everything about her had been designed to entrance, to beguile, to consume.

Anne knew how this worked. She had seen it before. Any time she interacted with the Goddess, something terrible happened. She held her head high, doing her best to pretend a confidence she did not feel.

"Well, I want you gone."

The Goddess pushed her face inches from Anne's, the creature's breath mingling with her own. A set of invisible fingers attempted to search Anne's heart, unwelcome and violating. It was all so overwhelming, so terrifying, and yet Anne had to find a way to block her out. It wasn't just for her own safety—but for Leonardo's too.

Anne took a breath. Rather than succumb to her fear, she leaned forward, pressing against the force that shimmered around the Goddess with a fiery energy of her own. Somehow, she found a way to summon this power from deep inside her belly, an instinct she hadn't used in years. And yet, it was there, lying in wait. And it formed a shield around her heart, her mind, burning with a heat of its own.

"I said...get...out."

Focused now, Anne inhaled deeply as the heat bloomed through her chest and into her arms and legs.

The Goddess hissed, but Anne stood her ground.

Slowly, the beautiful woman before her was disintegrating, the edges of her body softening, the contours of her face blurring, until she was nothing more than vapor. Anne watched with revulsion as the creature became sinewy and serpentine. Now, she snaked around Anne's torso, tickling the skin on her neck.

"Are we not friends, Anne? I have done so much for you."

"You have done nothing for me," she replied, steadily this time.

"Oh, come now," the Goddess purred. "I saved Claude's first child during her birthing. Didn't I?"

Anne's composure cracked for a second at the mention of Claude, but she hoped the Goddess did not notice.

Anne and Marguerite had helped to deliver Claude's firstborn daughter, Louise. It had been a difficult delivery, and they had worked hard to bring the child into the world. Yes, the Goddess had come to Anne's aid that night. And yes, the babe had lived. But not for long. Less than twelve months later, the Goddess had taken baby Louise, striking her down with a childhood fever before her first birthday.

Anne didn't like to think upon that memory. Louise's passing had broken Claude's heart. She was almost certain it had been the reason the friendship between Claude and Anne had been severed. The day Louise died, the Queen had retreated from Anne, asking for her less and less.

The creature shrugged. "Perhaps that is not a good example. How about your beloved Henry? I brought him to France for you. And he made a most wonderful proposal of marriage. That was my doing too. Was it not?"

Instinctively, Anne touched the necklace at her throat. She still wore it every day. Henry had given it to her the first time he had visited her in France.

It had been a promise of his love and a proposal of marriage. Two pearls, to represent Henry and Anne. The third for the son they would have one day. But that was many months ago, and Henry had not called her home after all.

This was the Goddess's doing as well, she was sure of it. Anne had received many letters from Henry, explaining the challenges with the church, and the snares surrounding the annulment of his marriage to Catherine. Of course, it had been this creature, destroying every opportunity for Anne to find happiness.

"You still love him, do you not?" asked the Goddess.

Anne bit her lip. Slowly the wall of heat returned, forming a protective cocoon around her heart.

"Henry is lost to me," she lied. "But you know that already, don't you? It is your pleasure to give me things and then take them away."

The Goddess glared, thrumming her sinewy fingers on the table now. The sound echoed in the room, eerie and haunted. "You act like you don't need me, my child. But our bond is etched through time, I'm afraid. There is no escaping it."

Something pierced Anne's chest, a million pinpricks igniting the fire within her. She never asked for this. She never wanted a connection to this creature. The Goddess was everything Anne detested.

"You are nothing to me!" Anne shouted, with all the vitriol she could muster.

To her surprise, the force of her words landed like a slap, and the Goddess recoiled.

"You are not as strong as you think you are, Anne Boleyn," the serpent seethed. "I have been delicate with you so far. You think I haven't noticed the old man in the bed? I could take him too if I wished."

Anne remembered this game now. She understood it all too well. Lies and deceit. It was the only way to win against this creature. She sank into a chair at the table and took a sip of her soup, ripping a piece of bread from the loaf.

"He will die someday, I suppose," said Anne mildly. "Take him now if you want."

The Goddess's gaze burrowed into Anne's like a hungry beetle, desperate to get past the wall. But this time Anne resisted. She would not allow the Goddess to search her thoughts.

"We may no longer be friends, Anne," the Goddess hissed, "but I have always loved an adversary. Friend *or* foe. It must be one or the other. That is the way of things."

On a roll now, Anne relaxed back into her chair. She did not acknowledge the paper and quill just inches from her stew, filled with sentiments of her love and heartbreak. Nor did she glance at Leonardo. Holding her spoon aloft, she glanced over her shoulder.

"I should like to eat my supper now."

The snake lingered by the door, glistening and ugly. When the creature finally spoke, there was something even more dangerous lurking there. She smiled slowly. "When you finish your meal, you might wish to be on your way..."

Anne's eyes betrayed her, and they flew to the serpent's face.

"Claude is in labor. Her babe comes early," said the Goddess, her slippery, forked tongue darting. "And I believe she is having difficulty with her delivery again. Pity I won't be there to turn the baby round this time."

The protective fire in Anne's belly spluttered like a flame in an open window, and her spoon clattered to the floor.

"This time the child might not live..." the snake hissed. "In fact, Claude might not live either."

PRESENT DAY
QUEEN'S UNIVERSITY, CANADA

The kitchen was covered in a thick blanket of snow. Fluffy and white, it didn't just cover the table and chairs, but every available cooking surface from floor to ceiling. The toaster oven, the microwave, the tea kettle, the cookbooks. Even Lily and the Titanium Trio were coated in a heavy layer of the stuff.

The usual sound of the Trio's bickering had amped up several decibels as they stood arguing in the alabaster wasteland.

"Ah," said Grapes cheerfully when she noticed John and I standing in the door. "We've been waiting for you two. It's almost time to start the family meeting."

Zach approached us with a wagging tail and gave John a sniff in the crotch. The black lab was covered too, and it had turned him an odd shade of grey. It wasn't until some of the powder rubbed off on my pant leg that I realized it wasn't snow. It was flour.

"What the hell is going on in here?" I asked, hands on my hips.

I glanced up at John with exasperation, but he was too busy laughing. If we needed a change of scenery to break the awkwardness between us, this was it. I stepped forward through the mess, trying to get my head around what had just happened.

An enormous paper bag that had once housed fifty pounds of flour lay sprawled on the ground. Lily had been closest to the blast and had suffered the worst of it. She was attempting to wipe clumps from her mousy-brown hair. Zach, having given us his best greeting, was sniffing along the linoleum floor, tracing a line through the flour with his nose.

John didn't bother inserting himself into the argument. Nor did he ask any questions. He simply pulled a broom from the cupboard and began sweeping. I, on the other hand, was having none of it.

"We were just making Dez's wedding cake. And there was a bit of an accident," said Grapes. She looked like a clown out of a horror film.

"Accident!" yelled Gerty, only too happy to start the argument again. "That was no accident. It was all Bernice's fault."

Bernice put her arms on her stout hips and frowned, a smear streaking the needlepoint hearts on her dress. "Oh sure, blame the blind one."

I raised my hand to stifle the squabbling. "Look, it doesn't matter whose fault it was."

But no one was listening. Lily had turned herself upside down in an effort to rid her hair of the powder. The dog was nipping at the clumpy locks as she shook it out, his tail sweeping clouds of talc across the cleaned parts of John's floor.

"Hey!" I shouted. "Why are you guys making Dez's wedding cake?"

I knew this would get their attention. Clearly, the Trio had come up with some ridiculous plan, and they would no doubt delight in explaining it.

"Isn't it a wonderful idea, Ellie?" said Bernice sweetly. "It's just like in the olden days when people actually *made* things for their weddings. None of this buying a wedding cake business. We're going to do it the old-fashioned way."

I rubbed my temples. A headache was coming on.

"But the wedding is in France." I sighed. "Last time I checked, you can't bring cake on the plane."

Grapes waggled her eyebrows. "We're going to mail it. If we get the fruit cake finished today, it should arrive in time. And then when we get there, we will prepare and ice it. It's gonna be a beauty!"

"The cake won't be a beauty anymore," chuffed Gerty. "It's all over the floor!"

Grapes wagged a cheerful finger. "No need to worry. I have another bag of flour in the basement. We'll get this cleaned up, and then we'll be off to the races."

None of this sounded like a good idea to me, but when the Titanium Trio set their minds to something, there wasn't much I could do to stop them. I was considering the best approach to containing these three crazy women, when Dez came around the corner, cheeks flushed pink. He held his phone in hand and I couldn't help but roll my eyes. He'd probably been speaking with Lucien in the living room.

Dez eyed the kitchen disaster with a smile, until his gaze landed on John and me, now standing on opposite sides of the kitchen. He gave me a disappointed look that was loaded with questions.

"Looks like business as usual, ladies," said Dez to the Trio. "Shall I get the other bag of flour?"

"That would be lovely, Dezzie," said Grapes.

Dez disappeared into the basement as Gerty lobbed a few new insults at Bernice. Lily grabbed a second broom from the closet and set about helping John clean up the mess. I, however, did not budge. I wanted nothing to do with this insanity.

Grapes waved a hand. "Don't worry about sweeping up. We'll get to that in a minute. Dez and I have been planning this wedding for weeks, and we need to go over the details."

I frowned. This discussion felt particularly awkward with John standing there. He was the only one not invited. To be honest, I felt a little sorry for him. Frankly, it was rather out of character for Grapes to overlook such a thing. She was usually the sensitive type.

"Oh good," said my grandmother as Dez arrived with a new fifty-pound bag over his shoulder. "Now that we are all here, we can begin."

Dez thumped the giant bag on the counter and turned to the group. "Grapes and I thought it would be easiest if we were all together to discuss things. There's a lot to get ready."

Gerty clapped her hands with more enthusiasm than usual. "Well, don't you worry, Dezzie. We've got our special wedding outfits ready. Don't we, girls?"

Bernice produced a conspiratorial wink. "All I can say is...cornflower blue. Bridesmaids need matching dresses, after all."

"And what will you be wearing, Ellie?" asked Gerty.

I shrugged off the question. I hadn't given it a moment's thought. There were still two weeks until the wedding, so I had plenty of time.

"How 'bout you, John?" asked Bernice. "What does a ring bearer wear these days?"

Dez and I exchanged glances. John hadn't been mentioned when we discussed the marriage proposal on our camping weekend, and I didn't quite know what to do with this new information. Given that John and I weren't even a couple anymore—not really anyway—I couldn't imagine what Dez was playing at.

John wiped his hands on his pants, leaving streaks on his dark jeans. "I'm not sure," he said. "Dez hasn't given me the instructions yet."

Heat flared in my cheeks, and I was sure they were a bright shade of red. Dez hadn't told me about John's role in the wedding either.

"Isn't the ring bearer something reserved for children?" asked Gerty.

Dez laughed. "Usually. But we're bending the rules a little. Lucien doesn't have a big family either, and the wedding will be small. So John is doing the honors."

He raised his hand, and John gave him a high five. "Always happy to help."

"That's wonderful, isn't it? Now we all have our roles," said Grapes. "John will be the ring bearer. Lily will be the flower girl. Ellie will be the best man. And we'll be the bridesmaids."

John put up a hand as though he'd forgotten something. "Oh, and the plane tickets have been organized too. We're leaving at nine o'clock sharp. No ifs, ands, or buts."

I gave Dez the deadliest glare I could manage. We had spent so much time arguing about whether he was ready to get married, he'd failed to tell me about any of the wedding plans. It was a slap in the face. I was supposed to be his best man, but I seemed to be the only one in the dark. Grapes had become his wedding planner in my place. And my quasi-ex-boyfriend was coming to France too.

Dez didn't seem to notice my reaction, but Grapes eyed me sideways. She looked a bit twitchy as she clapped her hands, presiding over this family meeting with her usual motherly authority.

"Alright, everyone, now that we have that settled, we can get back to the cake. But first, we need to get this mess cleaned up."

John grabbed his broom, but Grapes shooed him away. "Oh no, darlings, we don't have time for that. We need something a little more efficient, don't we, girls?" She surveyed the kitchen. "Ellie, dear, you will need to get out of the way. Just go stand over there. As far away from the stove as possible."

I hung my head and carried out her orders. I shuffled into the corner. There was nothing for me to do now that the Trio were planning to use magic. Everyone knew my fire talents were unreliable. If I tried to help, I would likely set the whole kitchen ablaze.

No one seemed to notice my hangdog expression except Zach, who sat on my foot and thumped his tail. Everyone else watched with bated breath as our favorite little old ladies formed a triangle, their thin voices rising and falling in a low-key chant. Arms outstretched, palms down, their words were indiscernible but their intentions clear.

I crept farther back into the corner and slid down, tucking my knees into a ball.

Slowly, the flour on the floor began to twitch, trembling on the olive-green linoleum. An odd popping accompanied the movement, like fingers flicking the surface of water. The jittering powder crawled up the kitchen counter, the microwave, the coffee pot, and the rubber plant by the window. Even the towels and the kitchen curtains wriggled as the flour prepared to take flight.

Dez nudged Lily, his eyes blazing with incredulity. He took her hand, as though somehow it would help make it all seem more real. I squatted in the corner, barely able to look. This was a spell I'd seen several times before when Grapes did the cleaning, but something about it always made me uncomfortable. Ever since I discovered my own witchy talents last fall, the Trio had started using magic around me. And yet, there was still something about it I couldn't get used to.

I gritted my teeth, knowing what was coming next. It wasn't so much that Dez and Lily were witnessing the Trio's witchcraft, but the fact that John was seeing it too made my guts squirm.

Grapes raised her hands to the ceiling, flipping her palms over. She blew hard, and the wriggling flour swirled into the air, forming a great, snowy tornado. A spritely wind accompanied the vortex, pulling at Lily's sticky hair and tousling the edges of Dez's T-shirt. The powder danced, sweeping through Zach's fur, then joining the funnel above. Even the flour that had been lodged in the toaster broke free and joined the slurry.

John, Dez, and Lily grinned from ear to ear as they watched. The Trio shifted under the growing gale, arranging and rearranging themselves under the snowy tempest, until they were centered around the kitchen garbage can.

"John," called Grapes, her hands still orchestrating the airborne powder. "Get the lid off the garbage, wouldn't you, darling?"

John almost fell over his broomstick as he dashed into the circle of witches. He grabbed the lid and flung it back, just as the three old ladies cast their hands toward the receptacle, their palms directing the powdery traffic.

I winced when John stumbled backward, trying to get out of the way of fifty pounds of talc as it swirled, hitting the garbage can with a heavy thud. The lid fell back to the base with a metallic clang and echoed through the now-silent kitchen.

"Holy shit," said Dez.

Lily giggled. "I love magic."

"God, I missed you guys," beamed John.

I put my hand over my eyes, still crouched in the fetal position. The headache that had started earlier was now a full migraine.

Grapes grabbed the spatula from the table. "Now then, girls, where were we?" she said in a no-nonsense voice. "I believe we were making a wedding cake."

MARCH 1519
CHAMBORD, FRANCE

The horses panted despite the cold, spit gathered at their bits. Anne edged them on from the driver's seat of the carriage, the snow swirling in her face. The animals' nostrils flared with exertion, but they continued to pull. They were midway through the darkest part of the forest, and getting stuck here would mean being vulnerable in the very worst place on their journey home.

Anne had insisted on leaving as soon as the Goddess told her of Claude and her baby. They didn't have the luxury of time. Childbirth was a dangerous business.

Leonardo had agreed. Though still weary, the bowl of stew had fortified him, and they had assembled the horses shortly after midnight. In his stead, the driver sent his son, a fifteen-year-old lanky boy whose face was still covered in spots. The young lad had done his best to drive the horses, but after a couple of hours sitting out in the blinding wind, he had become too chilled to function.

Anne had taken pity on the child and had sent him inside the litter, taking over the reins. The night was frigid, but she was glad of it. The air stung her cheeks and froze her airways, but it allowed her to think. Her fingertips still tingled with heat, and when she spoke to the horses, they seemed to understand her. She had been calling on a power she hadn't used since the night of King Louis's death, and she had to admit it felt good. It was the same power she had summoned when she spoke to the Goddess, and she was going to have to use it tonight if she were going to get back to Claude in time.

"Come on," she said to the horses. "We need to get past this snow drift. I know it's high, but it clears over this hill."

The brown bay snuffed in response. Its partner, a well-muscled gelding, surged on.

Anne peered into the blackness, a single lantern lighting their way. The road here was knotted with thick branches, allowing only the narrowest passing. The trees seemed to glare at her, the darkness taunting. Night was the time for a different sort of creature. Certainly not for courtiers and royals who were supposed to be tucked into their soft featherbeds.

A branch broke up ahead, and Anne snapped to attention.

The horses pulled, sweat glistening on their rumps, and she willed them forward, desperate to be free of this place.

A louder crack sent her gaze into the woods, eyes squinting. Her skin prickled. She couldn't be sure, but she thought she saw movement. Something large, something human, skittered through the trees.

"Who goes there?" she called with as low a voice as she could muster.

A figure darted through the forest as one human form became two. Soon, a couple of large men were advancing upon the litter. Their faces loomed in shadow as they swung branches at the horses. The mare and gelding reared, and the wagon jostled backward.

"No," Anne pleaded with the animals. "Please don't stop. Keep going."

But this time the horses did not listen. They stood, nostrils flaring, eyes rolling, refusing to budge.

"Let us pass," Anne called to the men with false bravado.

The bandits stopped for a moment, heads tilting at the sound of her female voice. They were wrapped in heavy furs, and it was difficult to make them out, but she doubted their intentions were anything but unkind.

She gripped the reins, forcing down her quaking stomach. "We travel under the protection of the king. You shall let us pass or you will pay the price."

One of the hooded men laughed. "Is that right, lady?" he said in lower-class French. "If you travel under the king's protection, then where are your guards?"

"If it's money you want, I'll give it," she said. "I have enough to find you warm lodgings for a fortnight."

The other man lowered his hood and approached. His beard was long and matted and a tattoo decorated his right cheek. "Enough for a fortnight, you say? Would you like to join us? I'll bet you'd be a lot of fun under a quilt."

Anne's hands trembled, but she held her chin high. "I make this offer only once. If you don't accept it, I shall have no choice but to call my guard."

The man with the tattoo drew closer. "What guard would that be?"

The second one, smaller and stockier, advanced around the other side of the transport until they both stood flanking the carriage. Her eyes darted between them and she realized there was no place left to run.

"What's a pretty young mademoiselle doing in the forest at night, driving her own royal carriage no less?"

She sat straight-backed, head high. Her heart raced, but she would not give in to it. "That is none of your concern."

"You must carry some precious cargo to be out here in this storm. Who you got in there? Someone important, I'll bet. Someone who might make for a nice ransom."

His friend snorted. "More coin than lodging for a fortnight, I'd wager."

The cab jostled and bumped. Leo and the young driver were obviously awake and wondering what was afoot.

"Stay aloft," she called over her shoulder.

But it was too late. The door opened, and the young boy emerged, thin-limbed and gawky. Leonardo followed behind, stumbling on the doorframe into the snow. The heavy quilts from the carriage hung from his shoulders, making him look even more decrepit than usual.

"Go back inside, Leo," warned Anne. "You'll catch your death in this cold."

The boy stepped forward, his movement as uncertain as a newborn calf. He looked scared, but to his credit he clutched a knife in his hand. He swung the blade at the tallest man but failed to connect, and the effort almost sent him crashing to the ground.

Anne winced.

The larger bandit roared with laughter. "This is your royal guard, is it?"

The boy tried again. He did not speak, and Anne was grateful. He was still at the age when his voice cracked. Uttering threats with those vocal cords would have earned him only more jeering.

This time, the lad set one foot forward and the other back to balance himself. But when he lunged, knife trembling, it was no more effective than his first attempt. The thieves simply sidestepped him, and they roared with laughter.

"I assure you," Anne threatened, standing now in the driver's seat, "I shall have reinforcements here at a moment's notice. Then you will be sorry for the trouble you have caused."

The tattooed bandit glanced back at Anne as the boy stabbed his arm, the blade finally connnecting. He yowled with pain, but it did not stop the man. Swiftly, he pulled the boy into a headlock and squeezed.

"I should kill you now," he seethed.

The bandit raised his fist and brought it down upon the child's head. The lad collapsed in a bundle in the snow, as limp as rope no longer taut. Anne's breath caught as she scrambled from the carriage and rushed to the boy's side. She put a hand to his cheek, feeling the breath that still came. The boy was alive, but he would have a good bump on his forehead. Tears welled behind her eyes, but she blinked them away.

"You can take my purse," said Anne, her throat thick with fear. "Let us be on our way. We have no trouble with you."

The shorter man moved toward Leonardo, still clutching the side of the carriage. The blanket around his shoulders rippled in the night air.

"Perhaps this old gentleman is the precious cargo you carry?" He advanced with interest.

Leo wore a nightdress, his twiggy legs poking out from beneath. Anne's master had become so frail, it almost broke her heart to see him like this. His long, white beard had yellowed. His shoulders were hunched. And he had lost so much weight, he might have blown away in a strong wind.

"I am a man of no consequence," da Vinci said calmly.

"I don't believe that for a second," said the tattooed man.

"Nor do I," said his counterpart. "You'll make a nice ransom, I'm sure."

Anne's world spun, her mind a frazzled mess of jitters. The protective wall of heat in her belly had gone cold and she could do nothing but watch. The stocky bandit seized Leonardo's arm. To his credit, Leonardo did not cry out, though his pain was obvious under the cruel vise of the man's grip.

But it was the sound of her master's head cracking against the door of the carriage that snapped Anne from her paralysis, sending shockwaves through her body, slamming through her torso and into her belly. Suddenly, her insides were boiling again.

"Let him go," she growled. "I warn you one last time."

"You warn us, do you, lady?" scoffed the tattooed man.

Anne stood over the boy, the snow collecting on his hair by the light of the lantern. She was not tall of stature, but something about her posture had changed. Shoulders back, chin strong, she glared at these thieves with a snarl.

"Do not press me, sir," she said. "You shall wish you hadn't."

The tattooed man picked up the branch he had used to startle the horses. "And what'll you do if I give this old gentleman a poke?"

The bandit thrust the stick at Leo, taunting him like a bully. Leo did not speak. He closed his eyes, spine bent, awaiting the blow.

Anne's belly flared white hot, searing and formidable. The panic that had held her only moments ago vanished. She narrowed her eyes. If she unleashed her full firepower, the bandits would be dead in seconds. It had happened that way with King Louis's dwarf. She had killed him in an instant. This time, if she were to use her power, she would need more control.

Leo moaned from within the man's grip.

She cracked her neck from side to side, and when she released her wrath, it shot from her with a long, enormous blast, one far greater than she intended. The branch the man was holding exploded with fire.

The thief screamed, thrusting the stick in the snow. He turned to Anne, terror snaking across his ugly face.

"What did you do?" he cried. "How did you do that?"

She clenched and unclenched her hands at her side, facing these men with brazen fury. The energy within her begged for release.

"I told you, leave us be," she said with a voice that was truly low and dangerous now.

"Are you some kind of witch?"

The muscular man twisted Leonardo's arm tighter behind his back. "That was a cheap trick is all. You've only made us certain of this old fellow's worth." He forced Leonardo into a headlock and pushed him to his knees. "Get the horses. He'll be easier to carry if we're not on foot."

Leo stumbled, unsure of his steps in the high snow. The tempest in Anne's belly surged, railing against its cage, but she could not let it fully take control. It would have to yield to her will. It was the only way.

She concentrated, slowing her slamming heart, smoothing her prickling skin. When she was ready, she imagined a small fire in the man's hood. Not a raging inferno, but something lively and red. Something that would send a clear message.

She blinked the thought into place.

Suddenly, the man's cloak blazed, a conflagration that crackled with otherworldly force. The man howled as he slapped at his robes to rid himself of the flames.

Free now, Leonardo pitched forward, grabbing the trunk of a grizzled tree to hold himself steady. Anne concentrated, straining to contain the beast within her.

The bandit wrestled with his cloak, desperate to get it away from his flesh. His scream split the night as the fire seared his skin. He threw the furs to the ground, stamping the pelts into the snow. His eyes bulged as he looked up at Anne, a patch of smooth, pink skin melted through a section of his hair.

"I told you no good would come of your effort," she hissed. "Now I suggest you run. Unless you wish to see more of what I can do."

Anne watched the men flee into the woods, cursing with terror, the sounds of their fear echoing through the darkness. She did not move, not quite trusting herself yet.

"Anne," called Leonardo from the tree line.

She ran to him now, dropping to her knees. "Are you alright?"

Her master closed his eyes. "No harm done. Just a bruise to an old man's ego."

She put an arm around Leonardo's waist and helped him to the carriage. The night was quiet, and he let her lead, leaning on her heavily. Her belly still burned. Her skin still prickled. Behind her eyes, tears wanted to flow, but she held them back. There would be time for that later. For now, she focused everything she had on restoring her master to the safety of the litter.

"Anne," Leo said softly. "Leave your purse by the road, alongside the furs. The men will need their coats. And the big one is badly burned. He'll need your coin for medicine."

She stopped. "But they tried to kidnap you. Why would I pay them any generosity?"

He placed a weary hand on her shoulder.

"Those men live in the wood, not in a comfortable castle. They are hungry. They are cold. And now, they are hurt."

"But Leo—"

Her master held up a hand, silencing any further arguments.

"They saw what you did, Anne," he said darkly. "They bore witness to your craft. You set them on fire. And that is a dangerous thing for us all."

PRESENT DAY
CHÂTEAU DU CLOS LUCÉ, FRANCE

The taxi driver piled our luggage by the steps of the château. It was no surprise that we'd brought more stuff than our group could ever need. Between the multiple suitcases, a large valise for our wedding attire, and the traveling trunk that housed the Titanium Trio's cake supplies, we looked like we were moving to the Clos Lucé for the entire summer. Dez had flown out a few days earlier to meet Lucien, so thankfully his extra baggage wasn't part of our growing pile on the lawn.

Lily checked the contents of her purse for the millionth time. She had been the most nervous traveler in our group. She lost her documents every time she went through a security checkpoint and set off the alarm three times because she refused to remove her shoes.

"I can't find my passport," she said with terror as the cab driver pulled away.

"I saw you put it in your side pocket," said John patiently.

She flushed. "Oh, right."

I had imagined it might be overwhelming to help three ninety-year-old ladies travel to France, but the Trio had been perfectly capable. Grapes led the charge through the airport, marching out front, thumping along with her walker. Bernice trailed behind her, happily whacking people with her white cane if they didn't respect her space. Gerty, who was a little hard of hearing, followed up the rear. She called out directions, a bit louder than necessary, as she navigated the complex terminal signage. It was obvious these women had spent a lifetime together, and this arrangement worked as well for them in their nineties as it had all their lives.

"Will you just look at this place?" said Grapes. "It's perfect for a wedding."

It was true. The Château du Clos Lucé was spectacular. The red brick of the manse was inviting in the midday sun, green lawns rolling in every direction. A surrounding forest rivaled any fairytale, with gardens along the east side of the property that boasted delicate wildflowers and an impressive horse barn.

Two faces appeared in one of the the front windows, and soon a tall gentleman wearing a fine suit with a cravat was striding across the lawn. He was accompanied by a strikingly beautiful woman who moved with the grace of a ballerina. I couldn't help but stare. The woman's cheekbones were high, her lips full, and her lustrous dark hair shone in the sunlight.

"Bonjour," said the man with an extravagant bow. "How lovely to meet you. I am Lucien's cousin, Maurice."

"Nice place you got here," said Gerty, cowboy-style.

"And this is Lucien's mother, Clarisse," he said with a little bow.

The woman smiled, revealing an exquisite dimple in her cheek. "It is wonderful to meet you all."

Grapes gave them each a hug and introduced our little party, assuming her role as head of the family. She took particular care to explain our relationship to Dez and the role each of us would play in the wedding. It felt a bit like a job interview at first, but her charm was infectious, and before long we were shaking hands and saying hello like it was a family reunion.

I had to admit, Clarisse wasn't what I had been expecting. Something about her was motherly and genuine, and she wore a lovely vanilla perfume that smelled like gingerbread cookies and Christmas. Maurice, on the other hand, reminded me of Lucien. Although his smooth-guy routine came off as more weird than polished. He was terribly formal, and there was something about the flashy gold ribbon that tied back his long ponytail that put him over the top.

"You must be the librarian," Maurice said, kissing Lily's hand. "Dez says you are very good with books and research...and solving intriguing puzzles."

Lily turned a ridiculous shade of red. Clearly, she was more impressed with him than I was. She dropped a bizarre curtsey in response, and I couldn't help but smirk.

"It's incredible you were able to secure the museum for Dez and Lucien's wedding," I said, hoping to help Lily out a little. "I would have thought it impossible."

Maurice's chest puffed like a peacock. "The Clos Lucé is a popular tourist destination. It is fortunate that we had a water pipe burst last month and had to undertake repairs immediately. We shut down all the buildings for the summer."

"A burst water pipe doesn't sound all that fortunate," said John.

"Oh, but it is. You see, only two administrative offices were damaged. No harm was done to the museum rooms themselves. And since Clarisse's family owns the château, we were able to repurpose this extraordinary setting for the wedding." He chuckled, exposing a set of little white teeth. "So you see, it has worked out. Because now you can stay in the home of the great Leonardo da Vinci and enjoy it as though it were your own."

Clarisse held up her hands in welcome. "And we have given each of you one of the rooms to sleep in. Of course, the matriarchs shall have Leonardo da Vinci's suite. John shall have the room of Marguerite de Navarre. And Ellie..." Her eyes flashed in my direction. "...you shall take the room of Anne Boleyn."

I glanced up at the château, electricity short-circuiting my brain, until I realized I was grinning like an idiot. I couldn't believe we were really here. And to think we were going to stay in the very rooms where Anne Boleyn and Marguerite de Navarre had lived. It was a dream come true.

I snuck a side-glance at John. He looked as cagey as me, shuffling on his feet as though an army of fire ants had nested in his shoes. Frankly, it warmed my heart, just a little. John had studied Marguerite de Navarre as part of his PhD comprehensive exams. It was the thing that had sealed our bond in the first place. It was only when he decided to focus his dissertation on the cultural traditions of the Māori in New Zealand that we had drifted apart.

Maurice raised a finger. "We mustn't forget the lovely Lily. I have personally selected the largest of the servants' rooms for you."

Lily blinked from behind her large frames.

"The chamber is well-appointed. And it is the room closest to the library."

Lily squeaked. "The library?"

He took her hands and gathered them in his. "Yes, and I would be happy to give you a personal tour just as soon as everyone is settled."

Clarisse turned and gestured for us to follow. Now that the room assignments were established, there was a lot of excited chatter among our traveling crew. As we walked across the lawns, I gave Lily's arm a squeeze, a silent promise we would explore the library as soon as possible. The Trio marched in their standard line format, Bernice swinging her white cane as they argued about who would get the biggest bed.

Maurice provided the tour, taking great joy in explaining the historic significance of the home. He covered every detail of the red and white brick exterior, the approximate building dates for each part of the castle, and the many monarchs who used this countryside château for a respite from their royal duties.

"The castle is made famous by King Francis the First," he said. "He was a true patron of literature and art. In fact, it was he who invited Leonardo da Vinci to live out his final years here. They even had a tunnel built between the Château du Clos Lucé and the Château d'Amboise so the two men could meet in secret."

Lily seemed to be hanging on his every word. "I read about the tunnel," she said. "But why did they need to meet in secret?"

Maurice raised a dubious eyebrow. "Brilliant question, lovely Lily. We have no record of what they discussed on these occasions. But we do know the two men had a strong bond." He put a hand over his heart. "It is even said that Francis held Leonardo in his lap as he died."

"How sad," said Lily, her glasses steaming.

At the entrance, Maurice produced another flamboyant bow. "I give you...the Clos Lucé."

The group grew silent as we shuffled inside. A gorgeous foyer gave way to a central hall. The red brick carried through the interior of the home, giving it a rustic yet elegant vibe. A heavy-beamed ceiling, darkened to a walnut patina, framed the space, making it look more like a hunting lodge. It was masculine and medieval and spectacular.

My head was spinning as we took the tour, until I realized I was holding my breath. Tapestries lined the walls of the great room, creating a welcoming ambiance. Polished leather couches and velvet green high-back chairs flanked an enormous fireplace. Several replicas of Leonardo's inventions stood in various corners. The space was resplendent, but it was the room's centerpiece that drew everyone's attention. A grand clock ran from floor to ceiling. Forged from white marble, hand-carved angels caught the light from the windows, making the marble almost shimmer.

"This is the château's most treasured piece. A clock built by Leonardo da Vinci himself," Maurice said with pride. "It is the first da Vinci clock of its kind. Are you familiar with the design?"

Lily's hand shot up like a star pupil in school. "A da Vinci clock is a Renaissance innovation. Most clocks in the 1500s only had an hour hand, but da Vinci's clock included a minute hand too."

Maurice blew out a long breath. "Yes, mademoiselle. What knowledge you have. Da Vinci designed it with springs rather than weights and pulleys. Something most unusual for the period."

"Does it work?" asked Grapes, checking her watch against the clock's time.

Clarisse grinned, picking up the thread of the story. "It does not. But not for a mechanical imperfection. Modern engineers have assessed its viability and insist that it would work, if not for the lost key."

"Lost key?" asked John.

"Indeed," said Maurice. "Leonardo made a key to wind the clock. He fitted it so perfectly, no other can replace it."

I could already see the Titanium Trio's wheels turning. I'd seen them exchanging the same sideways glances, loaded with adventure, too many times before. The idea of a long-lost key would be too intriguing for them to leave alone.

"It is said the key went missing right after Leonardo's death." Maurice's voice had transformed into something low and mysterious. He might as well have been telling scary stories over a campfire. Although, I had to admit it was well-delivered, and all eyes were on him.

Clarisse scoffed. "Oh, that key is something of an obsession of Maurice's. Although I suppose it's a natural preoccupation for a museum curator."

Lily giggled. "It would drive a librarian crazy too."

Maurice produced one last grandiose bow for the group. "It is true. It's been lost for centuries. But now that we have the infamous Bowlan research crew here, perhaps we shall finally find it."

APRIL 1519
CHÂTEAU DU CLOS LUCÉ, FRANCE

The men worked day and night on the marble that would become Leonardo's clockface at the Clos Lucé. Leo had drawn each angel in exacting detail and would allow the carvers no room for deviation. Despite his illness, da Vinci supervised the workers with an eagle eye, assessing every rosebud lip, every chubby cheek, and every rounded belly, insisting on perfection for the grand reveal. Even King Francis was to attend the event in honor of the clock's official installment, and much anticipation surrounded the celebration.

Anne knew Leo considered this clock his final masterpiece, and he would not rest until it was done. She was grateful for it in a way, for his health had improved since their return from Chambord under the trance of this great obsession.

She herself was less focused on this invention. Of course, she ran Leonardo's errands and followed his instructions for the final preparations, but her mind was elsewhere. Anne's thoughts went back, again and again, to the night they had met the bandits on the road. Once they had been free of the kidnappers, Anne had been able to coax the horses home. Following their plan, she and Leo delivered their tale about being robbed in the wood. Anne told her story about the courageous boy fighting to defend them and how she had left her purse in exchange for their freedom. And she had told it well.

As soon as she had been able, Anne had raced through the secret tunnel, determined to get to Claude. She was certain she would find her best friend dying with a lifeless newborn in her arms. But when she arrived, Anne discovered a large crowd gathered outside the queen's rooms, full of gaiety and cheer. The merrymaking was so boisterous, she would not be permitted entrance. Anne pleaded, but the maid would only say that mother and babe were doing well.

It was that memory that haunted Anne. She hadn't been visited by the Goddess in years. So why had the creature decided to come to her that night? And why had the Goddess threatened that Claude would die, only to allow her friend to live?

"Come, child. And don't forget the key," said Leonardo with a hand on his cane. In the last few weeks, he'd had little choice but to use it.

She tapped her waist. "It is safe in my pocket. You mustn't worry."

Leonardo set a stern look upon her. "I worry about it daily."

As patient as she was trying to be, she was tiring of this old man's intensity. "Leonardo, you asked me to be responsible for it, and I have been."

He bristled. "I am building this clock for you. It is you who shall have need of it. And so it is you who must bear the burden of its care. I hope you understand that."

Anne understood it all too well. Leo had sent her back and forth from the goldsmith for weeks. It had been exhausting, arguing fine points of the blueprints at Leo's insistence, quibbling over things that seemed so insignificant it had almost become embarrassing.

"But we are still waiting for the last spring. Why are we having the clock's grand reveal when the device isn't finished?" she asked, hoping to distract him from another lecture.

"You know why," he barked. "The double helix spring we await has nothing to do with the clock's timekeeping function."

The idea for the final spring had come to Leonardo after designing the staircase at Chambord. An almost impossible concept, and even more difficult to draw, he had conceived of two springs intersecting, coiling within one another in perfect unison. He was certain this was the piece that would allow the clock to bend time.

She thought on her most recent discussions with the goldsmith, their endless disagreements over the design. "But the jeweler said he didn't think it could be built. I told you that."

Anne didn't like thinking about the clock's true purpose. Building a clock for timekeeping, especially a device with an hour and minute hand, had been enough to contend with.

Leonardo leaned on his cane, his long fingers flexing on its crown. "The final spring shall arrive shortly," he said tightly. "And then we will set things right. Until then, you must trust no one."

* * *

When Leonardo used his cane, he was strong enough to walk on his own. So Anne contented herself to strolling beside him down the long, wood-beamed corridor. The Clos Lucé was comfortable and welcoming, not like the Château d'Amboise, where they spent much of their time on court business. It made sense that this would be the place where Leonardo would leave his greatest legacy. Despite his cantankerous ways, Anne was proud of what he had accomplished, and she was looking forward to seeing him reveal his masterpiece.

Voices floated up the stairs, workmen calling orders as the clock's pieces were being assembled. Leo extended his arm. He could no longer handle the steps by himself, so Anne hooked her arm through his, like a daughter accompanying her father to a feast in his honor.

When Domenico noticed them, he halted the workers. "It is the great Leonardo da Vinci," he called with admiration.

Anne's mouth twisted into a knot. Domenico was back to his courtly ways, all smiles and flattery, and she could barely stand to watch. With his work on the build site in Chambord, she hadn't seen much of this new Italian architect. But in the last few days, with the finishing touches imminent, Domenico had developed an unusual interest in Leonardo's clock.

As she and Leonardo descended the stairs, the men broke into raucous applause. Anne squeezed his arm in hers, as the old man produced a light bow for the crowd. Though Leonardo was critical of any flaw in the work, she knew these men respected his genius. After all, da Vinci was almost as famous as the king himself.

"I hope things are in order?" Leo inquired of Domenico, without the slightest hint of animosity.

"They are, indeed. It has been an honor to oversee these last finishing touches," said da Cortona smoothly. "We installed the internal mechanism just this morning."

Anne forced a pleasant smile, though it was an effort, as she watched this man exchanging pretty words with her master.

"And thank you for the spiral staircase drawings for the Château de Chambord," Domenico purred. "They are as impressive as you promised."

Anne stood at Leo's side, hanging on a little tighter to his arm. Domenico continued with his flattery, his voice dripping with false praise. This man was such a snake. Some days, he was smooth and flattering. Others, he was sharp and envious. But always, he was a perfect courtier in public.

"All hail for the king," announced the herald. "All hail for the king."

A hush fell over the workmen, and Anne was glad of it. At least she didn't have to listen to anymore of Domenico's simpering drivel.

King Francis sailed through the great hall, followed by the grooms of his household, their rich velvet robes trimmed with exquisite fur trailing behind. The king's chamberlain followed in their wake, an officious formality rippling off him in waves. Anne had seen chamberlain before, though they had never met. He was dour-faced and ancient, and he brandished his stave of office with an ominous clack on the floor.

Anne unlocked her arm from Leo's and melted into the crowd. These were the formal airs of the royal house, and she had a role to play as Leonardo's apprentice. Besides, it wasn't King Francis she was eager to see. She scanned the door, her stomach tightening. She had been secretly hoping that Claude and Marguerite would attend today. She'd had no news of the queen's new babe since that strange night, and a dark ache was starting to grow in her chest. It grew a little larger when she realized only the king's usual entourage was in tow.

"Shall we begin, sire?" asked Leonardo. "The clock is finally ready.

The only thing left is to put the key in the slot and bring the device to life."

King Francis turned his eyes to the magnificent piece at the room's center. "It is magnificent."

Leonardo clapped his hands, calling the workers to action, clearing the remaining scaffolding away and removing the heavy tarps from the worksite. Anne fought the urge to assist Leonardo as he made the finishing touches. She knew better. This was his moment, and she would not coddle him today.

The king and his grooms took the front row as the crowd assembled, an enthusiastic buzzing carried through the hall. Anne arranged herself at the back of the group, trying to blend in as much as possible. She dropped her eyes and assumed a subservient stature, a perfect apprentice.

"The queen sends her greetings," said the king's chamberlain discreetly.

Anne's eyes snapped to his. "I am sorry, sir?"

He gave her a watery nod, his jowls sagging so low he could have been a basset hound.

"Claude asked that I speak with you."

Anne's pulse quickened. She had heard nothing from her best friend since that night. Not a single message. And now, this stranger was bringing news of Claude in such a public forum?

"Does she fare well, my lord?" she asked, voice quaking slightly.

The man nodded. "Aye, she does. Her newest child was born safe into the world. It has just been announced. She named him Henry."

Anne's belly fluttered with warmth. It wasn't a fiery heat like the night she scared off the bandits, but a soft, sunny glow that made her want to hug this stranger. It was the first sign in months that Claude might have been thinking of her. Was it possible that her best friend named this child for Anne's beloved Henry Tudor back home?

"Claude knows the story of your return home from Chambord," the man continued carefully. "That you were rushing to her side. She sends her thanks."

"I...I...should be happy to go to her," Anne stammered, "if the queen is in need of some company?"

The chamberlain frowned. "I'm afraid that will not be possible. You are needed here, with Master da Vinci."

The warm glow retreated, and Anne felt her shoulders sag. She wanted to press, but the doughy-faced man turned away. She watched the back of his bald head as he retreated through the crowd. Now was not the time to trail after him, but still, she had to stop her feet from following.

Leonardo held his hand aloft, its stubborn tremor still apparent, but the room quieted all the same.

"Thank you, everyone, for coming today as we unveil the clock of the Château du Clos Lucé, made especially for our beloved King Francis. Such a timepiece has never been invented before. This device shall not only call out the top of every hour, but a second hand on the clock's face will track every minute of every day, from this day forward."

The workmen's voices grew steadily through the hall, the din mounting like thundering horses. The king's chamberlain clacked his stave on the floor.

"Before we begin, I shall need my apprentice," said da Vinci. "Anne, do come forward."

Anne bobbed a curtsey and made her way through the crowd. As she approached, Leonardo reached fast for her arm, and she was surprised at how heavily he leaned against her.

"We shall require the key," he said.

Anne pulled it from the pocket in her dress. She held it out dutifully, but her master did not take it.

Leonardo cleared his throat ceremoniously. "I wish to acknowledge my master pupil. Anne Boleyn has worked by my side to bring this design to life. Without her great mind, I could not have created this masterpiece."

She flushed at his words, and the crowd murmured its appreciation. Leonardo leaned harder into Anne, and she braced herself to hold him upright. She could only hope no one else noticed how exhausting all this was for him.

"You shall do the honors," he whispered.

Anne's eyes widened. They had not discussed this request. But she saw that dark look in his gaze, the same frightened, weary look she'd seen earlier. Leonardo gestured her forward. For a moment, she was afraid to let go of Leonardo's arm for fear he would fall. But everyone was watching, and Leonardo's gaze was pleading.

She unhooked her grip from his, double-checking that he was steady on his feet. Then, with all eyes upon her, she opened the glass frontispiece. Her fingers found the small circular hole in the clockface easily, just big enough to accommodate the key. She inserted the golden fishhook with steady fingers and turned the key three times. Anne was grateful she knew what to do. Leonardo had explained the steps so often, she realized, she could have done it in her sleep.

Soon a modest sound of the gears turning inside the clock's mechanism sputtered to life, and a strong and steady heartbeat thrummed through the room.

"The clock lives!" announced Leonardo victoriously.

Anne raced back to her master's side as the workmen broke into a new round of applause. The king beamed, his groomsmen nodding their appreciation as well. Anne couldn't resist a smile. She had to admit it felt good. After these many months of working and reworking the design, Leonardo had actually done it. *They* had done it.

Sunshine fell across the clock's face, reflecting off its iron hands, marble cherubs glistening in the sunlight. Da Vinci stood back as the others admired his work. But after several minutes of revelry and congratulations, Anne noticed he had grown oddly quiet.

Leo's eyes flicked to hers just as his weight gave out. Anne felt him lose the strength in his legs even before he fell. But she wasn't quick enough to stop him. The old man collapsed in an unceremonious mound, limp as a ragdoll.

"Leo!" she gasped, crashing to her knees beside him.

Everything else fell away as Anne ran her fingers across his cheek, begging him to be alright. The workmen, the great hall, even the majestic clock, none of it mattered. In that moment, it was only Leonardo.

Alarm spread through the crowd, bodies pushing to get a view, but Anne took no notice. She could hardly think. She could hardly breathe. Leonardo lay curled on the floor like a helpless child, and all she could do was cling to him, pleading for him to wake up.

"Call my physic this instant," commanded Francis.

Anne heard the king's words from somewhere far away, but they were part of another world. One that didn't matter anymore.

She could focus only on Leo. Right here and now. She pulled at his robes, as if it might stop her from losing him, a way to keep him close. As she did, her hand stumbled upon it, that heavy vellum card. The card of death. She didn't need to pull it out and look at it. The moment it connected with her flesh, she felt the wriggling maggots.

Death...Death...Death... It inched across her skin, up her arms, along her collarbones.

"What happened!" cried Domenico, arriving at her side.

She could not drag her eyes from her master, her hand still fixed on the card within his pocket. The maggots crawled up her neck, into her mouth, her nostrils. The stink of death was inside her now, sweet and rotting.

Domenico tried again. "Anne, you must let me help."

"Is he alive?" asked King Francis from somewhere above.

Domenico was gentle as he shuffled Anne aside, but his movements were determined. She found herself watching helplessly as Domenico put his head to the old man's chest.

Everything went quiet for a pulse, and Anne found she couldn't breathe. Finally, Domenico made a noise that was somewhere between a guffaw and a whine, relief dawning across his face like thin rays of light through a shuddered window.

"Thank the heavens," he cried, "Da Vinci's heart beats strong."

Domenico laid a hand over Anne's cold one. His touch was gentle and reassuring now as he caressed the sixth finger on her right hand. She couldn't be sure if it was his usual theatrics or if something genuine lingered there.

"He is only exhausted, Anne," he soothed. "He's going to be alright. But we need to get him back to bed."

PRESENT DAY

CHÂTEAU DU CLOS LUCÉ, FRANCE

John and I walked the halls of the château in awe, too fascinated by the castle to notice the strangeness between us. The place was sprawling and beautiful, preserved beyond my wildest expectations. It had been so carefully curated, we could have been walking those halls five hundred years ago. The aged red brick, the black-and-white marble flooring, the deep-seated windows framed out with thick, rippled glass. It truly was a relic of the past, of a time when things were simpler, life was harder, and creature comforts and luxuries were out of the ordinary.

We studied the tourist map we had picked up in the great hall. According to the arrows, our rooms were located in the west wing, on the other side of the castle from Leonardo's suite. Clarisse had kindly offered to escort the Trio, and Lily and Maurice were doing a tour of the library, so with everyone else taken care of, we found ourselves alone.

John and I had kept our distance in the weeks leading up to the wedding. We hadn't been avoiding each other exactly, but somehow we always managed to be assigned to different family projects. John helped Dez write his vows while I had gone dress shopping with Lily. John assisted Grapes and Bernice with the herb garden while I had taken extra-long walks with Gerty and the dog.

But now that we were here, something had changed, and I didn't know how to make sense of it. The back of my neck prickled, and I couldn't resist a scratch. I wasn't sure if it was the tension between John and me or just the sheer pleasure of having finally arrived at the castle that had been the focus of my academic career, but my nerves were firing in all directions.

"Can you believe this place?" I asked.

John shook his head. "It's incredible. Would you have ever believed we would stay at the Clos Lucé?"

"Not in a million years."

John's voice sounded distant. "It reminds me of writing our comps."

My stomach flip-flopped. It was our PhD comprehensive exams that had brought us together in the first place. I was working on an exam that looked at the witchcraft proclivities of Anne Boleyn, while John was studying Marguerite de Navarre's infamous *Heptaméron*. At the time, we hadn't known the two women were connected. It was at our first romantic dinner we discovered they were both witches. That was the first time he kissed me. I flushed at the memory.

"It does," I said, scratching the back of my neck again, a little harder this time.

His amber eyes flashed. "You sure you're okay?"

"Oh, I think the airplane pillow gave me a rash or something."

When we arrived at the rooms we'd been searching for, I was gripping my hands so tightly, my fingernails had made purple half-moons in my palms. Our chambers were right across the hall from each other, and I found myself wondering if Dez had been the mastermind behind this little coincidence.

"We're here," John whispered.

"Holy shit," I whispered back.

We stood in the hall, not quite ready to head in different directions. We used to do this a lot. John would walk me home after a date, and then we would linger on the doorstep, treasuring our last few minutes together. But this time it was different. We were hanging on to our past, and about to connect it to our futures. Wherever things were going to go, it felt big somehow, and I could tell by the look on John's face, he felt it too.

John took my hand in his. It was the first time he'd touched me since our embrace in the garden back home.

"Look, El. Let's not do this weird thing anymore." He gestured to the invisible wall between us. "We'll just be friends, okay?"

The muscles in my shoulders relaxed at the idea, grateful John had put it out there. Actually, I needed to hear him say it. There were no easy answers, but we didn't have to hate each other just because we didn't have the solution. Besides, it would make life easier if we could put aside the oddness between us while we were here. Maybe we could actually enjoy this vacation.

I nodded. "Friends."

He gave me a quick "friends only" hug, and I could tell he meant it. There wouldn't be any guilt trips or forced discussions, just a clean slate.

"You ready?" he said with a grin.

"Ready Freddy," I replied, matching his smile.

"See you on the flip side." He winked and then disappeared.

Standing at the threshold of Anne Boleyn's room, an errant finger trailed up my spine, and I sucked in a breath, every hair on my body standing on end. Anne's chamber was filled with her things, her furniture, her world. I couldn't believe I was going to sleep in the very place my great-great-grandmother had all those years ago.

"This is soooo cool," John's voice floated from across the hall.

But Anne's room crackled with an energy that held me and wouldn't let go. Long beams of sunlight poured in from the large window onto the rich velvet curtains of the four-poster bed, a thick, red canopy sweeping along spiraled posts. The air seemed sharper here, more alive somehow. A power bowed and flexed in this room, and in some ancient way, my body responded.

I was immediately drawn to a fine mahogany desk resting under the windowsill, and I ran my fingers across its grainy, dark surface. The scar on my hand surged with heat. It was the first time I'd felt it in months, and I gave it a quick rub.

An antique inkpot and feather quill stood aloft, situated around a parchment scroll. It was the perfect museum prop. These tools wouldn't likely have been Anne's specifically, but they returned me to the time she might have written a letter or composed a poem. I imagined her sitting under the window, looking out onto the lawns.

I continued my exploration, touching all the objects, every nook and cranny. The rough plaster walls, the thick beams that ran the length of the room and down the corners to frame out the high-ceilinged space. The muted blues and greens of the woven rug. Even the creak of the floorboards made me think of Anne's feet as she passed over them.

In some way, it was as though she was here with me, in this place where our two worlds collided. Where it was impossible to know the difference between them. The cells of my body seemed to vibrate with just the right frequency, with a timeworn connection that I could feel but I did not entirely understand.

Suddenly, I was exhausted, a haze settling over my brain. My feet were swollen, and my back ached. I hadn't realized it until now, but the trip had taken a lot out of me. The overnight flight had been sleepless. And there had also been the two-hour train trip with the squabbling Titanium Trio and Lily's constant panicking.

I needed to sit. To lie down.

Moving to the bed, I sank like a stone. The mattress didn't bounce on springs the way a modern one might. But it was soft, the stuffing made from down. The ropes beneath me squeaked slowly as the bed absorbed my weight and assuaged my weariness. To my surprise, it was the most comfortable bed I'd ever laid upon. The small pillow cradled my head in just the right way. The lumps in the stuffing fit my shape exactly.

Though the bed curtains were not drawn, I was in shadow, and it lulled me into a state of relaxation. I was tired but I didn't want to sleep. Somehow, I wanted to understand Anne's room from here. To see it from her perspective.

My eyes slid over the suitcase and traveling bag tucked in the corner. They drifted past the desk and the golden beams of sunlight. And finally, they landed on an oil painting, framed in gold gilt. In my haze, I almost didn't recognize her.

The medieval woman in the portrait watched me with an alluring smile. She wore a double string of black pearls, a gauzy veil fitted over her hair, and a deep green gown with split sleeves. In her lap, she held a large, white ermine.

"Hello, Ellie," she said matter-of-factly.

I scrambled backward, the mattress ropes screeching beneath me. The Lady's voice was so clear, she may as well have been on the other side of an open window. Whenever I had seen this painting at the Sleeping Goat back home in Kingston, her voice came through as a whisper. But this Lady was speaking to me directly, commanding my attention.

I scuttled across the mattress and leapt from the bed, shaking my head to clear it of the cobwebs.

"Did I startle you?" the Lady asked.

I rubbed my eyes, hoping I had just been sleeping. Hoping this woman would go back to being a normal inanimate painting.

The Lady studied me with a cool curiosity, her white ermine sniffing the air.

I scratched my neck again, raking red streaks into my skin. My weird world in Kingston had followed me here to France, and I wanted nothing to do with it. That familiar desire to be normal was rearing its ugly head. I didn't want to be some crazy fire witch who spoke with talking paintings, and I could feel the sweat moistening my armpits. Suddenly, I yearned to be with John, standing in the doorway, worrying about our relationship issues, wondering what our regular old nothing-out-of-the-usual vacation might bring.

The Lady smoothed the ermine's fur with a pale hand. "You know who I am, Ellie. We have met before."

My tongue stuck to the roof of my mouth, and I had to pry it away before I could speak.

"You're the Lady with an Ermine." I sounded stupid but it was all I could come up with.

She sniffed with pride. "Most tourists call me the Lady, for short."

"But...why are you so real?" I choked out the words. "Why is your voice so clear? At the Sleeping Goat back home, you sound far away."

The Lady produced a self-satisfied grin, as though I had just paid her a great compliment. "I am the original Lady with an Ermine. Painted by the great Leonardo da Vinci himself. Of course, I would seem more real than any replica."

My heart was thrashing in my chest. I couldn't help but think about all those months ago when I discovered I was a witch. When Tattoo Carl showed me how to light a candle with my mind. I had been so freaked out, I had almost burned down the house. Even now I ignored the scar on my hand that seared whenever I was around an open flame. I side-stepped the Kingston coven gatherings each month on the full moon, despite regular harassment from the Titanium Trio. I avoided Grapes's lessons about how to make healing potions and tinctures.

"What do you want with me?"

The Lady played with her string of black pearls. "I have an important message for you."

Suddenly, I was suffocating. I couldn't face her, not when the Lady was this close, this real. I backed away, grabbing a woolen blanket from the bed, and threatened to throw it over the painting.

"I don't want your message. Just Leave me alone."

She leaned forward, her body emerging from the gilt frame. "But it is vital."

Memories of the Lady with an Ermine in Kingston swelled through my brainstem. That Lady had told me to use my fire talent. And look how that had turned out. I had almost killed a man. I shook my head. I wanted no more of this talking painting's messages.

"Come closer, Ellie. You need to hear this..."

"I said leave me alone." My hands flexed around the blanket, and I brandished it like a weapon.

"Ellie Bowlan..." The Lady grew stern, speaking to me as though I was a naughty child. "You must hear this message. It is a matter of life and death."

I raised the fleece and advanced on the painting. She could give me the scolding tone, her narrowed eyes, the disapproving frown. But I wasn't buying it.

"You must listen," she insisted.

In full combat mode, I threw the blanket over the portrait, the scratchy fabric sticking on the gold gilt frame. My feet were already in motion as I sprinted from the room, muscles flexing in full flight.

The Lady called after me, her voice now muffled from behind its woolen prison.

"Ellie...Ellie Bowlan...you must hear this..."

VOLUME 2

"For there are three kinds of suspicion—a light suspicion, a serious suspicion, and a grave suspicion."

— Montague Summers, The Malleus Maleficarum of Heinrich Kramer and James Sprenger

MAY 1519
CHÂTEAU DU CLOS LUCÉ, FRANCE

The skin of Leonardo's hands was paper thin, blue veins snaking beneath his swollen knuckles. Thick white linen bandages encased his wrists. He lay sleeping, arms crossed over his chest, his breath so shallow he could have already been in a coffin.

Anne had not left the old man's bedside for days, except to wind his precious clock. She had cared for his every need since he'd fallen. When he hungered, she'd fed him broth. When he was cold, she'd brought him blankets. She had even started brushing his long, white hair so it wouldn't become tangled.

Most days she did battle, too, with the king's physic, who insisted on bleeding Leonardo to balance his humors. Anne was certain this only made him weaker. The doctor wrapped his wrists daily, and she thought she could see the makings of infection growing along the underside of his bandages. Only yesterday, she had sent the physic away, insisting he was causing more harm than good.

Anne sat on the edge of Leo's bed, stroking Salaì. Somehow the little feline had become her only ally in her quest to bring Leonardo back to health. She had been so consumed by the prospect of losing Leonardo over these last long days, it had pushed everything else away. She didn't even have the energy to be angry with Marguerite or Claude. Neither of them had come to pay him a visit. In the past, they would have rushed to Leo's side—at least, she thought they would. She had sent letters requesting that they come, but not a single message of sympathy had arrived.

"The spring..." Leonardo's eyelids fluttered. "Where is the spring?"

Anne's breath caught at the sound of his voice. She yearned to hear it now, and every time he woke, she was flooded with relief, only to have that ease vanish once he fell asleep again. She didn't care about the spring anymore. She didn't care about anything but Leonardo.

"Can I bring you some ale?"

"You must fetch the spring and make the installation," he said, his voice still thick with sleep. "It must be done today."

She dabbed his forehead with a cool cloth. They had been through this before.

"Leo, you must be fortified. You need your strength."

He blinked, settling his gaze upon her, as if seeing her clearly now. "I need only live long enough to know you have it right. Have you been winding the clock daily?"

She worked the cloth along his forehead. "Aye."

"And have you been counting the clicks of the gears? How many in one full rotation?"

Anne pursed her lips, determined to be patient with him. She had wound that infernal clock every day, and every day he had asked her to count. At first, she had been too distraught to pay attention, but at his insistence she counted sixty. One for every minute of the hour.

"I told you, the number is always the same." She kept her voice steady, reassuring.

"Good girl. Always sixty. And there shall be sixty beggars in my funeral procession..."

She went in search of the ale. He had been speaking a lot about his funeral too, but none of his wishes made much sense. Besides, she didn't like talking about such things. She was going to nurse him back to health if it was the last thing she did.

"There is an algorithm inside my desk," he said. "Go and fetch it. It is locked in the secret compartment. You'll need to push the button on the inside to access it."

Anne considered arguing but she knew better. He would only grow more insolent, more determined. And her master was clearer today, there was a brightness in his eyes. She would go along with him, at least for a little while.

She padded to his desk. It was covered with scripts, journals, and sketches. She had not thought to clean it. Leonardo would have taken it as an insult.

"It hides inside the left door," he advised, his voice sharper, clearer still. "Open it as far as the drawer will allow and run your fingers along the outer edge. Feel for a small peg etched in the panel."

Resigned to her task, Anne followed his instructions. She pulled open the drawer and felt along its edge. It was a bit of searching, but as sure as Leonardo promised, she soon found a round button. When she pressed it, out slid a side drawer at the back.

"Well done," said Leonardo. "Now retrieve the parchment."

She reached into the sub-compartment and pulled out a tiny scroll tied with a fine red ribbon. Bringing it to Leonardo's bedside, she offered it to him.

He shook his head. "It is yours to protect now, along with the key. Open it, and I shall explain its meaning."

Anne sighed as she removed the ribbon, the tiny parchment uncurling. Staring at the paper, she tried to make sense of the words and the mathematical formula written there. Of course, it was composed in Leo's usual backward mirror-image script, and she had to think about what she was looking at.

"It's the formula for the clock," he said. "Your studies in mathematics and engineering will be critical here."

The world of algorithms and formulas had always come much easier to Anne than to Claude when they were both his pupils that first summer. Her mathematical talents were one of the reasons Leonardo had asked her to stay on as his apprentice. She could remember explaining one of Petrus Ramus's principles to the Claude on a hot lethargic summer day at the Clos Lucé. Her best friend had been so ripe with her first child, she could concentrate on little else.

"Do you understand it, Anne?" asked Leo.

"Of course. But I still don't know what it's for."

Leo relaxed into his pillow, stroking Salaì behind the ears. The little cat purred, low and satisfied. "When the final spring is installed, this formula shall give you the coordinates you require to move through time," he said. "It requires that you turn the key counterclockwise. But the mathematics are complex."

She raised an eyebrow.

He gave her one of his old quirky Leonardo smiles, the kind he used to give her all the time when she was his star student. The one that said she was special, that she was his favorite. She hadn't seen that grin in months, and it made her want to please him so badly she could almost taste it.

"When you turn the key clockwise, it rotates sixty clicks in one full rotation, for every minute of the day. A clockwise rotation keeps the clock's heart beating. But beyond that, it is of no further consequence." He waved the thought away as though it were too simple to waste any more breath. "The counterclockwise rotation is more complex. You can move forward or back in time, into the past of the future. The algorithm will help you determine the precise time of your destination. But do your arithmetic well, for a poor calculation can put you in a time you do not understand."

Anne could feel herself getting caught up in his intrigue, in his brilliance. It was a magnetic force that pulled them together when they worked, master and apprentice. When he spoke to her like this, she would run to the end of the world and back for him.

"There is one simple rule," he said, wagging a thin finger. "One click counterclockwise will return you one hour in time. But any other destination, forward or back, requires the precise application of the algorithm. So double-check your numbers before you travel."

Anne found herself holding her breath. He was finally explaining things, after all these months. But the edges of her world were also fraying, splitting in two. She was torn between her desire to go down this mathematical rabbit hole with him and her need to play nursemaid. He was too old, too frail for this right now.

"I'm not traveling anywhere," she insisted. "I'm going to stay here with you."

"You must seek the girl in the future," he said, laying his hand over hers. "I have dreamt of nothing else."

It was true. Anne had been witness to his nightmares as he slept. He always seemed to be working something through in his mind but having difficulty doing battle with the horrors playing out in his dreams. Often, he awoke in a fitful delirium that rendered him useless most of his waking hours. Now a sinking feeling was settling upon her, heavier than stone. She squeezed his hands, a silent request that they could talk about this later.

But he continued. "The girl will be here at the Château du Clos Lucé in some five hundred years. There shall be a wedding. A wedding between two men. That is the date you must seek."

Anne wondered, not for the first time, if Leonardo was losing his mind. Not only was he proposing time travel, but a marriage between two men? Such a wedding would be impossible.

She pushed the ale toward his lips, trying again. He would feel better after he'd taken a sip. But Leonardo grew agitated with her effort. He pushed the drink away with a forceful swipe. It caught her off guard, and the goblet skittered across the floor.

"Do not ignore me, girl!"

Anne stared at him, her dark eyes flashing.

"I'm not ignoring you!" she snapped like a quill flexed too tight. "You are making no sense!"

She regretted it the minute she said it, but the goblet was still spinning behind her and his outburst had been most unfair.

He glared at her for a beat, and she wondered if the tantrum was going to grow worse. But when he finally spoke, his voice was once again logical and calm.

"I understand your confusion, Anne. But I assure you, what I am saying does make sense. We cannot use magic to find the girl in the future. If we do, the Goddess will know of our plans. She is still working against you. The only thing she cannot control is an object crafted from science alone. That is why the clock is so important."

Anne forgot her frustration at the mention of this vile creature. The Goddess had lied to her only a month ago, and she had declared herself

Anne's enemy. No one knew better what a formidable opponent she could be.

"Alright then, if we do get the clock working," she said, her mind spinning out a new idea, "perhaps we turn back time to return you to good health instead? We could go back to last year, just before you fell ill?"

Despite his weakness, Leonardo raised himself on his elbows. "When I pass, you must not attempt to change the order of things."

She stared at him.

"Death is natural. It comes to all of us. When death is unmolested, when it comes at the end of a long life, it is a gift. Something to be cherished and respected." Leo spoke slowly now as if to see if she was grasping his words. "It is only premature death, when life is stolen from someone too young, that we must concern ourselves."

Anne went to the window and looked out across the gardens, desperation pushing her there. She didn't entirely know what to think about what Leonardo had just told her. She didn't want to believe him.

"Find a way to meet the girl," he said. "Her fate is connected to yours. Her happiness as well as her suffering. I want you to live, regardless of what the Goddess has in store for you. It is the reason I painted Lady with an Ermine. It is the sole reason I built the clock, to keep you safe. Because I will not be here to protect you."

She turned.

He lay back on his pillow, tired from his effort. "Domenico's card of Mortalité has foretold it. I do not fear death. I only fear leaving you unguided in this world."

Her skin wriggled, the maggots inching upward. It was that card, that horrible card, gagging her. Death. Death. Death. A tear spilled down her cheek.

"Please, Leo."

He held up a hand. "There is no time for sentiment. I am clear of mind today, and I must tell you the rest. There is more to say. But before I do, you must burn the clock's final blueprint. And then return the algorithm to the hidden alcove."

Anne wiped the tear away and returned to the desk, the compliant apprentice once again. She sorted through his mess of papers until she found the clock's designs. It was complex, but she knew it well.

He nodded his encouragement. "Burn it, child. No one can know the clock's full design. Not the key nor the spring you shall install later today."

Anne couldn't handle another fight. Burning these documents seemed like a terrible idea, but against her better judgment, she folded the parchment and set it to the flames. She winced as she watched the corners curl into nothing.

"Now the algorithm," he urged. "Return it to its hiding place in the desk."

She fumbled as she tried to place the scroll into the hidden compartment. Anne had just burned Leonardo's greatest design, his final masterpiece, and she didn't even know why. But she wanted to get it over with so she could sit by his side and dab his forehead with a cool cloth.

"Close the drawer, Anne."

She searched for the peg on the side of the desk. It was hard to concentrate as the maggots continued to crawl. The drawer clicked shut just as Domenico arrived at the door of Leonardo's suite. Anne's gaze snapped to the Italian artist standing there.

Domenico issued a graceful bow, grey ringlets swinging at his neck. "Forgive my coming unannounced," he said smoothly. "I come to offer my assistance. It is said your recovery goes slow. I thought you might require someone who could help settle your affairs. Perhaps there is paperwork that needs tending?"

"That is kind of you," said Leonardo, "but Anne has things well in hand."

Anne's gaze slid to the desk. The chaos there didn't look like things were well in order. But she remained silent, not sure yet how to play this.

"Everything is as it should be," said Leo with a smile. "My apprentice knows the purpose of every document, of every journal."

"Are you sure?" said Domenico, scrutinizing the mess. "Perhaps someone with more experience would be better?"

Leo waved a bandaged hand. "I have faith in my apprentice. She understands me. A messy desk is a sign of a working mind. And my mind is not yet finished."

Anne's master had told her nothing of what to do with his papers. He'd given her no hint of how to settle his affairs. But she knew Leonardo da Vinci well enough to understand him. He wanted his old adversary at a safe distance.

"All is in order. I assure you," said Anne carefully.

Domenico pulled at the corners of his moustache, one of the bull horns sticking up a little higher than the other. "You are lucky to have someone so young and so competent at your side, Leonardo."

Leo beamed. "That I am."

"Then perhaps I shall only proffer the clock's key, so I can bear the burden of its maintenance," said Domenico. "It is too much to ask Anne to be responsible for everything. At least allow me to relieve her of that burden."

Leo narrowed his eyes.

Domenico chuckled. "Come now, old man. Can you not see the impracticality of your proposal? Anne shall not be able to care for the clock indefinitely. She will one day return to England. Let me bear its burden. As one of your oldest friends. I shall see that the clock lives on."

Leo did not return Domenico's smile. Neither did Anne.

"Let me be clear," said da Vinci, slow and cold. "I have declared Anne Boleyn the keeper of the key. She alone will care for the clock. She alone will tend to its upkeep."

"But that is not rational, da Vinci," said da Cortona.

"Do not press me further," Leo bellowed with a voice louder than Anne had heard in weeks. "And you shall not attempt to take the key from her."

Anne watched these two men, their eyes locked. There was so much beneath the surface, she couldn't begin to understand it. There was certainly anger on both sides, that much was obvious. Distrust too. But somewhere below that, she thought she also saw something that looked like pain. Maybe even a lingering vulnerability.

"As you wish," said Domenico finally, with a softness that felt like obedience, called to his master's side to heel.

Leo closed his eyes, strangely peaceful now.

"Come and sit with me, Domenico," he said. "Anne has an errand to run."

Anne raised an eyebrow. It was unlike Leo to ask Domenico to spend any time with him. They detested one another, didn't they? She had been certain of it. But something had just transpired between these two men. Something she did not comprehend.

"Go now, child," said Leonardo. "I should like to spend some time with my old friend."

Anne edged toward the door, stinging at the dismissal. Domenico lowered his head and pulled a chair alongside Leo's bed. She couldn't help but glare as he tucked the old man back under the blankets with a tenderness that seemed entirely out of place.

"Perhaps I could read to you?" he asked. "Would that be pleasing, Leonardo?"

"Mmmm, yes," Leo whispered. "That would be nice."

PRESENT DAY
CHÂTEAU DU CLOS LUCÉ, FRANCE

I sat at the table, fiddling with a piece of dry toast. Earl Grey tea steamed in a china cup beside me, a white linen napkin placed in my lap.

It was bizarre to be sitting alone in this grand hall, picking away at a soft-boiled egg, wondering where everyone else was. But I had slept late and my traveling companions had already started their days. I had avoided my room because of the talking painting, and by the time I returned, it was almost three in the morning. The Lady had mumbled endlessly from behind the woolen blanket, so it was hard to get any rest. As a result, my sleep schedule was a bit of a mess.

I had thought about asking for another room, but I didn't quite know how to explain it without insulting Clarisse. She had been so pleased to give me Anne Boleyn's room. Besides, what would I have said? The Lady with an Ermine portrait keeps talking to me and I find it a little off-putting?

The dining room was vast, and the sound of my cutlery clinking against the delicate plate was rather loud in the otherwise silent space. Tapestries adorned with foxes and hounds hung on either side of a wide-mouthed fireplace. The white stone mantel set into the red brick of the wall gave the room a majestic ambiance. Ten leather-studded chairs flanked the mahogany table, thick beeswax candles and a silver bowl piled with fresh apples decorating its center.

"There she is," said Dez, sweeping into the room. "Miss Sleepyhead."

He and Lucien were fresh-faced, each of them wearing pressed white tennis attire. I, on the other hand, was a hair-sticking-up mess.

"Good morning, Ellie," said Lucien, silently judging the smudged mascara beneath my eyes.

I could smell Lucien even before I saw him. The musk of his cologne was so strong it almost gagged me. Lucien d'Amboise and I had never been close. There was a polite formality about our relationship. I think he had always been jealous of my best friend status with his soon-to-be husband. Lucien liked to have Dez for himself. It was the reason I had backed off when they started dating.

"Good morning, Lucien," I returned, jamming a huge piece of toast in my mouth, determined to be the savage he probably thought me to be.

Lucien was nice enough, of course. He was exceedingly handsome, exceedingly smooth, exceedingly irritating. I had never found a way to break through his carefully polished veneer. He was too coiffed, too polished, especially for a guy like Dez.

My best friend was like me—a "no frills" kind of person. He was a cantankerous, messy scientist whose fingers were always a little bit purple from the gentian violet stain in the biology lab. Lucien's hands were manicured, his outfits immaculate. To be honest, I never understood what there was between them.

"Where is everyone?" I asked, swallowing down the mouthful with a loud slurp of tea.

Dez shook his head. "Didn't get up in time to be on the planning committee, eh?"

Lucien winced at my poor manners and turned away. He poured a couple of fluted glasses of ice water from the sideboard and passed one to his fiancé. "We have a full day, don't we, Desssmond? We are going to play tennis and then head into town for our suit alterations."

I frowned. I didn't like that Lucien used Dez's full name either. He pulled the "z" sound a fraction of a second too long, and it made him sound like a snake. Besides, nobody called him Desmond. It sounded ridiculous.

Dez raised a glass. "That's right, El. We won't have time to babysit you. So you're going to have to hang out with someone else today. And it's not going to be the Trio. They started working on the wedding cake this morning while you were sawing logs. They said they'd be in the kitchen all day."

"And Lily?" I asked. "I was thinking we could explore the library today."

"Lily and my uncle are planning to do that," said Lucien with a careful smile. "They seem quite fond of one another. It might be good to let them spend some time alone getting to know each other. If you catch my meaning."

Dez gave me a devilish grin. "Guess that leaves John."

My heart sank. Suddenly I regretted taking such a big bite of dry bread. It sat like a sponge in my stomach, sucking up all the liquid inside me. I hadn't been planning to avoid my boyfriend-ex-boyfriend. In fact, I was grateful we'd had the discussion in the hall yesterday, agreeing to be just friends. But spending the entire day together seemed a little intense, given the status of our relationship.

"That leaves John what?" asked John, looking as rumpled as me. His hair poked up from his crown, and there was a big white blob of toothpaste in the corner of his mouth. He wore the pajama pants I'd given him for Christmas last year. The ones with the reindeer pattern and a big grinning Santa Claus on the bum.

I had to admit, the sight of him made me smile. Lucien looked as unimpressed with John's state of disarray as mine.

"You guys can explore the place," said Dez with a cheeky grin. "There's a ton to do outdoors on a beautiful day like this. There are bikes in the building on the north part of the property. And horses in the barn if you want to go for a ride."

John rubbed the back of his head, and more hair stuck up. My heart fluttered despite myself. It made him look even sexier than usual. I pinched my leg to get my thoughts under control.

"That sounds fun, doesn't it, El?" said John in his usual good-natured way.

There was a hint of shyness there, but the stiffness was gone. Clearly, he'd meant what he said yesterday.

* * *

The pedals circled beneath my feet as I sailed down the dirt road, the wind caressing my skin. The trail encircled the poppy fields of the Château du Clos Lucé. John was ahead, and I made a point of not falling behind. Despite our casual sightseeing fun, I was not prepared to let him win.

We had cycled all over the area, transfixed by the scenery. Elegant sailboats drifted along the sparkling water of the River Loire, their white sails picking up the gentle breeze. The Renaissance town of Amboise was spectacular, with its French shutters and rustic lanterns, as though it, too, was preserved in time.

We had only planned to go out for a couple of hours, but somehow the day had disappeared. We had stopped at an open-air café and indulged in strawberry crêpes and cream for lunch. Later, we enjoyed lemon gelato on a wooden bench in town while watching the boats go by.

The day had been wonderful, just as Dez had promised. Being tourists in this magical place made it feel like old times. And now that John and I were just friends—and we didn't have to talk about what had happened between us—we didn't have to reach into that dangerous emotional territory. We kept it light, and it felt good.

Now that we were returning home to the Clos Lucé, John looked over his shoulder and smirked, picking up his pace. There was something playful in his gaze, and we both understood the game.

Before I knew it, I was pedaling as hard as my legs would allow, wind whipping through my hair. I would not let him beat me. He was in the lead, but I forced the pedals into a frenzy until I overtook him just past the bridge over the babbling brook. I swerved hard, cutting him off, so he couldn't get across the narrow bridge before me.

"Nice try," I yelled over my shoulder. "But you're not going to win!"

I could hear him laughing as I left him in my wake.

I continued to push, driving full steam ahead. Feet flying, muscles surging, heart revving like an engine. I howled with victory, the sound echoing through the forest.

When John finally arrived at the bike barn, I was standing beside mine with a gloating smile.

"Was that the best you could do?"

He pulled up beside me and hit the brakes. "You cheated."

I crossed my arms, still breathing hard. "You've got to up your game, John. I mean, you're dealing with a crazy person here."

He leaned back with a smile, straddling his bicycle. "So true. Crazy, but cute."

I cringed at the reference to our past relationship, but I was invigorated from the race and only willing to return the playful banter. We had agreed. No heavy stuff.

"Hey, do you think we're allowed to take out that paddleboat?" I asked.

We returned the bicycles to the racks and took the footpath to the duck pond. Weeping willows spilled like waterfalls along the walkway, and we enjoyed the shade as we passed. John bumped me with his shoulder, body-checking me into the heavy leaves of a willow, and I screamed. I gave him a playful shove in return.

"It looks like you two are enjoying yourselves," said Clarisse from behind a curtain of branches.

I smelled the vanilla scent of her perfume before I saw her behind the tree. An elegant, floppy straw hat covered her head. She cradled a large basket of wildflowers—pale blues and whites in the afternoon light.

"Clarisse," said John, surprised. "We didn't see you there. I almost threw Ellie right into you. Sorry about that."

She laughed. "Oh heavens, don't apologize. I love to see young people enjoying themselves here. And besides, I heard you coming up the laneway."

My cheeks turned pink. I was the one who had been howling at the top of my lungs as I cycled toward the barn.

"We were having a race," I blurted, a little louder than necessary.

"That's right," said John with a shrug. "Ellie beat me—for the first time ever." He bumped me again with his elbow.

Clarisse's dimple almost completely covered the confusion behind her smile. She must have been wondering what the deal was between the two of us. I gave her a nervous laugh, grateful she was too polite to ask.

"Well, try the paddleboat next," Clarisse suggested. "We had it made from a blueprint we found in the library. It is a Leonardo da Vinci design. If you walk through the woods, you will see several inventions we commissioned, so tourists can better understand his genius."

"That's amazing. Thank you," said John.

"Did you say you found a blueprint of Leonardo's in the library?" My academic instincts were kicking in. "Could we see it?"

She turned toward the château, the low basket loaded with wild-flowers hitched over her arm. "But of course. We have many of Leonardo's text. I believe Lily and Maurice have been there all day. You are welcome to view them any time."

"Holy shit," I said as she walked away. "Can you believe that? We've got to check it out."

John gave me a goofy grin, the same one that had made me fall for him in the first place. He grabbed my hand and pulled me toward the duck pond. "Not before we try the paddleboat."

There was a clip in Anne's stride as she returned to her master's chamber, an excitement she hadn't felt in weeks. For some reason, she had a good feeling about this version of Leonardo's final spring.

A wall of stale air collided with her nostrils as she entered, so thick with illness it almost stopped her in her tracks. The doctor had ordered the windows shut and the curtains drawn to manage the old man's decline, and for the last week, they had been forced into darkness, breathing only damp air and foul smells. Still, Anne reluctantly had to admit it might have helped. Leonardo was sitting up in bed, waving her over.

She picked up a run when she saw him motioning. At his bedside, she placed the spring in his hand and produced a ceremonious curtsey. She might as well have been giving him the queen's priceless crown jewels.

Leonardo did not match her optimism right away. His brow was furrowed as he inspected it, lenses perched at the end of his long nose.

Anne bit her lip as she waited. The spring was such a complex little thing, it made her head spin to look upon it. The goldsmith had insisted it could not be made. If not for her regular pestering, she doubted it would have ever found its way into existence. A regular spring formed a swirling outer coil, curling clockwise from top to bottom. But inside the larger coil lay a thinner, more delicate one snaking up in the opposite direction.

Leonardo had explained its logic several days ago when a previous version, once again, had failed to pass muster. The main coil would adjust time into the future, while the smaller one would adjust time into the past. They worked in harmony, forward and back, an exacting balance of science and genius. As Leo had promised, it was a device crafted at the very edge of magic itself. Anne still had trouble believing it would actually work. But if it really could bend time, it was the most incredible device she'd ever seen.

She watched him, not daring to breathe. His petulant tongue curled into the dimple of his lip as he scrutinized it. After a long moment, he let out a little whistle.

"You've done it, Anne," he said, his eyes flicking to hers.

She took a step forward, still unable to believe it. This was usually the moment when there was a follow-up to this statement. A "but" or a "however" that would clarify the little improvement or modification that remained.

"Do you mean...this is it?" she asked incredulously. "The final spring?"

Leo grinned. "The final spring, indeed."

He laughed now, low and hacking, and she threw her arms around his neck. He hugged her back, groaning under her enthusiasm. His thin body flexed as he roared, a sound so infectious, soon she was howling along with him. They laughed like it was old times, like they were both healthy and the whole world was theirs to enjoy.

"I can't believe I'm holding this spring in my hand," he wheezed, when he could catch a breath. "You've actually done it, Anne Boleyn."

"Did you doubt me?" she giggled.

"Maybe a little," he said, falling into fits once again.

When she could finally catch her breath, she blinked away tears that were streaming down her cheeks. "Do you think you are strong enough to come with me to install it? I could assist you down the stairs. We could manage it together."

His laughter wilted at her question, and then died between them.

Anne found herself wishing she hadn't suggested it. He looked at her then, his eyes awash with disappointment. He didn't need to respond. They both knew the answer.

She took his hand. "Never mind, Leo. I shall go install it now, and I will tell you all about it when it is done. We can celebrate together."

"Thank you, child," he said softly. "For this spring...for everything..."

She was suddenly unsure of what to say. He wasn't normally one to flatter. More often than not, she'd thought him overly critical. But in this moment, his words made her cheeks burn with pleasure.

"Before you go, there is a bit more business to discuss," he said, restoring some of his usual bravado. You need to fetch the key for the clock from the drawer of my night table. Right at the back."

Anne frowned. She already had the key, hidden in the secret pocket in her dress. He had insisted she carry it with her every day. But the time for arguing had passed. There was no point in asking questions. It was easier if she just did as he asked.

She rummaged through his night clothes, feeling for the item the old man insisted lay within. Sure enough, at the back of the drawer, her fingers fell upon it.

"What is this?" she asked, pulling out the key with a look of concern.

The key was elegant in its design, but nothing like the fishhook style of the one she kept in her pocket.

Leonardo gave her a watery gaze, a little grin pulling at the corners of his mouth. "That," he said nodding at the thing in her hand, "is the false key. The one written about in the scroll I showed you. Every day, you must set the false key upon my desk when you are away winding the clock with the true one. We shall use it as bait."

Anne was no longer following. She had not read the verse on the parchment in the secret drawer when he had showed it to her. The mirror writing had taken too much effort to decode. Besides, it was the algorithm he had wanted to discuss.

"Bait for whom?"

"Domenico da Cortona, of course," he said simply. "He plays a false game, but we still don't know what it is."

Anne nodded. She was delighted to know Domenico hadn't been successful at playing Leonardo for a fool. It had been difficult to tell these last few weeks, when they had been acting like long-lost friends.

But now she understood. Leonardo was playing his own game. And he was far smarter than da Cortona.

"Tell me about him, Leo. I find him so duplicitous, so difficult to understand."

He nodded. "Domenico is an agent of the Garridan's Trifecta."

"What's that?"

His gaze darkened, and he gestured for her to come closer.

"The Trifecta is a magical faction, made up of the three most powerful witches in the world," he said. "Their power is so profound, they have been able to shield their identities for years. But it is well known that their purpose is very dark, very black magic."

"Then we should confront him. We could force the information from him."

He shook his head. "It would do no good. Even the Garridan themselves do not know who the Trifecta are. And besides, whatever Domenico's true intentions, he will never tell. It is best to play along with his game and catch him at one of our own." He jutted his chin in the direction of the key in Anne's hand. "If Domenico takes the bait, then you know he understands the clock's secret function. And this particular clock, in the hands of the Garridan's Trifecta, would be most disastrous. Most disastrous indeed."

* * *

Anne glanced over her shoulder as she gripped the spring. The hall was empty, and for that she was grateful. At midafternoon, the servants were attending to other parts of the castle. The groundskeepers were out trimming the hedges. The cook and his people were in the hot kitchens preparing for dinner. A few minutes ago, a page boy approached her, and she had shooed him away with a handful of coins with another letter for Marguerite.

But for a group of monks that had passed through on their way to chapel, the great room was deserted.

Anne peered into the clock's inner mechanism, the gears clicking away with a happy rhythm. The location of the spring was not obvious, and for a moment Anne found herself wishing she had not burned the blueprints. Did the top of the spring affix to the lattice hammer on the left or the right? Was the spindle hitched to the log wheel or to the cog of the drive train?

"Come on, Anne," she whispered to herself. "Don't panic now."

Leonardo had designed the clock so the piece's placement would not be obvious, and she had to concentrate as she felt along the underside of its ticking heart. She held the final spring in her left hand while searching for the hidden spot with her right. Thankfully, the images of the design came back to her in flashes, and she navigated her way by touch.

The little hole took some time to discover, but when she realized the design was upside down from her position above, and she would have to do it all in reverse, her movements became more certain. Her sixth finger grazed the hidden place for the spring, and she flipped up the latch with her nail. She bit her lip, letting her eyes gaze up at the heavy-beamed ceiling as she concentrated.

"Okay, Leo," she whispered. "Let's hope this works."

She exhaled slowly and used her right hand to attach the spring's top end. Then, holding that in place, she snagged the bottom of the spring along her thumb, bending it forward until *snap*—the little device clicked into place.

Before Anne could even be sure of her success, the great hall began to swirl, spiraling inward and down, sucking the air from her lungs. The floor opened into an impossible helix, all the objects in the room falling into it. The chairs, the tables, the candelabra, all tumbled downward, circling like objects in a drain, then vanishing through the blackened center. A deep indigo light pulsed from within the void, and she felt the pull of the floor coiling in on her too.

Her arms were no longer solid, no longer made up of muscles and bones. They flexed and twisted like coils of rope funneling downward. Her hair, her body too, corkscrewing into the ground.

The vortex ticked like an enormous metronome, spindles and gears clicking wildly, lattice hammers nattering. Bells chimed, deep gongs echoing down, down, down the eddy. Anne couldn't get enough air to scream, not even to whimper, as her whole body became part of the spring itself, drilling deeper into the earth.

Just as she thought she might be pulled into the oblivion completely, the cavernous coil reversed direction. It bounced back on itself, vomiting her from the void. Now Anne was being thrown, feet first, her malleable body spiraling backward, toward the surface. A low bass note rose in pitch, like a finger sliding up the neck of a lute, as she was jettied from the deep blue vortex, along with the furniture and the candles and even the clock.

She gasped as her lungs became whole again and the air was restored around her. Her stomach roiled, and she put a hand to her mouth to wipe the spittle from her lips.

When it stopped, the great hall was just as it had always been. Leonardo's clock stood majestically at the center of the room, the marble cherubs shimmering in the sunlight, the device's hour and minute hands steadfastly keeping time. Only a faint indigo light shimmered from the underside of the mechanism where the new spring had just been installed.

PRESENT DAY
CHÂTEAU DU CLOS LUCÉ, FRANCE

The duckweed in the pond was thicker at the edges, and a mother mallard and her babies trailed a line through the green. The sun was shining, the air was warm, and for the first time in months I felt relaxed. Amazingly, I hadn't thought about my research or my usual obsession with academia for days.

The town of Amboise had a magical quality to it that I couldn't quite put my finger on, but it soothed the edges of my frayed nerves. The Loire Valley was not only filled with medieval castles and quaint lace shops but also with fields of heather and little farmhouses dotting the countryside. It wasn't pretentious or grandiose, but comfortable and quaint, and every day it beckoned to us to explore.

John and I had become inseparable over the last few days. We were the late risers of the group, and somehow the two of us always found ourselves alone at the breakfast table, hair mussed and bleary-eyed, making plans about what we wanted to see next.

Despite our rocky start in the garden back home, we had fallen into a comfortable rhythm here in France. We'd had leisurely picnics on the castle grounds and taken the horses out for a gallop in the poppy fields. We had gone for long hikes to check out Leonardo da Vinci's many inventions. The forest path that surrounded the château was filled with his contraptions. A set of enormous bird wings hung from the trees—a creation intended to be a flying apparatus. A hexagonal tank meant for military encounters loomed large in a clearing. There was even a wooden bicycle by a fountain in the gardens—apparently, the first of its kind ever developed.

Our favorite spot was the duck pond. Every day, just before lunch, we paddled around the mucky water and fed the mallards. There was something about the way we sat facing each other in the little boat, John's muscular upper body flexing as the craft bobbed left and right. I would sometimes catch him staring at me with a faraway look, and it made my cheeks burn despite our strict friends-only status.

"What did you think of Lucien's serenade to Dez last night?" John asked, pedaling casually as the paddleboat cut a line through the green.

We'd gone out to an open-air karaoke festival as a pre-wedding event, and Lucien sang some horribly romantic French love song to Dez in front of an adoring crowd. Lucien turned out to be a surprisingly good singer, and he wandered among the tables with his microphone as the other French tourists sang along. When he got to the verse, he dropped dramatically onto one knee in front of Dez and belted out, "I love you, Dessssssmond." Frankly, it was the most nauseating thing I had ever seen.

"It was nice," I lied. "But I liked the Titanium Trio's song better."

John laughed. "Yeah, they got a standing ovation and everything."

The Titanium Trio had ended the evening with a choreographed performance of a disco song by some obscure band from the '70s. Three thin voices belted out the disco tune and mimicked John Travolta's finger-pointing hip thrusts in unison. I'd seen their act before, but it always made me smile. They had won first prize at the Kingston community center talent show three years back for the same number, but they threw in some new stuff for this performance. Bernice did an impromptu mashed potato, while Gerty performed the robot. Grapes stole the show when she did a surprisingly good moonwalk across the castle's lower ramparts. It was so smooth, it would have made even Michael Jackson proud.

"What do you think of Lucien?" I asked.

I hadn't confessed my true feelings about Dez's fiancé to anyone, but I wondered if John, too, had noticed how obnoxious he was.

"He's great," John said cheerfully. "I don't know him very well, but he seems to make Dez happy."

"Do you think so?" I heard myself saying a little defensively. "Don't you think he makes Dez...different?"

John tilted his head. "What do you mean? Dez isn't different, he's just happy."

I threw a piece of bread to the mallards at the side of our boat, determined to hide my disgust. Dez *was* different around Lucien. That much was certain. Even if John was too kind to notice.

"I hate how the same ducks always take the bread," I said, changing the subject. "They are the pigs of the duck community,"

We watched as the largest mallards shoved the smaller ones aside and snatched up the food. I tried shooing the biggest ones away, but they still made off with the best scraps. If John was surprised by the abrupt change in conversation, he didn't seem to mind.

"You've got to throw it farther," he said. "Here, give me a piece. Let me show you."

I passed him some crust, and he lobbed it across the pond. The larger ducks scrambled to get to the food, but the young ones were faster. The babies scooped up the bits before the older ones could steal it, and John whooped with triumph.

"How'd you throw it that far?" I asked, happy that we had moved away from the subject of Lucien. "I can't get it past three feet."

He winked. "You've gotta use those pipes, El."

I tried again, but the bread landed in the same place.

John stopped pedaling. "Maybe if you get on your knees, you can get a little height."

I frowned. The idea seemed rather dangerous, but something compelled me to do it. I had never been one to back down from a challenge, and I didn't want to look like a chicken. Besides, I was determined to feed the babies. They were the ones who needed to grow after all. Gripping the sides of the paddleboat, I shifted my weight until my knees were in the seat. The boat pitched and wobbled, but John steadied us with his hands across the bow.

"Raise yourself up a little," he coached from below. "And throw it as hard as you can. Trust me. It'll work."

I gave him a skeptical look but followed his instructions all the same. Now that I was committed to the idea, I wanted to see if I could do it. I pulled myself upward until I was kneeling in the seat.

"Like this?" I gripped the edge of the craft as it wobbled.

"Yep," he said encouragingly. "Now throw it."

I pulled my arm back as far as it would go and heaved the scrap of bread, determined to get past the pig ducks closest to us. As I threw, my weight shifted under me and the momentum carried me forward. The boat bobbed left and then right, as I screamed. Before I knew it, my body was pitching over the edge, and I made a heavy splash in the water.

I sucked in a mouthful of pond scum, startled by the sudden cold. I was a decent swimmer, but the water in my lungs was terrifying.

"Ellie!" John's voice floated from above, mottled and murky through the water.

I tried to right myself and push toward the surface, but my chest was tightening. I clutched at my throat, coughing into the water, but that only had me sucking in more pond scum on my next breath. I began to sink, desperate to grasp what end was up. Panic paralyzed my arms and legs, and there was nothing I could do but descend through the slimy depths.

There was a splash nearby, and then someone was dragging me upward. I sputtered, choking and coughing again to expel the stinking water from my lungs.

John held me steady. "I'm so sorry. Are you okay?"

I heaved in my first full breath of clean air, relief flooding through me. My feet found their footing on the squishy pond bottom as I took another gulp and then another. I wiped the goo from my eyes, John's muscular arms still firm around my waist.

"I'm okay," I gasped.

"Oh God, I feel so bad. I didn't think you'd go overboard."

John picked a long, green weed from behind my ear. As he flung it into the water, it stuck on his finger. He had to flick it a few times before it came away. Despite my quasi-near-death experience, I found myself giggling. The whole thing seemed so ridiculous. I would never have drowned. My feet were actually touching the bottom.

"I must look fabulous right now," I said, slime trailing through my wet hair.

"You look beautiful," he returned. "But you don't smell that good."

Now both of us were laughing. The intimacy of the moment, both of us covered in duckweed, John holding me in his arms in a smelly pond. Of course, I had fallen in the water, and of course, John had pulled me out.

I wasn't sure how it happened but something inside me went quiet. That nagging voice that questioned everything in my life finally shut her mouth, and the only thing inside me was warmth. The brick wall I kept so high around myself just didn't seem important, and I let it fall away. I wrapped my arms around his neck and pulled him to me. Right then and there, I wanted John more than anything in the world.

We stopped laughing. There was a yearning in his gaze, a tenderness that made me remember a time when we had been happy. A time when I thought nothing would ever come between us.

I kissed him tentatively, exploring his mouth, his tongue. He returned it with a longing and a hunger I hadn't felt in months. The water rippled around us as our passion ignited, keeping us warm against the cold.

John hooked his thumbs through the belt loops on my shorts and drew me closer. I pushed into him, eager to feel his strong body against mine. We stayed like that for a long time, kissing in the duck pond, without a care in the world.

"Ellie?" called a voice from the water's edge. "What are you guys doing in there?"

John and I looked over, our romantic interlude interrupted. Lily was dressed in a fine orange silk gown, a large, white feather in her hair. She wore an extra-long string of pearls that came all the way down to her waist, and she carried a peacock-blue handbag.

"Lil?" I frowned. "Why are you all dressed up?"

She squinted, pushing the glasses up her nose. I had seen so little of Lily all week, I had almost forgotten she had come with us to France. She hadn't even joined the gang for karaoke last night, begging off with some excuse about how she and Maurice had to explore the library.

"Have you forgotten the pre-wedding brunch?" she called. "It's already started."

My hand flew to my mouth.

"Oh shit," I said, disentangling myself from John's embrace. "Dez is going to kill us."

MAY 1519
CHÂTEAU DU CLOS LUCÉ, FRANCE

"Leo, we've done it," called Anne as she dashed through the door.

She had run the whole way from the great hall to Leonardo's room, and she was having trouble catching her breath. A line of perspiration had collected on her lip, and she swiped it away in a most unladylike gesture, but she didn't care. Her master was going to be thrilled with her news.

A single candle burned at Leo's bedside, and she had to step over the books and papers that littered the floor. The shadows danced along the curtains of his four-poster bed, shimmering like apparitions in the sputtering flame. Leo lay sleeping, long and deep, his little cat curled up in the crook of his arm. His lenses lay on his pillow, with a book butterflied across his chest. It was common for him to nap now to keep his strength up for the other parts of their day when he needed the full force of his mind.

Anne lay a hand on his nightshirt and gave him a gentle jostle.

"Leonardo," she said, "I installed the spring. And you won't believe what happened next."

The old man did not stir. For a moment, she couldn't even be sure he was breathing.

"Leo?"

She stopped, the room's shadows suddenly growing in on her. Her mentor lay as still as a stone, as fragile as she'd ever seen him. His yellowed beard had become patchy. His cheeks were sunken. And the smell of death shimmered around him like a shroud.

Dread swept over her, a winter frost settling on her skin.

"Please wake up," she begged.

Anne poured him into her arms, desperate to hold him, to have his reassuring whisper in her ear. Breathing in his scent, she was filled with a sense of standing at a precipice. This couldn't be the end. She wasn't ready.

Something sharp exploded in Anne's chest, and she found herself choking on tears. She couldn't help but think about all the times they'd spent together, the endless months of collaborating on ideas for Leonardo's blueprints and engineering designs. The sporadic arguments, the passion for science, Leonardo's petulant sense of humor. The earlier days of walks in the meadows, of chasing Salaì through the fields, having picnics by the duck pond as he sketched the landscape.

Most of all, she loved the quiet evenings, when no one else was around. The hours they spent by the fire talking about the possibilities of the universe, looking into the night sky, and wondering what lay beyond.

She cried now, deep, rasping breaths she could no longer contain. Her whole body shuddered as she buried her face in his beard, letting the little hairs of his moustache tickle her skin with the feeble rise and fall of his chest.

"I shall never know another soul as brilliant, as kind as you," she whispered.

Leo's eyes fluttered. "I should think it was about time you noticed." He spoke so softly she almost didn't hear it.

Anne looked up.

He dragged a tongue over parched lips. "There isn't much time left, my child. Death is coming for me."

"No." She moaned, gripping his night shirt with clawed fists.

Anne broke into another puddle of sobs, but Leonardo did not shush her nor tell her to stop. He simply patted her back and waited patiently for the tears to come to their natural end. When she was done, he brushed a stray hair behind her ear.

"I always wanted a daughter. Did you know that?" he said tenderly. "But for someone like me, that was never a possibility."

She sniffed. "Why not?"

"Life is complicated, I suppose." He gave her a weak smile. "But instead, I found you."

Anne wiped the wetness from her cheeks. She'd always wanted a father like him too. Her own father was more focused on matters of court than matters of his own family. And whatever effort he did apply, he spent it on her brother George. For Thomas Boleyn, daughters were nothing more than obligations. Leonardo, on the other hand, had recognized Anne's talents and helped her grow. He had believed in her, in spite of her sex.

Leonardo took her hands into his, his eyes sweeping over her sixth finger.

"I remember the day I discovered your little secret," he said with a melancholy smile. "This wonderful extra digit. It was the reason I knew you would be special."

She allowed the warmth of the memory to bloom in her mind. It had been a warm spring morning when she'd met Leonardo riding his bicycle on the front lawns of the Clos Lucé. He'd been so vigorous then. So full of life.

"What I didn't realize was how I would come to love you," he said. "I am so very proud of you, Anne. Do you know that?"

Her eyes met his, but she didn't respond. She couldn't. There were no words.

Anne could only sit with her hands in his, looking upon this man she loved more than anything. They sat for a time in silence, allowing the pain to lay itself bare between them. There was nothing else to do but accept what they had to face together.

"I have left my last will and testament on the desk. I should like you to oversee the funeral."

Anne forced a nod. She would do whatever he asked.

Leo touched her cheek now with such tenderness, it could have been the caress of an angel. "There is one last thing, my child. You must promise not to use the clock to try to save me."

Her eyes grew wide. She didn't want to promise that.

"Please don't ask that of me, Leo."

She knew now, that clock was the only thing that might actually save him. Perhaps she could go back in time and do something to change the course of his illness. Maybe she could prevent it from happening at all. It wasn't something she had truly believed could be possible, but now that the clock's spring had been installed, maybe there was a way.

"No, Anne," he insisted. "That would require a twisting of the universe, a tempting of the fates. It would give the Goddess a way to deepen your curse."

She bit her lip, trying to stop the ache that was rising through her chest like floodwater, threatening to drown her in it.

Fatigue was making grey circles beneath his eyes, and his breath hitched. "As a father loves his daughter. Promise that you'll not try to change the course of my death."

Her gaze locked with his, but there was no stubborn man looking back at her any longer. The only thing that remained were the benevolent eyes of the father she loved.

"I promise," she heard herself say.

Leonardo relaxed into his pillow and closed his eyes.

The exchange had clearly worn him out, and so she waited, allowing him to rest. She would wait for him forever if he wanted. She would do anything he asked. Anything at all.

Anne gathered him in her arms again and held him, smoothing her fingers across his weathered skin.

"Can I get you some ale, Leo?"

His lips parted. "Find the girl."

He went still in her arms, a lifeless weight. Nothing more would come from him. She knew it the moment he passed. The light had left his eyes.

She did not move. Her arms cradled his body, but his life force was gone. The room fell silent, just the lurching shadows in the flame of the candle for company.

Her soul ached to join his, wherever it was heading, and it yawned and stretched against its living edges. But she could not. No more than he could stay with her. And she found she had no choice but to set him free and leave a gaping hole in her heart that could only ever belong to Leonardo da Vinci.

A darkness crept into her heart as she let him go. Her beloved Leonardo was gone.

Anne breathed in and out in the quiet of the room, waiting for the wave of emotion that would wash her away forever. But it didn't come. As the seconds turned to minutes, and the minutes turned to nothing, the room seemed to harden around them. The air, the brick walls, the wood-beamed ceiling, they were stiff, inflexible, depleted of life. And as the shadows crawled across the wall with the setting of the sun, sinking behind the horizon in a crack in the window shutters, she felt herself harden in the same way. She had become an empty vessel, as empty as the one she held in her arms.

They were a frozen picture of grief, forever etched in the memoirs of time.

PRESENT DAY

CHÂTEAU DU CLOS LUCÉ, FRANCE

Debussy's dulcet piano music played from small speakers on the sidewall of the garden. Clarisse had decorated the space with soft white paper lanterns that hung like fairy charms in the trees. Tiny silver lights trailed the trunks of the most ancient oaks, as though magic had been born in this very place.

The white linen tablecloth fluttered in the breeze, set with blue earthenware dishes just a shade darker than the sky. The hues of green in the gardens surrounding the picnic site shimmered with life, celebrating their luscious varieties. The emeralds of the manicured grass, the darker hunter greens of the thickened forest, the soft, earthy shades of the frizzy ferns and mosses that climbed the weathered tree trunks.

"Everything is so beautiful, Clarisse," I said, picking a stray piece of duckweed from my wet hair.

John and I had managed to run back to our rooms and change, but there hadn't been time to shower, so I was still sporting a few green lovelies in my dark hair. Thankfully, we had made it to the party just as the others were having drinks.

Lucien's mother smiled, her dimple flashing. "I wanted it to be perfect for my son and his new husband."

We raised a glass of champagne for the impeccably dressed wedding couple, with lots of oooohs and ahhs from the Titanium Trio. As usual, Lucien was dashing in a tailored striped suit with a white V-neck underneath. Dez, too, was perfectly dressed in a slim-fit vintage floral dress shirt and pale linen pants. Clearly, Lucien had selected their attire.

I took a large sip to hide my scowl, the bubbles fizzing my nose. I had never seen Dez wear anything other than jeans and a pair of comfy sneakers. And I had to look twice to make sure it was really him.

"You smell a bit funky, El," whispered Dez when the toast was over. "And why is your hair wet?"

"Never mind," I said, giving him a nudge with my elbow.

"My mother has an aptitude for more than decorating," said Lucien boastfully. "She is also an accomplished cook. Everything she makes is delicious. Isn't that true, Dessssmond?"

Dez grinned. "Clarisse has been feeding us nonstop since we arrived. I think I've gained five pounds."

I gritted my teeth against the sound of Lucien's long "s" and tried to breathe past the wafting scent of his cologne. My goal was to be pleasant today, no matter how obnoxious Lucien was.

"Sounds like you have Grapes's talents in gastronomy," I said, trying to be affable. "It's a gift I wish I had. I wasn't lucky enough to inherit it."

Clarisse flushed at the compliment. A whisper of crow's feet at the edges of her smile only made her more beautiful. "We all have our talents, Ellie. Perhaps yours just lie elsewhere."

"Oh, Ellie's got talents," snorted Dez. "She can make a mean bonfire if you ever go camping with her."

I flashed him a warning glance.

"That's enough, Dez," I said, keeping the false smile plastered on my face. I wasn't interested in disclosing my witchy aptitudes to these people.

Clarisse glanced between Dez and me, curiosity on her brow. But once again, she was too polite to ask.

"And what about you, John?" she said. "What is your special talent?"

He shrugged in his good-natured way. "No special talents for me. Other than my research."

"John's doing his PhD dissertation on the Indigenous cultural traditions of the Māori," said Dez, a boastful note of his own coming through.

Clarisse sipped her champagne. "The Māori in New Zealand, do you mean? That's quite far from Canada for a PhD dissertation, isn't it?"

John nodded. "Yep, it's pretty far. But it's an incredible subject. I sort of just fell into the opportunity."

His eyes slid to mine, and I felt the muscles in my shoulders stiffen.

Dez continued. "John was the only student chosen from Queen's University to do an international exchange. It was the opportunity of a lifetime."

My stomach clenched. That marvelous feeling I had enjoyed in the duck pond was sinking away faster than a soggy crust of bread.

"It does sound fascinating," said Clarisse. "And do you plan to move there once you have defended your thesis? I'm assuming you'll be pursuing an academic appointment at a university in New Zealand?"

John glanced my way again, but this time I didn't return his gaze. I was having a hard time maintaining a neutral expression. John's eight-month trip to New Zealand was the one topic we had been avoiding since we arrived in France. And now we were discussing it in front of a group of people we barely knew.

"I'm not sure yet," he said, fiddling with a napkin.

Lucien leaned forward, a sly smile turning up his lips. "Dessssmond and I have been talking about something similar. After the wedding, we will most likely move here to France. Between the Université de Sorbonne and the École Polytechnique, there will be plenty of academic opportunities for us both."

"What?" I blurted.

Dez shrugged mildly. "It's just something we've been talking about. We haven't made any firm plans yet."

Lucien reached across the table and took Dez's hand. "That's true. But I'm working on him." He winked at his mother. "We all do special things for those we love, isn't that right, Desssmond?"

I glared at Lucien. "There are plenty of academic opportunities in Canada," I said evenly. "Dez will find a post-doctoral fellowship at Queen's once he has defended. That has always been the plan. Isn't that right?"

I waited for my best friend to agree with me. We had talked about this for almost ten years. We were going to stick together. Always.

The freckles on Dez's cheeks twitched, a pink flush growing behind them.

Lucien chuckled. "Of course, my fiancé is brilliant. He could work anywhere. But it's not like you'll be staying in Canada either, Ellie. No doubt you'll be packing your bags too."

I set my champagne glass on the table with a tight click. "What is that supposed to mean?"

He blinked with surprise, pretending at his own misunderstanding. "I just assumed you would be following John to New Zealand next year. No?"

My teeth were clenched so tight I couldn't even open my mouth to reply. In that moment, I hated Lucien. In less than a minute, he had managed to expose the deepest pain in my heart *and* threaten to take my best friend away from me.

Clarisse put a hand on her son's leg. "Now, Lucien, we mustn't meddle. Every couple must decide things for themselves."

The tension was so thick it was creating a green smog in the garden. The Titanium Trio stood listening to the exchange with wide eyes. Grapes's caterpillar eyebrows had become two white, unmoving straight lines. Even Lily looked uncomfortable. She had pulled the rope of pearls so tight around her neck, they had left deep red circles on her skin.

John cleared his throat. "I still don't know what my plans are," he said awkwardly. "We...don't...well, Ellie and I haven't thought that far ahead."

I snatched up the wine glass and emptied it now. As the liquid slid down my throat, bubbles stinging my sinuses, I imagined smashing the champagne flute over the top of Lucien's head. Shards of glass flying everywhere. But as soon as I conjured the image, my mind switched and suddenly I was smashing the glass over John's head too. He wasn't exactly an innocent party. He had left me for one academic pursuit, and I knew, in that moment, he would do it again.

"We're not a couple," I said fiercely. "And I will certainly not be moving to New Zealand."

Clarisse lowered her eyes, the strain of the discussion making a blue vein pulse in her forehead.

The brunch party went silent. John stared at the table, and I chewed a thumbnail. Lucien wore the tiniest of smirks. We sat in the garden like that, tense and stormy, for what felt like an eternity. Dez's eyes bore into the side of my head, as though I was the one who had ruined things. Like it had been all my fault, and not his nosy boyfriend's for poking at a wound he knew had been there all along.

Grapes pushed her walker between Dez and me. She shuffled me back a little, feigning an imbalance that was clearly not real, before bumping Lucien out of her path too. Eventually she made her way to a nearby tree.

"Clarisse, I have been meaning to ask you..." Grapes pointed to a stubby grouping of pale yellow toadstools. "I think that is aphalloides. Is it not?"

Clarisse frowned. "Oh?"

"Yes, you should be careful of it when you collect your wildflowers. It is quite poisonous. In fact, that stuff will kill you."

Thankfully, a group of servants dressed in crisp white aprons descended upon us now, and everyone cooed appreciatively that there was something new to focus on. The group began chattering with enthusiasm as the beautiful meal was served. A plate of fresh, buttery croissants arrived along with a lively garden salad. The smell of the fresh bread mingled with the ever-present scent of Clarisse's Christmas vanilla perfume and pulled the group into a heady swoon.

"Jesus Christ, Ellie," Dez said under his breath. "Get it together."

My cheeks went hot. "I *am* trying, you know."

My stomach rumbled, but I wasn't hungry anymore. Guilt pressed down on me, and I could tell by Dez's posture that he was miffed. And then there was John. The champagne glass crashing down on his head was replaying in my mind.

Lucien. *Smash.*

John. *Smash.*

The conversation in the group became easy again, a happy chattering rose through the gardens amid the silverware clinking against the blue stoneware. Even the birds had resumed their singing, and frogs chirped from far away in the duck pond. Clarisse's fairytale party had been restored.

Steaming quiche, beef bourguignon, ratatouille, and duck à l'orange. The dishes went on and on. Everyone was so engrossed with their meal, my little argument with Lucien had faded into the background. For everyone else, that is. I was still fuming.

It was annoying the way that Lucien held up his little pinky when he took a sip of wine, how he cut his food into tiny pieces and dabbed at his mouth with a linen napkin every time he took a bite. It was so nauseating, I couldn't eat a thing. But no one else seemed to notice. By the time the dessert arrived, even Lily had found her way into the conversation, the red spots on her neck almost entirely faded.

"We have been looking for Leonardo da Vinci's lost key," she said. "It's said to have magical powers."

She nodded at Maurice for him to explain further.

Maurice dabbed a napkin to his lips with a dramatic flourish. His movements were so similar to Lucien's, I had to bite back a snarl.

"The key to da Vinci's clock is hidden somewhere in the Château du Clos Lucé. I am certain of it," he said with his usual melodrama.

Lucien waved off his uncle with a dismissive flick of his wrist. "Maurice has been looking for that key for years," he said, sounding a little bored now that he wasn't creating emotional drama at the table. "He has already searched this place, high and low."

"What kind of magical powers?" asked Grapes.

"Oh, it's just a silly rumor," said Clarisse, waving it off. "The people of the Loire Valley are superstitious. They say when the key is turned backward, the clock can bend time..."

"According to the legend," Maurice continued, "there is a special formula for determining how it can be done. But that has been lost too."

Lily nodded. "We've been looking in the library. We were thinking we might find something in one of Leonardo's notebooks."

I had to smile now, despite myself. Of course, Lily would start with the library. She made a practice of hiding anything of value in the library at Queen's University. It was where we had concealed all my father's research last year. So, if the key was going to be somewhere, it would be the best place to start looking.

Maurice raised an eyebrow. "Yes, Leonardo's notebooks are an excellent possibility. Given that it was his apprentice who is said to have hidden the key."

"And who was that?" asked John, apparently fully recovered from the awkwardness earlier.

Maurice's dark eyes bored into mine, and I found myself blinking at him, hanging on his story along with the rest of them.

"I thought you would have already known, Ellie. Given your research on this subject." His moustache twitched beguilingly. "Da Vinci's star pupil was the infamous Anne Boleyn."

MAY 1519

CHÂTEAU DU CLOS LUCÉ, FRANCE

Leonardo da Vinci's funeral was a somber affair. Anne had made it so. Despite the best horses pulling the king's gold-frame carriages, and the throngs of mourners who came to pay respects, the day was brittle with sadness. There was no music, no feasting, no festivities of any kind. Just a long funeral procession that progressed in utter silence.

Anne had attended to every detail of Leonardo's last will and testament. He had requested a burial in the Church of Saint Florentin. So she had arranged it. He had requested a procession of substantial proportion. So it had been the greatest march France had ever seen. The cortège began with the royal family, followed by the chaplain and the rector. Behind them followed the prior and the vicars, as well as the chaplains and the lesser friars of the Church of Saint Denis d'Amboise. Three grand masses were given by the deacon of Saint Florentin, and thirty lower masses were performed at the four surrounding churches of the Loire region. It was the last tear France would shed for Leonardo da Vinci, and all the people of Loire had acknowledged the loss.

Leo had requested sixty beggars to walk behind his casket carrying sixty funeral tapers. And so she arranged that too, opting to walk beside them in allegiance to her master. Leo's request for the beggars had been unusual, but Anne had understood it. Sixty beggars for the sixty clicks in a full rotation of the clock. It was his way of sending her a message, even in death. A message that reminded her she was the one keeper of the key.

"Sixty...always sixty..." Leo's voice lilted through her mind with a ghostly echo.

It was important to him. But in the days since the funeral, she found herself wondering why. Leo had never fully explained the number. Nor what it had to do with the clock's secret function. Nor how to find the girl in the future. The obligations Leo had set upon her were overwhelming, and now that her mentor was gone, she feared she would never understand.

Not that any of it mattered. She wasn't up for the challenge anyway. In the fortnight since the burial, she hadn't left Leo's rooms, except to wind his clock. True to her word, each time she left the chamber, she placed the false key on his desk. Although this had been fruitless too, because each time she returned, the key remained untouched and untaken.

No one had entered Leo's rooms since the day of his death besides Anne. Not Domenico. Not anyone. Only a servant brought her food and ale, but she had refused all other care. She ate little. She slept little. It was all she could do to just sit and stare out the window.

Leonardo's suite was becoming more cluttered by the day. Silver dishes and goblets dotted every surface, half-spilled and discarded. Anne's fine black funeral gown lay on the floor, and she stepped on it each time she crossed the room.

The only thing she preserved with care was Leonardo's desk. It remained strewn with parchments of his writing and blueprints of his unfinished inventions. She didn't want to touch it. That space had been his alone, and it comforted her to see his things as disorganized in his death as in his life.

Anne lay upon the trundle bed looking up at his larger one. It would have been unthinkable to sleep in her master's bed, though it would have been more comfortable. But she no longer cared about those things. She wore her nightgown and Leonardo's velvet dressing gown over top. It still smelled of him, and it was the only comfort she wished for. She had no friends, no family. She wanted none of them. Not even the thought of Henry could stir her heart.

A knock came at the door.

"Go away," she called. She was not interested in a meal this morning.

The knock came again, harder this time.

"I said go away!"

Anne was never one to shout at her servants. Da Vinci had taught her too well that respect was a virtue. But she couldn't help herself.

Despite her acerbity, the door opened a fraction.

"I do not want breakfast today," she yelled, balling her fists like a petulant child.

But the maid did not appear. Instead, the calm dark features of Marguerite de Navarre graced the doorframe. Her old friend stood with her hands gathered at her waist. Her hood and gown were a rich black velvet.

Anne stared. For a fortnight, her mind had been empty, frozen shut, a void of darkness. But now, as she looked upon the king's sister, bile rose in her throat. This woman, dressed in black, was a fraud. She had no right to wear the color of mourning, to feign grief. She knew now that Marguerite hadn't cared for Leonardo da Vinci at all.

"Did you not hear me?" Anne hissed in a low voice. "I said... go...away."

Marguerite approached, her intrepid steps clicking on the stone floor.

"I wish to speak with you, Anne."

"Well, I do not wish to speak with *you*!"

Marguerite sat at the edge of Leonardo's bed, the way she used to when they had been friends. She looked down at Anne on the trundle, her dark hair tangled, night clothes musty and soiled.

"It is time I explain things," said Margueritte. "I owe you that."

Anne refused to look at this woman. "You owe me nothing."

Marguerite reached for Anne's hand, but she jerked it away.

"Listen to me," said Marguerite. "I owe you an explanation. And once you have heard it, you may not forgive me, but it will help you understand."

Anne leapt to her feet and scurried across the room. "I need no explanation. I know what you are."

"And what is that?"

"A pretender!" Anne spat. "You and Claude and Francis are all snakes in the grass. You enjoyed the glow Leonardo cast upon you. He brought you greatness. He brought you enlightenment. But when it mattered, you treated him like one of the dirty beggars from the funeral procession. When he needed you, you did not come. And for that, you do not deserve my time nor my friendship."

Marguerite looked down, regret flashing in her eyes. "Aye, it is true. I did not come. Not even when you sent letters." She shook her head. "But the truth is, there was nothing I could do to save him."

Anne felt her cheeks burn. "That is a convenient excuse, isn't it? I suppose it didn't occur to you he might have taken comfort in your visit?" She pounded her chest. "That it might have comforted me too?"

Marguerite rubbed her forehead. "It occurred to me, yes. It occurred to Claude too. She has done nothing but cry for you since your letters started coming."

Anne crossed her arms. It was one thing for Marguerite to offer her own regrets. But to make excuses for the girl who used to be her best friend? The one who had promised to remain steadfast, no matter what. It was unconscionable.

"Do not speak to me about Claude."

Marguerite voice was steady and careful now. "My words may sound like excuses, but I offer them as comfort now. I shall not come again. It is too dangerous."

Anne crossed her arms.

Marguerite's eyes softened on Anne's face. There was a look of such tenderness it almost killed Anne to see it. "The reason we did not come, is because of your curse. You are a danger to everyone who loves you, to everyone who comes near."

Anne huffed. The only reason for her curse was because she had defended Claude against her horrible father. It had been Marguerite who was supposed to kill him. But when she could not, Anne had done the deed in her stead. And this was how they repaid her?

"Look," said Marguerite. "Claude's firstborn, Louise, died because the

Goddess wanted to punish you. The Goddess has no interest in Claude otherwise. If we continued as friends, all of Claude's children would suffer the same fate. Can't you understand she had to protect her babies?"

Anne's stomach clenched. She had always wondered if it was her fault baby Louise had died. The Goddess had implied as much.

"The same holds true of myself and Francis," continued Marguerite. "The Goddess would come for us all."

Anne turned her gaze out the window to the ornamental gardens below. "You're lying," she said coldly.

Marguerite pressed on. "Even Leonardo could not be saved. It is true, I might have prepared a draught for him. It might have mended him, at least for a while. But he was doomed, Anne. He was doomed because of...you."

The color ran from Anne's cheeks, but she did not turn. Somehow, the ire she held so tight in her core drained away. Beneath it was only a trembling, gruesome horror. Was she responsible for Leonardo's death? Had she killed the person she loved most of all?

"Leo understood this. I have the letters to prove it." Marguerite pulled a package of envelopes from a pocket in her dress. "He was determined to stand by you. To give his life so you might be spared."

Anne snatched the letters from her hand, still unwilling to believe this woman's lies. She scanned the pages, looking for the evidence to verify the story. Anne alone would know the veracity of Leonardo's handwriting. And she would know if Leo had been part of this whole thing.

As she read page after page, she realized Marguerite was speaking the truth. Leo had given his life to protect her. The Goddess had come for him, and it was all Anne's fault. Her world melted, and she felt herself sink into the chair by the window. No longer able to stand.

"I didn't know," she whispered.

Marguerite touched her cheek. "He didn't want you to know. He didn't want you to bear that burden, when you have so many others on your shoulders."

Anne thought about all those conversations, all those times she had seen him poring over books, whispering in his dreams, trying to find a solution to help her. Anne Boleyn, the fire child cursed by the Goddess. Anne Boleyn, the master apprentice who Leonardo loved as a daughter.

"It is the sole reason he built the clock," said Marguerite. "He built it for you. Not for Francis, as he would have had others believe. It was Leo's last attempt to save you from yourself."

Anne put her head in her hands, unable to believe what she was hearing. The hardened shell she had so carefully built over the last few weeks came away, and the only thing left was the fragile broken heart beneath. She began to weep, slowly at first, then dissolving into great, racking sobs. Marguerite pulled her into her arms and hugged her, the way she used to all those years ago.

Anne cried for Leonardo. She cried for Louise. She cried for the loss of her friends. But mostly she cried because it was all so hopeless.

Marguerite held her as she bawled, wrapping her in a motherly embrace, patient and kind. When Anne's tears subsided, Marguerite pulled away.

Her old friend hastened to the door. "I must take my leave," she said. "But for the sake of yourself, for the sake of Leonardo, you must try to use the clock to make things right."

Anne's cheeks were still wet with tears. "But how?"

Marguerite shook her head, her hand on the latch. "I do not know. Leo did not tell me of the clock's secrets. He feared the knowledge would fall into the wrong hands. You are the only one he confided in."

Anne shook her head. "Leo did not tell me what to do. Not exactly anyway. I really don't know how."

Marguerite winced, pity written in her eyes. "Perhaps that is the case, Anne. But, you must try."

PRESENT DAY
CHÂTEAU DU CLOS LUCÉ, FRANCE

The note affixed to my door was in Grapes's tidy handwriting. *Meet us at the clock for a family meeting, 8 a.m. Bring John.* Grapes had likely snuck it there last night, not wanting to disturb my sleep.

The brunch yesterday had left me unnerved, and I wasn't sure if Dez had entirely forgiven me. After the meal, he and Lucien had gone into town for pedicures, so it was hard to know for sure. Dez was not the beauty spa type, and I found myself wondering if he had enjoyed his foot massage. I imagined him accidentally kicking the aesthetician in the face when they scrubbed the bottoms of his feet. I knew it was terrible, but the idea gave me an odd sense of satisfaction.

John, on the other hand, had been good-natured about the whole pre-wedding debacle. I might have thought he would be embarrassed too, but after the spat, he had just rolled with the punches. It was clear the story of Leonardo's key was as intriguing to him as it was to everyone else, and he quickly fell under Maurice's spell along with the rest of them.

I had to admit, despite my determination to maintain a good sulk, even I had been pulled into the plot. My dreams last night were filled with flitting images of da Vinci's timepiece and that funny little keyhole in its face that was meant for winding.

My tongue still tingled with toothpaste, and I checked my watch before knocking on John's door.

I wasn't sure how to make sense of the butterflies in my stomach. Was it nerves? Resentment? I didn't know. Our kiss in the duck pond lingered in my mind, but it collided with the very public, very awkward conversation at brunch yesterday.

When John opened the door he was shirtless, and I tried not to gawk at his developed biceps, the square of his pecs, his six-pack abs.

"Hey, sorry to wake you," I said stiffly. "Grapes and the rest of the Trio have called a family meeting."

He glanced at the note in my hand and laughed. "Never a dull moment with the Titanium Trio."

It was amazing how John could make everything better with his cheerful outlook on life, acting like nothing had changed between us. To my surprise, I found myself relaxing as we walked down the corridor. We chatted about our plans for the day like we usually did and contemplated what the Titanium Trio might be up to. If John was willing to go on pretending everything was fine, that was alright by me. Two could play at that game.

In the great hall, we found Maurice and Lily helping themselves to the croissants on the sideboard. The Trio were there too, wearing jungle outback gear with floppy hats and khaki pants.

"It's simple mathematics, Bernice," scolded Gerty, pointing at the clockface. "For goodness' sake, have you forgotten the basic geometric principles of a circle?"

As a young woman, Gerty had been a high school math teacher, and she was clearly unimpressed with Bernice's arithmetic right now. I cringed. I had dealt with a few of Gerty's well-intentioned lashings as a youngster, and I knew how it felt. It looked like Bernice was about to rebut with a snide remark of her own, when Grapes noticed us approaching.

"Good morning, sleepy heads," she said. "You're right on time."

John poured a cup of coffee from the sideboard and passed me an Earl Grey tea. As usual, it had just the right amount of milk.

"What are you guys up to?" I asked with a suspicious tone. These three ladies had talked me into some ridiculous schemes over the years, and I always approached family meetings with a healthy dose of wariness.

"We've had an idea, and we need your help," said Grapes cheerfully.

"Help with what?" asked John.

Grapes's eyebrows danced. Bernice stared up into the rafters. Gerty bit her lip in a familiar guilty snarl. I had seen it a million times before. These three had conned me into synchronized swimming tournaments, tap dancing contests, and even a face-painting disaster at the Kingston Fair that left my skin rashy for a week.

"Okay, spill it," I said, crossing my arms over my chest.

Gerty put her shoulders back and raised her hand in a Boy Scout salute. "We're organizing a search party for the key."

John and I exchanged glances.

"Told you," he said under his breath. "You owe me five bucks."

I couldn't resist a giggle. I had placed a bet that the Trio was going to pull us into some crazy baking plan for the wedding cake design. Grapes had been going on about it for days. But John was certain the Trio wouldn't be able to resist the story of the clock.

"We're going to split up into teams," announced Grapes.

I shook my head, sliding John a fiver. "Grapes, the castle is huge. We'll be looking forever."

"It'll be fun, Ellie. We just have to get started," she said. "Maurice and Lily will continue their work in the library. You and John will give Anne Boleyn's room a thorough going-over, and we will take the gardens. We'll make a competition out of it."

I bit back a smile now. This was the Titanium Trio's go-to move. They made everything into a competition. From gardening to dance-offs, it was always more interesting if it was a game.

Lily's cheeks flushed. "It does sound like fun."

Maurice's smile broadened. "It would make faster work if we all helped. We might have a real chance of finding the key."

I took a long sip of tea, thinking it over. It wasn't the craziest idea they had ever come up with. Still the key had been lost for five hundred years. There was no way we were going to find it.

Grapes's blue eyes sparkled with adventure. "It's important, Ellie.

Historically speaking. You could even say it would be irresponsible to not at least try," she said with her best convincing voice, the one I found almost impossible to resist. "We wouldn't be doing it for ourselves. We'd be doing it for Anne Boleyn. She's one of our kin, Ellie. She's family."

* * *

John opened the ancient drawer and peered into the dark void. The drawer, though sticky with oil, held nothing inside. He blew out a disappointed breath.

"God, there's nothing here either," he said.

"That's okay," I called from beneath the desk's underbelly. "A drawer is too obvious for a hiding spot anyway."

We had been searching Anne Boleyn's room for over an hour, now fully engrossed in the Trio's game. If the key had been missing for hundreds of years, then its location would not be obvious. Leonardo was one of the most secretive scholars of his time, so it was going to be harder than opening a sticky drawer. We needed to look for hidden spots, trap doors, that sort of thing. A place so secret no one else could had found it in the castle's long history.

From beneath the desk, I ran my fingers over the wood grain. I don't know why I had decided to get down on my hands and knees and crawl underneath, but something pulled me to it. And every time I ran my fingers over a series of smoothed carpenter's pegs, a little burst of heat tingled through my scar.

Usually, the scar on my right hand only flared up when I was close to an open flame. It was only last year I had learned my parents had my sixth finger removed when I was a baby. After a lifetime of keeping our family's witchy talents a secret, Grapes had finally explained that my scar was the thing that conveyed my fire power. And so, as a general rule, I made a point of ignoring it any time it burned. Still, there was something about one particular carpenter's peg. It made me wonder.

I felt it again, and the same flash of heat trilled up my arm.

"There might be something down here," I heard myself saying.

I hadn't wanted to tell John about the burning sensation. It would have been too hard to explain. But the words sort of fell out of my mouth. Now I was regretting it.

John got to his knees and crawled under the desk with me.

"What is it?" he asked, his face close to mine.

"I-I don't know," I stammered. "It's just...a gut feeling."

The scar on my hand and my talents with fire were subjects I didn't like discussing with John. He had always been supportive, even enthusiastic, about my gifts. He had been there when I had learned to light a candle by blinking the thought of a flame into place. Actually, it was John who helped put out the blazing fire with an extinguisher when it had all gone wrong. Nevertheless, I didn't like talking about it with him. When I was with John, I just wanted to be normal.

"It's these funny little wooden circles," I said. "They seem a little out of place. Don't you think?"

In the shadows, I pushed one of the pegs a few more times. But other than a sharp pain on the side of my hand, nothing happened. John shone the light from his phone at the circle, trying the peg a few times too.

"I'm not seeing anything," he said.

He turned to face me in the small, cramped space. The flashlight highlighted the dimple in his chin, and my stomach whirred with familiar butterflies. I wanted to run my finger over that delicious little cleft and plant a kiss upon it, but I resisted the urge. The sweetness of his breath and the closeness of him made me remember lying in bed, tangled in the sheets, after making love. It made me think of our kiss in the pond yesterday.

But Lucien's obnoxious voice stabbed through my mind, his snide smile cemented in my memory.

"I just assumed you would be following John to New Zealand next year..."

Not bloody likely.

"Forget it," I said. "I was wrong."

We climbed out, both of us frustrated in so many ways. My scar still burned, and I rubbed it with irritation. John slumped at the end of the bed, beside the red velvet curtains tied back around the spiral sconces.

"Wait a second... What is that?" he asked.

He pointed to the blanket strung over the painting on the wall. The Lady with an Ermine painting had stopped mumbling from behind it over the last few days. She had been unhappy about her woolen cage at first, hysterical even, but with a bit of stubborn determination to ignore her on my part, she had eventually given up. After that, I had slept like a baby. To be honest, I had almost forgotten about her.

"Don't!" I shouted.

But before I could stop him, John was on his feet, pulling the cover away. The Lady with an Ermine stared from behind the covering, her lips formed in a thin, angry line.

"I have never been treated so rudely," she sniffed. "Not in all my years."

John stumbled back to the bed and dropped onto the mattress, his legs giving out beneath him.

My hand flew to my mouth, horrified by the animated Lady in all her otherworldly creepiness. But it was John who surprised me more than anything. Could he actually hear her?

"Sweet Jesus," he said. "Did that painting just talk to us?"

I paused a beat.

John's eyes were wide, terrified even, and I struggled to find the words to explain. Obviously, there was a line of impossibility, of insanity, between what he was seeing and what was true. And I was sure, he'd seen nothing like it before. I didn't want to have to be the person to explain it to him. Frankly, I still didn't quite see how she could be real either.

"Of course, I spoke to you," the Lady said with a serious sulk. "I've been trying to give Ellie Bowlan an important message ever since she arrived. But she threw a dirty blanket over me and refused to listen."

John looked at me, his eyes demanding an explanation.

My mouth fell open. How would I explain this strange, enchanted painting? How could I tell him the same painting talked to me back home at the Sleeping Goat?

"Did you put the blanket over this...thing...so it couldn't talk to you?" he asked warily.

I shrugged. "Maybe."

"You see?" she spat. "Ellie Bowlan is disrespectful."

John massaged his temples, clearly struggling to process what was happening. I couldn't blame him. The first time I'd heard the Lady whisper my name, I almost passed out. In fact, I was feeling a little dizzy right now.

"Look," I finally snapped at the supernatural portrait, "I don't want to hear your bloody message. Okay?"

John blinked, disbelief turning to incredulity. "Ellie, are you saying you've been ignoring this possessed painting for a whole week? We have spent the entire morning searching the castle for Leonardo da Vinci's lost key, and there is a talking painting in your room?

"Exactly!" said the Lady. "It's unconscionable."

My shoulders sagged. It did sound ridiculous when he put it like that. Suddenly, I felt stupid. He was right, of course. I sank down on the bed beside him, scratching the scar on my hand.

"Fine," I mumbled begrudgingly. "What do you have to say?"

"I'm inclined to keep the message to myself, after the way you have treated me," said the Lady. Her white ermine hissed. "But Leonardo would not permit it."

My lips pinched into a line as thin as hers, daring her to continue.

"Leo was determined to protect Anne Boleyn from the Goddess. And as the last in her bloodline, he was determined to protect you too. Though I can't imagine why."

At the painting's mention of the Goddess, the blood pooled in my feet and I was glad I was sitting. The Goddess had cursed all the women in my family for generations. But I thought we had gotten rid of her last year.

"I don't understand," I said weakly.

The Lady gloated at my reaction, a flash of teeth in her smile. "Aren't you glad you've decided to listen to me now?"

John leapt from the bed and approached the bewitched portrait, standing only inches from her face. "Is Ellie in danger or something?"

The Lady produced a nonchalant shrug. "She may be, though I don't know for certain. I only know that it's a matter of life and death."

John leaned in further, putting his hands on the gold gilt of her frame. "What is a matter of life and death?"

She ran her fingers through the rodent's fur again, a full pout on her lips. "I only know something shall happen at the wedding between two men."

"You mean Dez's wedding?" said John. "That's in two days. What's going to happen?"

Her eyes flared as she poked a finger into John's chest with haughty disdain. "I don't answer to just anyone, sir. And I will thank you to take your hand off my frame."

John took a slow step back, rubbing his chest in the place where her ghostly finger had connected with his shirt.

The Lady turned to me and cleared her throat. "As I said, I have a message specifically for you, Ellie. From Leonardo da Vinci himself."

"Fine," I muttered. "What is it?"

She closed her eyes and delivered her ghostly missive. "The key that winds the clock is the answer. Find it and protect it. That is your fate. But beware the Garridan."

"Oh yeah? And why should I do that?"

I thought I saw the Lady's lip curl, but she continued. "It is the only way to keep the Goddess from your bloodline."

I threw my hands in the air. "What the hell is that supposed to mean?"

I stared at her now, waiting for an answer. Something to clarify this whole business. But she did not reply.

John stared too, shaking his head as though struggling to clear his vision. We watched as the Lady tilted her head back into its original position, retreating into the oil painting like she had never been animated in the first place. Her body was now frozen in her frame, her voice shimmered through the air with an ethereal electric energy.

Her voice came off in a whisper. "Use fire only as a last resort..."

John blanched. He touched the oil surface, but it was just a regular canvas now.

"Wait. A last resort for what?" he asked.

But the Lady with an Ermine had returned to her inanimate form, a medieval woman, draped in a gauzy headdress, strings of black pearls at her neck, and an oversized white ermine motionless in her lap.

AUGUST 1519

CHÂTEAU DU CLOS LUCÉ, FRANCE

Anne sat in the library, spinning a globe with a half-hearted finger. She had spent many hours with Leonardo poring over the books in this room, and it soothed her to be here now. She remembered the day Leo had come up with the idea for this special little device. How he had ordered a dozen ostrich eggs from the merchants who traded the Africa route. How he had been happy with only the largest ones, demanding flawless shells for his latest invention. It had been weeks of watching him split the eggs and then forming two exacting halves into a perfect sphere. And more weeks after that of Leo carefully etching a map onto the egg's delicate surface. Even the new continents to the east were drawn in. At least, the parts that had been mapped by the king's cartographers.

Leo had been a much younger man then, so full of vigor. How she ached for those times. Those were the days before the Goddess had ruined their lives. Before Claude and Marguerite had abandoned them both.

It had been months since Marguerite's visit to Leonardo's rooms, and it had taken Anne most of that time to find her way back from her heartbreak. When she had learned of the truth from Marguerite, that Leonardo had died for her, it had almost crushed her. For weeks, she didn't even know how to breathe. But as the days passed and Anne recovered a little, she realized it did help to know the truth.

Over the summer months, some of her spirit returned, enough so she could go about her day-to-day business. But mostly, what had emerged was a hardened resolve for her master's vision. If he had given his life for hers, she would carry out his wishes, no matter the cost.

And yet Leonardo's plan had been so vague, it was hardly a plan at all. She was supposed to use the clock to find a girl who could be her twin some five hundred years in the future. But there were many problems with this idea.

First and foremost, she did not know *when* to find this girl in time. Leonardo's algorithm was complex. It required its traveler to know the precise date on the calendar to make the calculations. It really wasn't a simple matter of turning the key at random. And then there was the math to return a person back to their own time. That was a much more serious problem, one she hadn't yet solved. It required consideration of multiple timelines at once, and on every attempt she had become entangled in a labyrinth of arithmetic.

She fiddled with the globe, running her hand along the sea monster etched in the shell. The landmass of South America was laid out, but the northern portions were missing. She considered what life might be like if she ran away to the New World. At least when the Goddess came for her, no one else would get hurt. But that wasn't part of her mentor's plan. Leo had spent the last months of his life designing a solution for her. And though she didn't understand it, she had to try.

The second problem was the girl herself. Anne did not know what message she would deliver, even if she could find her five hundred years from now. She had no idea what terrible thing might befall her, nor how to protect her from it.

The third problem was Domenico da Cortona, of course. He was a Garridan who worked for a powerful Trifecta of witches, but she didn't know what their interests were in the clock. Leo had asked her to discover Domenico's true intentions by leaving the false key on the desk, but even that had failed. Months had passed and Domenico still hadn't taken the bait.

Her heart ached for Leonardo. She thought of him when she awoke.

She thought of him when she crawled into her trundle bed at night. But he was dead, and she had promised not to try to change that. And so she made her way to the library every day, to pore over books, trying to think her way through her master's impossible puzzle.

The volumes of black leatherbound books at the Clos Lucé drew traveling monks and clergymen from all over Europe. Francis preferred to fill his court with scholars and the learned, and there were often scribes and illuminators sitting at the simple wooden carrels, copying texts on all kinds of subjects. Over the years, she had often wondered what they were copying, what knowledge they sought. But Leo had always cautioned her not to speak to them. These men were part of a closed and quiet sect, and they would not have liked to speak to a woman in such a place. Much less on matters of science, mathematics, or the planets.

As she looked upon the men now, one young scribe caught her eye. His tonsure was that of an apprentice, and his shoulders were slumped. She looked a little closer. His master was giving him a silent scolding with a look in his eye that could have been the devil himself.

Anne bit her lip. She had been an apprentice too and knew how it felt to be admonished by her teacher. Though she'd never felt the need to cower the way this boy did. Leonardo had loved her and that was the difference.

She considered paying the young lad a kind word, but she did not. Anne couldn't afford a friend, old or new. She didn't want to put anyone else in danger.

A few scribes shuffled to the exit, the young apprentice among them, and Anne followed them out. She would wind the clock and then perhaps return to Leonardo's chambers to search through his personal notebooks again.

Midday was a good opportunity to tend to the clock because so many of the house staff and courtiers were busy with daily duties. When she approached Leonardo's masterpiece, she was pleased to see the hall was empty. Opening the frontispiece, she gave the gears a cursory review, ensuring they did not need oil. Then she put the key in the lock and wound it clockwise three times.

As she completed her task, something flitted through her mind. An idea that tickled her brain like the tip of a feather. Could she make a small experiment? What if she turned the key counterclockwise, just one click? According to Leonardo, it would take her back only one hour.

She still hadn't determined how to return to her own time. But what did it matter? If she couldn't figure it out, she would live her life an hour behind the one she lived now. The more she thought about it, the more she liked the idea. It might mean making progress on Leonardo's unsolvable problem.

"What do you think, Leo?" she whispered. "Should I give your clock a try?"

She had taken to talking to him. He never answered, of course, but it comforted her to imagine he was there at least in spirit. Anne glanced over her shoulder to be sure she was alone and then turned the key counterclockwise.

A strange shade of indigo blue shot from the clock's internal gears and engulfed the room in a cerulean haze. It was so thick it could have been a fog on the Scottish moors. She squinted, trying to adjust to this strange new light, just as everything began to spin. The great hall coiled, round and round like a tornado, pulling everything inward and Anne along with it. Her arms, her legs, her whole body circled, bending at impossible angles. The sensation was so disorienting she almost vomited.

Inside the vortex now, the physical world fell away, blue murky objects melting into nothing, her body disintegrating into vapor, until she thought she could see the threads of time themselves. They swayed like a woven blanket in a breeze, a rainbow of strings twisting and turning in on themselves, creating and recreating the surrounding objects. They grew like vines, weaving and winding together, and then undoing themselves all over again. Things existing and not existing simultaneously in an eerie void of blackness and color.

Somewhere far above, she could see the stars in the sky. The moon orbiting the earth. The earth orbiting the sun. She could see everything all together, and yet she could see nothing. Only a million tiny threads entwining, braiding into a growing and regrowing fabric.

And then, without warning, it stopped. The threads of time simply ceased to exist. The great hall was the same as before, the room was empty, the towering marble clock reaching up into the high-ceilinged rafters. It was so seamless, she couldn't be sure it had happened at all.

Anne blinked, trying to make sense of it. She checked the time. It read forty-nine minutes after ten. Precisely sixty minutes backward in time. Leonardo's favorite number.

Sixty, always sixty.

She peered at the frontispiece, thinking to retrieve the true key from the winding mechanism. She didn't want someone to find it while she was exploring. But to her horror, the key was gone.

With her heart in her throat, Anne scrambled across the black-and-white floor, hoping maybe it had fallen. Panic pushed the air out of her lungs as she circled the clock's marble façade, scrutinizing every cherub, every artistic curve and line. Her heart lurched as she scanned the floor, the furniture, even the mechanical lion Leonardo had presented to the king last year.

When something jumped in the secret pocket of her dress, she let out a long breath. Her fingers grazed the golden fishhook key's smooth surface. It had returned to the same place she always kept it. Of course, it had. She was its keeper, after all.

Anne imagined her mentor now. He would have given her an encouraging nod and then urged her to complete the experiment. Determined to validate her progress, she returned to the library. Just as she hoped, the monastic scribes were hunched in their carrels, copying their texts. And the young apprentice was being scolded by his master.

Leonardo's globe spun on its axis, as though someone had just dragged a finger along it. She held a hand in front of her face, as solid as the former version of herself. Yet her former self had vanished.

"So, I can only exist in one time or another," she noted.

Anne padded from the library, wishing to make further study. Leonardo would have insisted upon it. As she returned to the great hall, one of the kitchen boys nodded his cap in greeting. She reached up to touch the clock's iron hands, as solid and functional as it was the day of its unveiling. But as she did, the tips of her fingers were already unraveling.

Her hair, her lips, her arms were turning into gossamer strings again, weaving and wrapping around themselves in an endless dance. The indigo light shone from within the clockface, and the threads of time unwound, unwound, unwound until it all went black.

* * *

Long, curly hairs tickled Anne's cheek.

"Thank heaven, she breathes," someone called to a group of courtiers standing above her.

Anne's eyes fluttered, her stomach roiling. Her vision was blurred, and a steady beat boomed through her ears, so deafening she might have been inside one of the bass drums in the king's marching band. She brought a limp hand to her scalp, and a bit of blood came away on her fingers.

"Are you quite alright?" Domenico asked from somewhere far away.

Anne struggled to right herself, but she found she couldn't sit up. Her body was still too fluid, too infirm to push against the floor.

Now two arms were wrapping themselves around her back, cradling her neck, gentle and steady. Her stomach lurched at the sense of being upright, the muscles in her body quaking. As she swooned, Domenico put a bolstering arm around her waist, holding her there until she could stand on her own.

"You gave us quite a fright, Mistress Boleyn," he said, the crow's feet around his eyes crinkling with an encouraging smile.

Anne couldn't help leaning into him. She wasn't sure what had gone wrong with her experiment, but she was certain she wasn't supposed to wake up on the floor in front of a group of strangers.

"I've not been feeling well lately," she lied.

Domenico's eyebrows creased with concern. If she hadn't known him better, she could almost see true sympathy lurking there. "I am sure you have been quite heartbroken by Leonardo's passing. He was a good man," he said gravely.

Anne frowned. Something about his voice, the reassurance of his arm at her side, confused her. Domenico seemed genuinely sad.

"I just need to rest," she insisted.

"Of course. I shall assist you back to your room."

Anne had no choice but to agree. She was still far too weak to make the journey across the castle by herself. Bobbing her head in thanks, she allowed Domenico to lead her from the hall, grateful at least to be away from the watchful eyes of the crowd.

"I'm staying in Leonardo's rooms," she said weakly, as he led her past the library, the brick walls of the castle still shifting this way and that.

Domenico gave her a wistful nod. "I understand. Being close to Leonardo's things, his life's work. It must be a comfort to you. Leonardo taught me so much when I was a young man. Did you know that? I owe him a great deal."

There was a softness in his tone, a humility she had never heard before. But Anne didn't encourage the conversation. She was too muddled to think. All she wanted was to get back to bed.

"I knew him years ago in Florence," he continued. "He was a much younger man then. Quite brilliant. Quite handsome. He was my teacher. He taught me about design, about art, about...life."

Anne frowned, struggling with this new version of Leonardo's nemesis. Had she misunderstood him all along? Leonardo had once been Domenico's mentor too. Although it was many years ago, it was possible there could have been a time when they had been friends.

When they arrived at Leonardo's chamber, Domenico helped her inside. She let him guide her as they passed the mess of dishes piled in the corner, her funeral dress strewn on the floor, and Leonardo's desk still piled with blueprints and textbooks.

"There now," he said tenderly. "You must get your rest. You need to be strong, now that you don't have Leonardo anymore."

She sank into the soft pillow. The bedding still smelled of Leonardo, and it comforted her.

"Thank you," she whispered. "I owe you for your kindness."

He patted her hand. "You owe me nothing. I only want to help. These are difficult times for you, dangerous even."

The bump on her head was still throbbing, but she was clear-minded enough to catch his last sentence.

"What do you mean...dangerous times?"

"Oh, only rumors, Anne," he reassured her. "There are those who question things out of the ordinary. Small-minded people, speaking of small-minded things, I'm afraid," he said sadly. "For example, there are those who question why da Vinci chose a woman for an apprentice."

Anne didn't like where this was going. Why was he telling her this?

"And some have noticed that sixth finger on your hand. Despite its beauty, there are those who find it...odd."

She pulled her hand under her sleeve. Anne had always made a point of hiding it, but in her grief she had become careless.

"There are even rumors that you are a witch. Imagine such a thing." He tutted at the absurdity of the thought. "But you mustn't worry about that right now, Anne. Just close your eyes and rest."

PRESENT DAY
CHÂTEAU DU CLOS LUCÉ, FRANCE

We perched on the edge of the bed, staring up at the talking painting. The Lady with an Ermine hadn't spoken a word since turning back into a regular portrait on the wall, but her self-important voice still rang through my ears.

John sat, hands on knees, waiting like he was watching the final scene of a TV show and didn't want it to end. But I knew she wouldn't have anything more to say. That was the trouble with magical things. They didn't operate within a normal set of rules. There was no logic. You just had to take what you got.

I wasn't sure where to go next with John, given how cringey it felt to talk about magic when he was around. I really didn't want to tell him about how this same painting spoke to me at the Sleeping Goat back in Kingston, nor did I want to discuss what she'd said about using my fire power as a last resort. I never used my witchy talents for anything, so the Lady's whole message seemed rather obvious. She had been so desperate to deliver her great wisdom, but in the end it was a no-brainer, and I couldn't help thinking it was all just a horrible waste of time.

"Ellie?" called Lily from the doorway.

She held a battered, brown book in her hands. Her cheeks were so flushed she looked like she had sprinted from the other side of the castle.

I breathed a sigh of relief. Lily had come to my rescue, and I wasn't going to waste the opportunity. Besides, there was something in the way she said my name. The tiniest hint of enthusiasm was lurking there.

Lily almost tripped over the woolen blanket on the floor, but I whisked it out of the way. She marched across the room to the desk. Maurice trailed behind her like a lost puppy, waving a silver-framed mirror.

"Our librarian is a genius!" he cried.

John was still staring at the painting, and I gave him a nudge. When he finally dragged his gaze away, I gave him a pleading glance. One that begged him silently to keep our exchange with the Lady with an Ermine between ourselves.

"I'm glad you turned up something, Lil," he said, rolling with the punches, "because Anne Boleyn's room has been a total bust."

I shot him a look of thanks, something soft nudging my heart. The Titanium Trio arrived now too, looking hot and flustered. Gerty's hat flapped over her eyes. The pink needlepoint hearts on Bernice's pockets sagged with perspiration. Even Grapes, the fitness queen, was a little sweaty. I smirked when I saw them. They had been so determined this morning as they had arranged our search teams, but now the lot of them were looking like it was time for a nap.

Lily set the timeworn leather book on the desk. Its pages were yellowed and water-stained, the edges tattered and jagged.

"I need to find the right page. Hold on," she said as she peeled through the journal.

Grapes pulled me aside, the rest of the family talking over each other as they compared notes.

"Did you find anything?" my great-grandmother asked quietly.

"No," I said. "How about you?"

I wanted to tell her about the painting, but now was not the time. I would tell her later when no one else was around, when we could puzzle over its meaning together.

Grapes frowned. "I just don't understand it. We used our best summoning charms, and I was sure we'd find something, but we came up empty."

Maurice clapped his hands amid the chaos and chatter.

"We found a clue in one of Leonardo's notebooks," he announced. "His notes are written in mirror image. But Lily suggested reading the text from this mirror and voilà...there it was."

The group went quiet.

Lily blinked from behind her large frames, her eyes finding mine. She pointed to an illustration on the page surrounded by notes scratched out in the margins. The handwriting was entirely indecipherable because everything was written in reverse. I wondered about the patience required to do such a thing in my own research. Writing from a mirror would double the time to get anything done. Leonardo was truly a genius, but his eccentricity couldn't be underestimated.

"It's right here," she squeaked. "Look. It's a design for a desk with a secret compartment."

"I recognized it right away," said Maurice with a puff in his chest. "This desk usually sits in Leonardo's chamber, but we moved it here when the wedding party arrived to accommodate the Trio."

Lily pulled me toward the notebook. "Ellie, look at the design. The desk has a hidden cubbyhole. Just on the underside."

Lily wore that "crazed librarian" expression, the one she always got on the verge of a discovery, and I felt myself being pulled back into the game. It was one of the reasons I loved having this woman as my research partner. She loved her books as much as me. And Lily had found a far more tangible clue than the useless message from the talking painting.

She passed me the looking glass and I studied the image, slowly adjusting to what I was seeing. The hidden drawer looked to be on the right because the image was backward. A special section on the desk's underside highlighted one particular area in greater detail. I nodded as soon as my eyes landed upon it. A modest carpenter's peg marked the trigger to access the secret alcove.

The scar on my hand sent a jolt of electricity up my arm and my mouth went dry. "Wanna give it a try?"

Lily grinned. This was our thing, and we'd do it together.

We crawled under the desk. It was easier with Lily because she was smaller than John, and we curled in together. She shone the flashlight from her phone onto the notebook as we sat underneath, discussing the correct location of the peg as we interpreted the mirror image design. Lily took a second to get herself oriented, but I already had a hunch which peg it was.

"I don't think that's right," she said when I tried pressing one of the buttons. "The one we want is behind the drawer. It needs to be pulled forward. See?"

She dragged me back to the notebook, her flashlight stinging my eyes. But as I studied it, I realized she was right. Everything was making sense now. John had the drawer half open when I thought I'd found the right peg the last time. I had been close, but not quite.

"John?" I called up. "Can you pull the drawer out all the way? Like you did before, but farther."

"You bet, boss," he said lightly.

I resisted a smile. I knew he loved this stuff as much as Lily and I did. It was the thing that brought us all together in the first place. He yanked the sticky drawer open with a few good jolts. I could feel him straining to get the last of it open, the underside of the desk bumping against Lily and me.

"Hang on, almost there," he called.

When the drawer finally came away, I slid my fingers along its outer edge, searching for the peg that would make my scar burn hottest.

"You want that one there," said Lily, pointing the flashlight to where I should be looking.

The back of the drawer was tricky, but as my fingers made contact, my scar exploded with heat. The peg was smooth against the wood's surface, exactly like all the others, but as I pressed it, a narrow chamber clunked opened from behind the drawer.

"There's something in there," I gasped. "Lily, you do the honors."

I held the flashlight for her as she reached in and pulled out a small roll of parchment tied with a frayed red ribbon.

"Holy moly," Lily breathed, the light reflecting off her lenses. "We found it."

We scrambled from under the desk, helping each other from our awkward squashed positions. Lily gave my hand a squeeze and pushed the scroll into my palm.

"You read it, Ellie."

I gave her a wicked grin and pulled the ribbon from the scroll. The yellowed paper was brittle, and I was careful not to damage it. Smoothing it out, Lily held up the mirror again as the family crowded around.

Two keys forged, one false, one true.
Da Vinci's clock starts time anew.
The Garridan shall pursue it well.
But the keeper of the key shall never tell.

Below the verse, a complex algorithm was written in the same meticulous handwriting.

"That's the formula for the clock," shouted Maurice with a hint of hysteria. "I've been looking for it for years!"

"Let me see," said Gerty, pushing her way through the group despite her birdlike proportions. She studied it for a moment with a scowl, a little hair twitching on her lip.

"It is a formula, alright," she said. "But it's complicated. I wouldn't mess around with something so complex. Make one mistake and you could find yourself in the wrong time, with no idea how to get back."

"Does anyone know what a Garridan is?" asked John.

Maurice snatched the scroll from Gerty. "It doesn't matter. Ignore the verse. We have found the algorithm. Now we just have to double our efforts to find the key."

Frankly, I didn't like the rudeness of his gesture.

"Actually," I said, making a point of sliding the scroll from his fingers. "I think it matters a lot. The verse goes together with the formula. You can't take one without the other. According to the message, there were two keys forged. One real. And one fake. So we are looking for two keys, not one.

Lily nodded. "I agree with Ellie and John. The verse goes with the formula. And if Anne Boleyn was Leonardo da Vinci's apprentice, then she was probably the keeper of the key. So we need to figure out who the Garridan was. Because I'm willing to bet the Garridan was the one who took it from her, and that's how it got lost in the first place."

AUGUST 1519

CHÂTEAU DU CLOS LUCÉ, FRANCE

Anne smoothed the russet fabric of her skirts, and they swished stiffly as she headed for the door. Her sleeves were slashed with luxurious ivory silk, Henry's pearl B necklace gracing the white of her neck. Today she was determined to play the part of a lady of the court, but the lace scratched her skin and the French hood irritated the bump on her head. She couldn't wait to return to her room and get back into her comfortable nightdress.

Domenico's words from yesterday clung to her like the stench of rotten fish. He seemed to be genuine, truly concerned for her welfare. And yet, his message was dangerous. Witchcraft was no laughing matter.

Anne was vulnerable, that much was clear. Now that Leonardo was gone, he could offer her no protection. And there would be no safeguard by the royal family either—Marguerite had made that plain enough. If Domenico was spreading rumors of witchcraft about her, there would be little she could do to stop it. And yet yesterday, Domenico had been kind. He had spoken of Leonardo with great affection and had been tender with her too. Perhaps he had simply been trying to help. Although every bone in her body told her this was just not so.

She pressed a stray hair into her hood as she strode to the desk to fetch Marguerite's letters. Anne had left them there when her old friend visited after Leo's funeral, and she hadn't thought of them since. But today she was planning to review them at chapel. Taking morning mass at Lauds was most common for the ladies of this court, and she wanted to be seen there. If there were rumors circulating about her being a witch, the best way to fend against them was to appear devout. One rumor might counteract the other. And with the letters tucked inside her lady's breviary, she could study them unnoticed.

Anne scanned the detritus on Leonardo's desk. Blueprints and notebooks lay half open, an inkpot gone dry sat with a ruined quill inside. As she reached for the stack of letters, the realization fell on her like a hundred-pound stone. The false key was missing.

She inhaled. Anne had laid her trap, and finally da Cortona had taken the bait.

Her world swung suddenly into focus. Domenico's interest was not in her welfare after all, and if that was the case, the rumors of witchcraft were weapons in his grasp. The worst thing about them was that they were all true.

Anne felt sick as the realization dawned. She was well and truly in danger. For a moment, the ground swayed beneath her feet, and she put a hand on the desk to steady herself. She could not panic. She needed to measure out her next steps carefully. If Domenico could make a move against her, she required a countermove. But what? She had no equally damaging information to hold against him. She needed his secrets, something she could trade in exchange for her own. But only Leonardo would have known such things, and he was gone, his bones turning to dust in the grave.

"Come on, Anne," she whispered. "You need to think."

When the true key twitched inside her pocket, the idea came to her, as swift as a gale on a bird's wing.

* * *

The great hall bustled with life this time of morning. A group of monks and several clerics shuffled through on their way to the library. Page boys delivered notes bonded with wax seals from all over the country. Men of the merchant guild, draped in furs from faraway lands, bartered their daily trades. A couple of ladies-in-waiting eyed Anne with curiosity, giggling behind their manicured hands.

She settled herself upon a chair and tried to blend into the scenery. Arranging her skirts demurely, she glanced down at the algorithm. It had taken her some time to check, double-check, and triple-check her math, but she had finally done it.

The problem had always been that the traveler required the exact calendar date of their destination. Bending time was only possible with this precise detail in mind. It was the reason she could not find the girl in the future.

But today she didn't plan to visit the girl at all. Anne planned to visit her master. Yes, she had promised Leo she would not use the device to try to change his fate. He was gone, and she meant to keep her word not to change the order of things. But what if she only wished to speak with him? She could seek a date in the past when she knew Leo would be at the Clos Lucé. If she could talk to her master, perhaps he could give her the information she needed to keep Domenico at bay.

The two men had known each other long ago, and they had once been close. That much was clear, Leonardo, she reasoned, would possess some knowledge of Domenico. Something that could give her leverage against the sly Italian architect.

When the last of the merchants left the hall, their booming voices echoing down the corridor, Anne opened the frontispiece of the clock. She wound it clockwise three times, as was her usual custom. And then she closed her eyes and listened. She had to concentrate to get the right number of clicks counterclockwise. The formula was complex, but she was sure the number was twenty-three. That would take her back to the first day she met Leonardo da Vinci, three years ago.

She wasn't sure why this was the specific day she had chosen. Perhaps finding a more recent date would have been easier. But there was something special about it. It was the day her life had well and truly changed, when she had become more than just a girl. That day, thanks to Leonardo, she had become a scholar.

She counted the clicks carefully. A minor miscalculation could send her thousands of years back in time. Or hundreds of years ahead.

"Come on, Leo," she whispered. "Where are you..."

A shimmering indigo light spilled from behind the gears, draping everything in a now familiar blue haze. The threads of time in their vast array of colors began to unravel, the physical objects in the great room spinning and spinning, unweaving themselves into nothing. The redbrick walls disintegrated into a mottling of crimson and brown strings, the black-and-white floor tiles crumbling into grey, until there was only an inky void with the sun and the moon and the planets under a dizzying canopy of stars.

The sensation was nauseating, but this time she was prepared for it. When it stopped, she took a deep breath. Though she was light-headed, this journey was easier than the first.

"Please, please, please," she whispered as she dashed through the hall toward the arched grand entrance. Pushing hard on the heavy oak doors, she took the stairs two steps at a time in a race toward the garden.

Her breath was ragged when she arrived, and the boning of her bodice cut into her ribcage, but she did not care. Because there, on a wooden bicycle, was an old man in a purple dressing gown, a bit of his white nightgown sticking out beneath.

Anne gasped. Leo was just as she remembered, thin and wiry like an elderly spider. His beard was tied with a piece of leather string, and he wobbled atop his latest invention. But the way he moved suggested he was still vigorous and spry. Healthier than he had been in years. She remembered this day well. Anne and Claude would meet Leonardo in several hours. And she would win the old man's affection by being the first to successfully ride his bizarre bicycle.

Right now, he was attempting to ride the contraption himself and having a terrible time of it. Despite her desire to run to him and throw herself into his arms, she knew she had to be careful. They had not yet met, and she needed to win his trust first.

Shoulders back, posture strong, Anne strode across the sunny lawn toward him, the rich green of the grass making a particular spectacle of this strange man in his aubergine robes. Leonardo was struggling to get up enough speed, so when his feet touched the pedals, he tipped over once again. It was just like the first time, when Claude and she had watched him from the upstairs windows.

"Master da Vinci," she called in a steady voice, anxious to conceal her nerves.

Leonardo looked up, his lips puckered with frustration. For a moment he didn't reply, but she thought she saw a ghost of recognition there.

"Do I know you?" he asked.

Anne swallowed. Her story was going to sound unbelievable, but she had decided to be direct. She was betting on this approach. Leo was a clever man, and rather open to surprises.

"Indeed, you do know me. I am Anne Boleyn. We just haven't met yet."

"Come again?"

She issued a deep curtsey. "I am your apprentice. We will meet here in these very gardens several hours from now. You will fall off your bicycle and crash into that stone wall over there."

Da Vinci glanced back at the collection of pink roses on the east edge of the garden whose petals would soon be scattered in every direction.

"I am sorry to be so direct," she continued. "But there isn't much time."

Leonardo studied her with intelligent blue eyes, as though he was trying to remember something but couldn't quite grasp it.

Anne's voice wobbled. "I am from the future.".

Da Vinci did not react with outrage the way a normal man might. Nor did he accuse her of lying. He simply dismounted his contraption and leaned it against a poplar tree, its canopy casting a welcoming cool shade. He touched his pocket briefly but pulled his hand away.

"There is something terribly familiar about you," he said softly. "I suppose you could be a memory. But one that is not from the past."

Anne clasped her hands, an affectionate warmth spreading in her chest. "Yes, that's it exactly. I will know you over these next three years at the Château du Clos Lucé. We will work together on everything. You will instruct me in math and science. You will teach me Greek and Roman literature." She lowered her voice. "And you will train me in the craft."

Leonardo tilted his head, but once again he did not react. She understood well enough that strangers didn't go around discussing witchcraft. But she was so close, she had to try.

"Please, Leonardo. It sounds strange. But it's true."

Anne pulled Marguerite's letters from her dress and handed them to him. He took them from her and pulled a pair of lenses from his pocket. Sliding them over his nose, he scanned the pages. His genius shone so brightly now, she could almost see the gears turning in his mind. He had aged so much these last three years. She had almost forgotten the sparkle in his eyes.

When he was finished, he fixed her with a suspicious look.

"How did you get here?" he asked.

Hope bubbled through her belly, daring to lift her spirits. She had Leonardo's full attention now and she wasn't going to waste it.

"You built a special clock, Leo. I helped you," she said carefully. "It took you an age to design it. A clock with an hour and a minute hand. A clock that can..." She paused. "A clock that can bend time."

Leo's eyes grew wide.

She stepped closer, wanting to take his hand but thinking the better of it. "It's true. You built a clock that can bend time. And it works. It's the reason I am standing before you right now."

The old man's mouth fell open. He staggered to a bench in the shade and sank onto it. It was a full minute before he replied. "I actually did it?"

Now she lay her six-fingered hand on his arm. "Yes, the clock works," she said carefully. "But you died before it could fully function."

Incredulity flitted across his features. "I have thought for years about such a clock. Ever since I was a young man." Leo's hand went to his pocket again, and he played with something inside. "Why have you come?" he asked. "What do you need? I imagine we only have about twenty minutes before you will be returned to your own time."

Anne was amazed at how he could know this. But then again, if Leo had been mentally designing the clock for years, it was likely part of the blueprint he had never explained.

"I'm in trouble," she admitted, a hint of her desperation gnawing at the edges of her voice. "With the Goddess."

Anne didn't have much time to explain, and she covered the basics as well as she could. She told him he had designed a wax poppet to kill King Louis of France. That the plan had gone horribly wrong. That instead of Marguerite committing the dark magic, it had been Anne herself. That it was this act that had set the Goddess's curse against her.

He closed his eyes as she spoke, listening intently.

She told him that he had made her the keeper of the clock's key. That he had dreamt of a girl before he died who would be born of Anne's bloodline some five hundred years in the future. And that Anne was supposed to use the clock to find her to save her from the Goddess.

"But I don't know how to do it," she said. "You only said I was supposed to seek her out during a wedding between two men."

His fingers worked the leather string in his beard as she spoke. When he started to hum a little tune, Anne knew he was well and truly processing her story.

"And what other tools did I leave you?" he finally asked.

Anne frowned. "What do you mean? You left me nothing else. I have been struggling alone to determine my next step. I have searched your notebooks and blueprints, but we threw it all in the fire to keep the clock's design a secret."

Leo crossed his arms. "No," he insisted. "I must have left you something. There must have been other tools. A legacy to help you when I was gone."

She shook her head. He had left her with no other devices. No books, no instruction. She had only the true key. Domenico had taken the false one. But that word Leo used—legacy. He had said it once before, three years ago, when they had defeated the king and his dwarf.

"My legacy for your legacy..."

The realization hit her square between the eyes.

"The Lady with an Ermine!" she exclaimed. "She is bewitched. You painted her for me."

Leo had painted the portrait when the Goddess first cursed her. He had explained that paintings were immortal in their own way. That the Lady would watch out for Anne when he was gone.

"A painting," he chuckled. "That *is* brilliant."

Anne had forgotten entirely about the Lady with an Ermine. The portrait hung in her chambers because Leo had insisted Anne always have her close by. But since his death, she had been staying in her master's rooms.

Leonardo raised a hairy eyebrow. "If this bewitched painting still hangs in the Clos Lucé five hundred years from now, would she not know of such an unusual wedding?"

Anne gasped. Why had she never thought of this? Of course, her master was right. If the painting was still there, maybe the Lady could help her determine an exact date.

"And if I can find the girl, what do I do? What should I tell her?" she asked, ready for more instruction. It was such a relief to speak with Leonardo. He would tell her what to do.

He pulled on his beard again, his gaze unfocused as he contemplated the question. "Unfortunately, I have no idea."

Anne's shoulders slumped. This wasn't the response she'd been hoping for. Disappointment threatened to pull her back into that familiar place of despair. Just when she almost grasped how she might carry out Leonardo's plan, she'd fallen flat.

"I put these in my pocket this morning," he said, producing a small pair of scissors. "Somehow I felt they would be of great importance today."

She took them from his outreached palm. "What are these?"

"Surely you know a pair of scissors when you see them, child?"

Anne was having trouble following again, although this was not unfamiliar when she was having a conversation with her master. "Why do I need scissors?"

He chuckled. "I don't know. But they do come in handy from time to time."

Anne nodded her thanks. It didn't seem like any other great revelation was going to come from him. He had nothing more to offer. Perhaps he just felt sorry for her and wished to give her a small gift. She slipped the scissors into the hidden pocket at her waist, the feeling of defeat weighing heavy.

"You can do this, you know," said Leonardo with a little smile.

She looked up, desperate to believe him. There was something about the tone of his voice. It was so reassuring. This was the man she remembered. The man who had taught her everything.

"I do not know you, but I do have a great deal of faith in myself," he said frankly. "And I would not have made you my apprentice if you were not up for the job."

Anne blinked.

"And that tells me you must be smart. I only select students with great mental prowess. So, my advice to you is, use your mind. Do not look to me for the answers. You must find them within yourself."

"But I have tried. I really have."

He shook his head. "I wish I could do this for you, my child. But alas, I cannot. Sometimes that is the way of the world. One must stop being the student and start being the teacher."

She frowned.

Leo pinched her chin with a fatherly nip. "We must have faith in ourselves, and in our students who will come after. I do not have the solution, but I have trust in you. Perhaps you should think on that, Anne Boleyn."

Anne's gaze flitted to the château, thinking now of the clock and when it might pull her back into her own time. She had been so distracted by the girl from the future, she had almost forgotten about Domenico.

"Leo, there is one more thing. I need you to tell me everything you know about Domenico da Cortona. Every story. Every offense. Every dirty little secret."

Da Vinci's eyes darkened. "Da Cortona...that's a name I haven't heard in years. Why do you ask such a thing?"

"Because he's trying to take the clock's true key."

"I see." Leonardo's mouth turned down, his long beard sagging.

Anne held her breath, waiting for more.

The old man's features grew black. "Actually," he said gravely, "there's plenty to tell."

PRESENT DAY
CHÂTEAU DU CLOS LUCÉ, FRANCE

The underpass that connected the Château d'Amboise to the Clos Lucé was a dripping, sopping mess. According to Maurice, it had been shut to tourists because it was close to collapse after five hundred years of disrepair. Dank water seeped through the cracks in the ceiling, heavy archways buckling under the force of the earth. John and I had already seen two rats running in the dim glow of the wall sconces, and that hadn't made it any more welcoming.

It was one of the only places we hadn't yet explored on the castle grounds. As the rest of the family reorganized themselves in their search for the key, I knew it was our next stop. There was something about the algorithm in the desk, and the weird message from the Lady with an Ermine, that made me want to see it.

Lily's theory about Anne Boleyn and the Garridan had played on everyone's sense of adventure, and Grapes's family game of find-the-key was renewed. The Trio were going to double their efforts in the garden, Maurice and Lily were going to search the dining room and then the kitchens. But I had a special feeling about the tunnels, and John and I took them at a run to see who could make it to the entrance first.

An iron grate installed around the opening in the rock framed a rusty staircase with a sign marked DO NOT ENTER. Under normal circumstances, it would have been impossible to snoop around the museum in off-limits areas. But as house guests, the rules of the game were different.

We descended the steps into the subterranean void, sticking close together now that we were down here. The musty air grew thicker as we went deeper. I wrapped my sweater around my shoulders, grateful I had brought it with me. A set of dim electric lamps, likely installed decades before, dotted the darkened shaft, making a long trail in the blackness like underwater jellyfish.

My logic was this. If Leonardo da Vinci had built a passageway between the castles to conduct secret business with the king, he might have hidden other things down here too. It was out of the way and would have been off-limits to most courtiers and servants. Since the scar on my hand seared with heat beneath Leonardo's desk, I wondered now if it might give me the same kind of sign that something was hidden here too.

"What a horrible place," I said, holding my nose as I trailed my other hand along the slippery rock walls.

John held his phone in the blackness, its flashlight beaming. The dim lamps were a meager help in lighting the trail. Especially worrisome were the slick black puddles, and neither of us wanted to step on another rat.

"It's definitely creepy," he said as we walked side by side. "I wonder what Leonardo da Vinci and the king were up to when they met down here."

The grit from the wall was sticking to my fingers, and I brushed it off before continuing again. I had my suspicions, of course, about the tunnel. Leonardo da Vinci was an enigmatic man, and there was plenty of legitimate literature to prove it. His mirror image writings were a great example of his secretive nature, but there were many others. Da Vinci's painting of the Last Supper, for example, could be superimposed on the original to produce a different picture altogether. I had even seen an analysis of his painting 'Lady with an Ermine' showing another creature had been painted beneath the oversized white rodent that was there today.

But there were social media posts and a few off-brand websites that took it one step further. Some advocated that da Vinci practiced witchcraft. I would never have believed it myself if I hadn't come from such a weird family too.

We walked along in silence, the sound of our steps splashing beneath our feet.

John shone his flashlight up at the arched ceiling. "What did you make of the Lady with an Ermine's message this morning?" he asked as he wiped a drop of water from his cheek.

My eyes shot to his silhouette. This was John's first mention of the bizarre encounter, and I was rather surprised to hear his matter-of-fact tone.

"I don't know," I said with a playful smirk. "But I've never seen you more freaked out."

He laughed, the beam of his torch blinding me for a second. "Hey, she was my first talking painting, okay? Cut me some slack."

I contained a giggle. "You did great. I almost puked the first time she spoke to me at the Sleeping Goat."

John stopped walking, our game of find-the-key suddenly shifting to something more serious. "What do you mean?"

"Oh, well..." I said awkwardly, unsure of where to go now that I had let this little secret slip. "Yeah, there's a replica at the Goat that talks to me too."

John's face was in shadow, but I could see his jaw stiffen.

The truth was, there was a lot I hadn't shared with him about my witchy proclivities. I hadn't mentioned the way my scar itched every time I even imagined a flame. Nor had I told him much about the night in the tower, when he and Dez pulled me from the burning building. We had just skipped it altogether and started dating. It had been easier to pretend I was normal, even though we both knew I was not.

"You mean you've talked to her before? The talking painting?" he asked, a hint of pain stitched through his question.

"Yeah, kind of," I said with a wince. We were treading too far into the deep end of the swimming pool, and I wasn't sure how to swim back. "The portrait in Kingston talked to me a lot last year."

The flashlight caught John's face, disappointment etched in his features.

I shrugged sheepishly, knowing I had to keep going despite my every instinct to change the topic. "She was the one who told me to burn Landon Fishburn last year. I hadn't understood her message until we got trapped together in the tower. But it was the Lady who gave me the idea to use fire."

The glow from the phone was dancing in the puddles along the pathway, and though it was dark, I could see that John's posture had changed.

"Why didn't you ever tell me that before?"

My stomach twisted. We had been through so much, John and me. He had saved my life. And I trusted him completely. There really was no good reason for keeping these things to myself. Maybe I didn't have the courage to tell him everything, because I actually didn't want it to be true.

"I guess, well, I'm not sure," I stumbled, trying to make him understand. "Being a witch is not cool, John. It's actually really scary. Terrifying even."

Silence sliced between us like a blade.

He didn't say anything for a while, but when he did, his voice dropped an octave. "Is that why you push me away sometimes?"

I stood frozen in the darkness, the water drip-dropping in the background, creating an eerie atmosphere between us. His voice lingered with the same vulnerability as the time he asked me if I loved him.

"I don't push you away," I said lightly, trying to take us back to safety. We were in the deepest part of the pool now, and there was no edge to grab onto.

John turned off the light and jammed his cell in his pocket. He walked up the pathway at a brisk pace, shaking his head in the gloom. Before I knew it, he was far ahead, his footsteps echoing through the tunnel.

"Hey, why are you going so fast?" I called.

"I'm not," he said, his spine as rigid as a flagpole. "I'm looking for the key. Isn't that what you want me to do?"

I ran to catch up with him. "John, stop. What are you doing?"

He turned abruptly. "Okay. I stopped! Now what?"

I drew my head back, silenced by his reaction. I had never heard him yell before.

John's jaw flexed in that familiar way. "I've done everything for you,

Ellie. Everything you've ever asked me to do." He was well and truly shouting now. "Whatever you want, I do it. I even went to New Zealand for you. What more can I do to make you trust me? What more can I do to show you I don't care that you're a witch?"

My blood ran cold at his outburst. I couldn't believe John was yelling at me about going to New Zealand. It was the one thing we'd so carefully avoided on this holiday. After months of following his social media posts about him with his super-exceptional research team. After wondering what he was doing every day. After missing him. After wanting him. After wishing I could be there too.

"Oh really?" I growled, my anger surfacing like a festering infection ready to burst. "You have really suffered, haven't you? *You* pursued your life's dreams. *You* got to travel all the way around the frickin' planet. *You* got to see things, to do things you never thought you'd get to do. Well, I'm sorry. But I don't think you can play your sad song for me."

I poked my chest hard. "I was the one who stayed behind. Did you forget that? I was the one who had to watch how much fun you were having on Facebook."

John looked at me then, his features ghoulish in the shadows. He seemed to be studying me, trying to find the person he thought he knew. But the regular me wasn't there. The green of my envy was finally rearing its ugly head.

He leaned against a wet wall and slid down on his haunches. His voice was so soft I almost couldn't hear him.

"You were the one who wanted me to go, Ellie."

"What?" I shouted, still itching for a fight. "Come on, John. Don't back down now!"

"You were the one who insisted."

But I wasn't interested in his broken-hearted whispers. My raw fury had been set free, and I couldn't put it back in the bottle. I didn't want to. It felt good to finally let it out.

"Come on, John. Mr. I-love-you-more-than-anything, Mr. I-missed-you-so-much!" I screamed. "*You* left *me*, remember?"

John looked up at me now, a slow gaze dragging toward my face. His expression was grim, and his words came low. "Maybe you should check your memory, Ellie," he said in a deadly serious voice. "You were the one who brought home the application forms. You were the one who badgered me, day after day, to apply. When I found out I won the scholarship, I told you I didn't want to go, that I didn't want to leave you. But I did because you insisted. And now, you're determined to make this my fault?"

"Oh please," I said, slamming my hands on my hips. "Don't start playing the victim now."

His mouth fell open. "I can't believe you!"

Maybe there was some truth in what he said. I had been toying with applying to the post myself, but I knew I couldn't go. Still, I was mad that John did. Vitriolic even. And a fire was burning in my belly that wasn't ready to be extinguished.

"I was trying to be supportive of your career, John! You can thank me for that later."

He scoffed. "Oh yeah, you've been really supportive. The minute I got on the plane, you started finding excuses about why you couldn't talk. Not tonight, not that night. Then the texts stopped coming. There was just nothing. You left me hanging, without even doing me the courtesy of breaking up. If that's your definition of supportive, I don't want it."

It was a slap in the face. But was it true? Had I been the one who pushed him to go? I suppose the exchange had been my idea. And maybe, once he'd left, I had been the one to make excuses. It was after he started posting on social media, with all those pictures of him and his team. It got me thinking about our relationship, how impossible it was going to be to have a future together.

"I can't follow you, you know," I said darkly. "I have my own career to pursue."

He stared. "I never asked you to follow me. I would never ask you to do that."

"But that's what it comes down to, isn't it?"

Tears threatened to flow and my insides felt raw, burned by the fire that had been blazing just moments before.

"You can go wherever you want, but I'm not leaving Grapes," I spat. "I'll never leave her behind."

There it was. I finally said it. The thing that was bothering me most of all. Grapes was the only real family I had left. And I would never abandon her.

He stood now, his shoulders hunched, his hands stuffed in his pockets. It was a while before he spoke, but when he did, his voice was empty.

"I can't believe you think I would ever ask you to leave Grapes," he said. "I love her too, you know."

He turned and walked away, back down the underpass toward the Clos Lucé. But this time I didn't run to catch up. This time, I watched as John Chelsea's lumbering frame disappeared into the shadows.

VOLUME 3

"But the devils cannot interfere with the stars."

— **Heinrich Kramer,** *Malleus Maleficarum*

AUGUST 1519
CHÂTEAU DU CLOS LUCÉ, FRANCE

Anne had been at the kneeler for forty-five minutes, and her knees were screaming with agony. She was alone but for a group of friars keeping their canonical hours, their muttered prayers echoing throughout the chamber.

Usually, Anne spent scant time in chapel because she and Leo found it boring, but also because the sanctuary was rather claustrophobic. A simple iron cross sat at the altar at the room's apex, draped in rich white linen and flanked by a dozen thick, tapered candles. Curved archways gave way to a ceiling painted with images of the saints. The window at the front arched into two, set between jewel-toned glass in the shape of knight's armor.

She had planned to only make a show of being here for a while, but she had lingered longer to let her thoughts settle. After what Leonardo had told her about Domenico, she needed a bit of time to process. His tale was rather shocking, and she hoped it would be enough.

Anne gripped the pew in front and tried to find a comfortable position, but it was impossible. Her knees would never be the same. At the kneeler, she had spent painful moments reading through all four of Marguerite's letters, but the last one was the most perplexing. Leonardo's spidery script lay bare upon the page. It was most unusual to see his writing when it wasn't in reverse.

> *Dearest Marguerite,*
>
> *I implore you to avoid using the craft to address the problem of the Goddess. It is only through witchcraft that she has a hold over Anne. More of it will only put her and yourselves in further danger. I understand how troublesome it is for you and Claude to know you cannot be with her. Anne misses you greatly. But it is necessary. You must keep your distance. Otherwise, the Goddess will come for you too. And the price will be your lives.*
>
> *I am determined to remain with our dear girl. She is like a daughter to me. The clock we are building is slow-going. We use no witchcraft whatsoever. With only science, we may keep the Goddess at bay. She has no jurisdiction here, and so the divine creature cannot access the power of the clock.*
>
> *If there is a way to save Anne, it will take place in five hundred years. I have seen the girl, the one born of Anne's bloodline. She possesses Anne's skill with fire. Alas, it is she who will have to end this—if it can be done.*
>
> *When the time is right, I will instruct Anne to go to her and try to change the course of things.*
>
> *Yours,*
>
> *Leonardo*

Anne had been over the note several times, but it still perplexed her. What exactly was the girl from the future supposed to end?

The monks, having finished their service, filed from the chapel, their tonsured heads bowed in silence. She noticed the young apprentice from the library among them. The boy lifted his eyes to meet hers and gave her a forlorn smile.

Anne wondered if he had joined the monastery of his own choice. She had been forced to leave England around the same age. Anne had been sent to France as a lady-in-waiting to Princess Mary. Those had been lonely times, her first days in this country, with its foreign customs and its strange language. That was before she met Claude and Marguerite and Leonardo, and they had become a family.

She tucked the letters into her prayer book and stood up from the kneeler, her joints howling with torment. Now that the chapel was empty, there was no need to stay. As she smoothed her skirts, she heard a click of fashionable men's shoes with a heel, not the quiet leather soles of a monk's.

From the shadows emerged a man with salt-and-pepper hair and a tailored waistcoat.

"Mistress Boleyn," said Domenico icily. "How interesting to see you at prayer."

Anne's heart thudded, but she forced herself to be calm. She smiled demurely, hands gripping her breviary in earnest.

"Monsieur da Cortona, I make my prayers every day," she lied. "Perhaps it is you who does not frequent chapel often enough."

He did not return her smile, nor did he pretend concern for her welfare. This was the Domenico she knew all too well.

"I'm not interested in your lies," he sneered. "I am here to demand the true key."

She blinked innocently. "Whatever do you mean?"

Domenico reached into his waistcoat and produced the simple golden key. "What do you think you are playing at?" he spat, throwing it to her feet. "Leaving a false key for me to find. Was it your idea or Leonardo's?"

She could feel the fury rippling off him, but she smiled coyly. "Perhaps you shouldn't take things that are not yours."

"I know you carry it on your person," he demanded, teeth gritted. "Give it to me or I shall take it by force."

The false key lay at her feet, and she bent to pick it up. Though it might not have been the true one, Leo had crafted it himself, and so it was still precious.

"You should think twice before you lay a hand on me," she warned.

Domenico looked around the empty chapel with mild amusement, the heavy oak doors closed tight. "We are alone, Mistress Boleyn. There are no witnesses here."

This was accurate enough. There would be no one to hear her cry if he planned to use violence against her. He was a tall and wiry man, not a well-muscled machine, but he could certainly inflict damage on her small frame. Except that she was no regular woman. Her sixth finger itched with heat. She wanted to set this man's heels on fire. But she maintained her resolve. She had a plan, and she was going to stick to it.

He towered over her now, the smell of his foul breath burning her nostrils. "Do you know what an accusation of witchcraft could mean for someone like you?"

He let his threat hang in the air.

Anne glared back.

"It wouldn't take much," he continued. "You would be placed under arrest. And the king would have no choice but to set the clergy upon you. They would use the Hammer of Witches to test you. The inquisitor would find the evidence to have you burned at the stake at the center of town."

A slow-moving dread began wrapping itself around her neck, but she could not lose her wit. She cleared her throat. "I'm not sure if you want to do that," she said, rotating the false key between her fingers. It glinted in the light from the altar windows. "You are not the only person in possession of incriminating secrets."

Domenico chuckled, but it was not a light and easy laugh. "You know nothing."

Her heart was clanging, but she needed to play her part well, if she wished to convince Domenico she was his equal. "You forget, I was Leonardo's apprentice too. He told me a great deal about you." She let the sentence dangle, mirroring his earlier threats. "About your...relationship."

His smile fell away. "You are a liar."

She prepared to take her first shot across the bow. "You think I don't know about your affair? That you were much more than Leonardo's apprentice? That you were wanton lovers. And that he bedded you for years?"

A twitch in Domenico's eye told her she had struck a nerve.

She stood squaring off against this tyrant, ready to shoot another cannon. "In the end, you were the one who reported Leo to the authorities. You had him sent to the stocks for sodomy. All the while, you ran off to a new city. You took everything Leonardo taught you and made a new reputation for yourself." Her lip curled with disgust. "He loved you, Domenico, and you betrayed him."

When da Cortona took a shaky step back, she knew she had him.

Anne closed her hand over the false key with a victorious snap. "What will you do, Domenico, if I circulate these truths? The way you circulated your rumors about me."

"You are a bitch!"

Anne slid the false key into the pocket at her waist. It would join the true one waiting there.

"That may be," she said calmly. "But alas, we both have a hand to play. Now perhaps we can come to an agreement."

He hissed. "And what is that?"

She bobbed him a pleasant curtsey. "My silence in exchange for yours."

* * *

Anne slipped through the upper hallway, hoping to go unnoticed. Her exchange with Domenico had been exhausting, but in the end, she thought she had managed it. Domenico was a devil, but she had surprised him and that was enough to buy his silence, at least for now. In some ways, the exchange had bolstered her, bringing back a little of that old confidence she used to enjoy when Leonardo was alive. She imagined her master looking down upon her with a knowing smile.

Anne's visit with Leonardo had not only given her what she needed to contain Domenico's threats; he had also given her the idea to visit the Lady with an Ermine. If the talking painting could help her determine the date of the wedding between two men, it would solve the second of her problems. And if that were the case, she would only need to figure out what to tell the girl from the future when she found her.

Slowly but surely, step by step, Anne was starting to wonder if there might be hope. In tiny snippets, she dared to imagine a time when she could have her life back, when she might be free of her curse. She knew things would never be the same again with Marguerite and Claude. And she wouldn't stay in France. Not without Leonardo. But maybe, just maybe, she could finally find happiness with Henry in England.

She fiddled with the little golden B affixed with three pearls in the hollow of her neck, the one that Henry had given her. Was it possible they might be free to marry one day and have the son they both dearly wanted?

Stealing into her chambers, she turned and locked the door. She didn't want anyone to see her while she was speaking with a bewitched portrait. Anne had been careful ever since Domenico told her about the rumors of witchcraft, and she wouldn't forget his warning, ill-intentioned or otherwise.

Her room was chilled, despite the summer heat. No maid had set the fire in the hearth for weeks, and the room was exactly as she had left it. The bed curtains were pulled around their spiraled mahogany posts, and the sun shone through the window that overlooked the poppy fields. The painting, Lady with an Ermine, still hung where Leonardo had instructed —at the foot of her bed, on a wall that befitted such a masterpiece.

Anne approached the portrait, her newfound confidence suddenly faltering. She wasn't entirely sure how to make the picture come to life. She had never actually spoken to it before.

"Hello?" she said softly, feeling rather silly about the whole thing. Only mad people spoke to paintings under normal circumstances.

To her dismay, there was no reaction. The Lady remained as still as any other portrait hanging in the castle.

Anne glanced back at the door, wondering what she was doing wrong. Trying again, she dragged a finger over the oil's bumpy surface.

"May we speak, my Lady?"

This time, the ermine's whiskers twitched.

"Oh!" cried Anne.

The woman in the portrait turned her head. "Hello, Anne Boleyn."

Anne took a step back. There was something terribly unsettling about a painting that talked.

"I hate to bother you," said Anne, pressing past the strange sensation. "I must ask for a favor. On behalf of Leonardo da Vinci."

The Lady smiled. "I wondered when you would come. Leonardo said you might."

Anne stumbled. "You know Leonardo?"

"Yes, of course. I speak with Master da Vinci often. Though it has been many months since our last parley. He cares for you, Anne. He is very proud."

Anne shook her head. To think Leonardo had been speaking with this painting all along and he'd never mentioned it. There were so many things Leo had never told her.

"He *cared* for me," Anne corrected. "I'm afraid Leonardo has died."

The Lady put a hand to her mouth. "I had not heard. I am so very sorry," she said, signing the cross over her chest. "May he rest with the angels now."

Anne studied the painting for a moment, her curiosity growing. The woman was so real, so lifelike. It was like looking at herself in the mirror. She remembered posing for Leonardo as he painted it. That gauzy veil headdress had almost driven her mad.

"Do you still hang in the Clos Lucé five hundred years from now? I know it is an odd question, but…"

The Lady drew her shoulders back. "Of course, I do. In the same place I hang today. No one would dare move me," she said with pride. "I am an original portrait by the great Leonardo da Vinci. I must have a place of honor."

"Have you ever seen a girl who looks like me? Like us, I mean?"

It was all rather difficult to explain to a painting, but Leonardo had created her in Anne's image. So the Lady would hopefully notice someone who looked like her if the girl had indeed come to the castle.

The bewitched painting appeared to require no further explanation. "Yes, I have. That is also what Leonardo wished to discuss on his last visit. He asked me to give the girl from the future a message."

Hope bloomed like a perfect rose in Anne's heart. Maybe this was the same message he wanted Anne to give the girl.

The Lady closed her eyes and recited the missive she had been asked to relay. "The key that winds the clock is the answer. Find it and protect it. That is your fate. It is the only way to keep the Goddess from your bloodline."

Anne frowned. This message was no more helpful than what Leonardo had told her. She didn't understand why Leo would want to give the girl from the future the same instructions.

"And," she asked, "did you deliver the message? Did you find her?"

The Lady scoffed. "I did. The girl was quite rude. But she really does look like you. Like us. Although she was dressed like a man."

Anne wasn't sure she could dare believe the portrait. "Why does she stay at the Château du Clos Lucé? Is she a princess?"

The Lady shook her head in disgust. "Heavens, no. That girl is far too vulgar to be such a thing. She does not live at the château; she is merely a guest at a wedding."

Anne shot up, straight-backed and alert. "A wedding between two men?"

"Indeed, strange though it is," said the Lady.

Anne took a breath to steady herself. "Do you know when it will take place? I need the precise date."

The Lady smiled, as though it was common knowledge. "Of course, Mistress. Let me fetch the calendar."

The woman left the frame, disappearing into the background. Anne could hear her shuffling through objects in her room, and Anne wondered what it looked like inside the Lady's world. As she waited, the ermine leaned out of the picture, sniffing at Anne with curiosity. Its shiny white fur glimmered in the sunlight, and she considered petting the creature, but seeing its sharp teeth she thought the better of it.

When the Lady returned, she held up the calendar and showed it to Anne.

"Right here," she pointed to a box on a grid. "It shall take place on this Saturday in May."

Anne had never seen such a timepiece. The dates were laid out in a simple white chart lined up in seven columns for every day of the week, each box marked with a number. It was so different to the scrolls the clergy kept. But that didn't matter. She had the exact date of the wedding between two men, and that was more than she had managed in months.

"Thank you, Lady. You have done me a great service."

PRESENT DAY

CHÂTEAU DU CLOS LUCÉ, FRANCE

The leaves of the willow cascaded like a waterfall, wispy and soft in the late morning light. Lying in the grass, I admired the tree from beneath its majestic canopy. Often, I sat under my favorite maple tree back home, its larger leafier patterns dotting the blue sky. Here, under the willow, there was only a screen of green and I was fully hidden from view. Which was perfect because I wanted to be alone.

Big old trees comforted me, they helped me feel grounded. Somehow, when things went wrong in my life, I always found myself under a tree. It made me feel closer to my father. The man I still missed every day. The man with whom I had spent so much time sitting and reading under maples as a child. I could almost feel him sitting beside me, happy to listen to my worries and woes. And I needed that right now.

John and I had never had even a minor dispute before, so the fight we had in the tunnel hit me hard. My skin felt scrubbed raw. My head hurt. And I was a little sick to my stomach. Ironically, even though the bewitched painting behind the blanket in my bedroom had stopped talking, I hadn't slept a wink.

I couldn't stop replaying our argument in my mind. John said I was the one who insisted he go to New Zealand. And I supposed that was true. I hated knowing that I might slow him down, that I might prevent him from being the best version of himself. I was proud of John's accomplishments and wanted him to succeed. But what I didn't foresee was my own jealousy when he chose to go.

The familiar sound of Grapes's walker on the lawn beyond the curtain of foliage pulled me from my thoughts. *Schlump bum bum...schlump bum bum...* The beat was more muted on the grass but unmistakable all the same.

"There you are," said Grapes, poking her head through the wall of willow.

I gave her a wistful smile. "How'd you know I was here?"

If there was anyone I could stand seeing right now, it was my great-grandmother. She always knew how to make me feel better, and I was secretly grateful she had sought me out.

She stepped into my private tree-fort, batting away a few stray leaves. "I saw John at breakfast and figured I'd find you under a tree today. He looked terrible. And you don't look too good yourself."

I had skipped breakfast this morning with the express purpose of avoiding John, but it made me feel even sicker to know he was upset too.

"Do you want to talk about it?" she asked.

I didn't really want to talk about John, about the fight, about any of it. Saying it all to a real person just made it seem worse. But Grapes was determined. She parked her walker against the tree and sat down. Even in her nineties, Grapes maintained incredible flexibility because of the yoga she did every morning. It really came in handy at times like this.

I sat beside her, and we perched like two cross-legged Buddhas in the grass. She pulled a croissant from her bag and gave it to me.

"Grapes, how do you know if you're in love?" I asked, picking up the conversation in the place I had left it with the memory of my father.

She tilted her head. "You just do, I suppose."

"That's what John said. But what if you don't know? How can you tell?"

"Is that what you were fighting about?"

"Kind of," I mumbled, biting into my breakfast, the flaky croissant melting on my tongue.

She leaned back on the trunk with her hands behind her head. We listened to the birds singing in the forest, the little black-and-white starlings tittering in earnest. I flicked away an ant that was trailing up my leg as I tried to figure out how to explain it all. But in the end, I didn't need to. Grapes already seemed to understand.

"Your Grandfather didn't know for a while either. When we first got together," she said. "He was a lot like you. Analytical. Smart. And maybe a little bit neurotic."

I laughed, my mouth jammed with a big bite of bread. "Hey, watch it."

Grapes stared up into the tree with a dreamy expression. "I remember it like yesterday. I said it one day while we were walking through the woods. It was such an exquisite afternoon, and we were having so much fun. When I said 'I love you,' your great-grandfather gave me a pleading, panicked look. His mouth opened, but no words came out." She chuckled. "He just gasped like a fish."

"So, what happened?"

Grapes shrugged. "I didn't let it bother me. We were going to be together and I knew it. I just needed to give him more time. And eventually, he came around."

I picked a dandelion gone to seed and blew its white tufts into the air.

"I wish I could trust my gut like you do, Grapes," I said. "You have such good instincts."

She frowned, her tone becoming a bit stern now. "Ellie, you have spent your entire life ignoring your instincts. Maybe you should try trusting yourself sometime. You won't be disappointed."

I lay back on the ground, splaying out my arms and legs like a beached starfish. "It's just that I have all these questions. Like, what if John gets a job on the other side of the world? How would that work?"

She raised a caterpillar eyebrow. "Well, I don't know. Maybe you would join him? There will be lots of job opportunities for you wherever you live."

I sat up with a start, my eyes as big as dinner plates. "But I couldn't. I wouldn't. I could never leave you behind."

Grapes smiled. "Ellie, I won't live forever."

We had never talked about this before, and the thought of losing Grapes was making me panic. Like a knife was suddenly hacking through

my gut, threatening to butcher me. I put my head in my hands, unwilling
to hear any more.

"You know," she said gently, "I always hoped you would find some-
body. So that when I'm gone, I'll know you are okay. I want you to have
someone to take care of, and someone who can take care of you in
return." She gave me a wink. "Besides, there's that little girl you're going
to have. The one who will be the center of your universe."

My daughter. My little Liza. I hadn't forgotten about her. She was
one of the best things that came from the debacle last fall. Bernice's
prophecy had foretold of the baby girl I would have one day, a girl with
dark hair and amber eyes. I didn't know when she would come, but I was
waiting for her with all my heart.

"I don't want you to die," I said, my voice trembling. "I couldn't
handle that."

She put a soft hand on my arm. "Death is normal, dear. It happens to
all of us. And when my time comes, you'll be ready."

"I'll never be ready."

A butterfly landed on Grapes's shoulder, and it sat batting its wings as
if it were waiting for more of her sage advice. "You never know what the
universe has in store. You don't get to decide how much time you have.
The one truth about life is that it's finite. That's it, that's all."

My heart sagged under this impossible truth. I knew better than
anyone how finite life could be. When my parents and grandmother were
murdered, I had been only eleven years old.

"As for John, don't overthink the love thing. Ask yourself one simple
question." She looked at me now, her blue eyes sparkling. "Can you live
without him?"

The butterfly took flight, leaving us alone again. I thought about her
question, turning it over in my mind. Though I didn't know the answer,
it was a new way to frame my thinking. I had always been afraid to let
people into my heart. I knew how hard it was to live without them when
I didn't have them anymore.

Somehow, thanks to our little heart to heart, I found I could breathe
again. The pain in my stomach was starting to subside, the blade of the
butcher's knife retreating.

Grapes stood to take her leave, pulling on her walker to right herself.

Getting up was hard for her, but I didn't help. She was stubborn about these things, fiercely independent, and would be insulted if I tried.

"I've got to get going," she said. "Today we're going to ice the wedding cake. It has to be perfect for the big day tomorrow."

I smiled. "Good luck with the Trio."

She shuffled away on her walker but turned back before passing through the leaves. "Oh, I forgot to tell you. I've been thinking about that word. *Garridan*. My own grandmother used to say it as a kind of insult."

I glanced up, intrigued by her new change in direction. Grapes always could keep me on my toes.

"Granny would say things like, 'That fella's a real Garridan. I don't trust him one bit.'"

"So it's just a simple slur?"

She scratched her chin, pulling at a little hair she hadn't yet plucked. "No, it means more like...keeper of secrets. It's another word for spy."

"Spy?"

She nodded. "Granny used to talk about something called the Garridan's Trifecta. They were an old sect in Europe, a group of agents who didn't practice witchcraft. But they were connected to the three most powerful witches in the world. The Garridan would do their bidding and sell them secrets."

A few dots connected in my mind as I let this new information sink in.

Grapes's eyebrows were dancing now. "It's got me thinking. If one of us finds the key, maybe we should keep it to ourselves. Just for a while. I mean, we don't know Lucien's family very well, do we? They seem nice enough, but..."

"But what?"

"I'm not sure," she said airily. "I've just had a funny feeling ever since we arrived."

AUGUST 1519
CHÂTEAU DU CLOS LUCÉ, FRANCE

Anne stole through the castle, an unlit lantern swinging in her hand. It was well past midnight, and she did not wish to be seen. She padded through the corridors barefoot to ensure her silence. Salaì trailed after her, his feline paws matching her stealth. Nonetheless, she checked every corner and every shadow. There were those who still might be about, and she did not want eyes upon her in the library right now.

If you insist on following me, she said in her mind's eye to the cat, *you must stay close. No going off to catch mice.*

Leonardo's little feline, once so loyal to his master, had finally taken a liking to her. She had cared for him for three years, but he had ignored her completely until Leo's passing. Now the cat could have been her shadow.

The moon cast a glow through the library's tall windows, but she would need the light of her torch if she was going to succeed tonight. Thanks to the Lady with an Ermine, she knew the date of the wedding between two men—a critical piece of information for finding the girl. But the problem was more complex than simple math. The algorithm itself was difficult to apply, especially when she planned to travel such a vast distance through time. But the trickiest part was adjusting the date into the future.

During a tutoring session last year, Leonardo had explained that calendars were adjusted through history to correct for minor modifications to the average length of the year. France adhered to the Julian calendar, which had a requisite pattern of normal years and leap years. But she had read about a mathematical drift, one that miscalculated time by a fraction.

She had to work according to the calendar used in the future, not the one of today, if she wanted to do it right. And so, she required a particular book, one that was chained to the shelves in the library, to adjust her calculations.

It had occurred to her this might be important when the Lady with an Ermine showed her the calendar from the future, with its grid boxes and words written in English. In her time, the almanac was written in Latin. The days of the month were listed alongside notes about the holy days, feast and fast days, along with the phases of the moon.

She had spent the last few hours applying different counts to the formula, depending on the alignment of the earth's orbit.

Creeping toward the bookshelves, Anne held her lamp aloft. She blinked a modest flame into life, and the candle danced in the gloom. It was rare that Anne used her natural talents these days. Leo had counseled against it, and the letter he had written to Marguerite had explained why. If she used magic, the Goddess had a connection to her. It was the reason Leo insisted the clock be designed with science alone.

The book sat on the bottom shelf, and she pulled it from its resting place. Dust had settled on its rich leather binding, and she brushed it clear of debris before setting it in a study carrel.

She paged through the tome. It was an enormous text, and it took some effort to find the new calculation. She had only discovered the volume because it sat beside the book of engineering principles by Petrus Ramus, one of the texts from Leonardo's early tutelage.

Anne searched the pages until she found it. It was a mathematical proof for the length of a year. A full year was actually 365.24 days long. It seemed a minor difference, just a few decimals. But it meant that every hundred years, the Julian calendar erroneously gained an entire day. And that error would have quintupled over five hundred years.

She slipped the book back on the shelf and headed for the door. Anne would make the adjustments to the algorithm when she got back to her room.

We found it, Salaì, she said to the cat, her heart thumping in her chest at the achievement. It was another piece of the puzzle.

But as Anne moved through the chamber, she detected a light click. It sounded like a small object dropping to the floor. Salaì heard it too, and his whiskers twitched with interest. Squinting into the shadows, she allowed her eyes to adjust to the darkness. Her heart lurched. If someone had been watching her, it could ruin everything.

The long bookshelves hosted a single study carrel at each end, shrouded in deep, inky shadows. Stepping slowly toward the noise, she lit her lantern once again and held it aloft.

"Who goes there?" she called with as much authority as she could muster.

A thin figure cowered in the obscurity, draped in a heavy wool cloak. Even in the gloom, she could tell it was not Domenico. Though a loose cowl cast shadows over his face, the tonsure of his hairline made it clear —shaved on top and a fringe around his head.

"Please, Mistress," said a soft voice. "I mean no harm."

Anne narrowed her eyes. Though she had never spoken to him, she knew this young monk. The cower of his shoulders, the trepidation in his movements. He was the apprentice from the library. The youth who had smiled at her in chapel yesterday.

"Why are you here in the dark?" she asked with suspicion.

The boy pointed at the high arched windows. "It is not dark. The moonlight guides my work."

"And what work do you do in the moonlight?"

He covered his papers with his sleeve. "Nothing, it is nothing."

Anne drew her torch closer, her wariness heightened. She had pitied this boy, even felt a kinship with him because he was so young. But it was possible this monk, who seemed so sweet, was one of Domenico's spies. The Italian artist did have a network of informants, that much she knew, although she couldn't imagine this shrinking young friar among them.

"Why do you follow me, Garridan?" she said, swinging the lantern his way.

The boy made a pleading gesture and Anne noticed blood on his fingers, along with a stain of black ink.

"Please, lady, I am no Garridan. I am a simple apprentice scribe."

"Then show me your work," she demanded. "Prove it."

The monk hung his head, the baldness of his pate reflecting in the candlelight. "Please, don't tell my master," he pleaded softly.

She held the lamplight over the offending scripts. To Anne's surprise, words did not fill the boy's pages, no notes nor transcriptions of any sort. Instead, as the light flooded the parchment she beheld images, so beautiful, so artistically crafted, they almost brought tears to her eyes.

"Transcription takes all my time during the day," he said, chastened. "It is only at night, after Vespers, that I can practice my true art."

She glanced from the pages to the lad and back again, an understanding dawning. This boy's drawings were exceptional. She thought of Leonardo's sketches and wondered if they could rival his own. Anne relaxed, relief trickling through her like cool spring water. This boy was no spy. He was simply trying to hone his gift, his God-given talent.

"Your work is spectacular," she said kindly.

He dropped his eyes. "Thank you, Mistress."

They were quiet for a time as she studied his pages. She couldn't take her eyes from his drawings; his talent was so vast the work could have shone without her lamplight. She thought of all the sketches in Leonardo's notebooks, how he simply needed to draw sometimes, to quell a storm within him.

"I know who you are," he said shyly. "You were the apprentice of the great Leonardo da Vinci."

She smiled now. She couldn't help but like this boy. His face was still round, no beard upon his chin. His eyes were like a doe's, almost feminine. In a small way, he reminded her of Claude when they first met.

"My name is Anne Boleyn."

He gave her a timid grin. "It is an honor to make your acquaintance. I am Matis."

"May I?" She gestured at his pages.

She examined the images again, drinking them in. She couldn't help it. Ink sketches of the saints and scenes of the rite of the Eucharist filled the sheets, exquisitely drawn and perfectly proportioned. Salaì leapt up on the desk in one sprightly stride and rubbed his face against the boy's arm. A rolling purr suggested this monk had passed the feline's test of confidence.

"Master da Vinci would have been most impressed," she said.

"Do you think so? I have admired Master da Vinci for years."

The cat nudged him again, demanding the boy's attention.

"This is Salaì," she said. "I think he likes you."

Matis stroked the cat with his scabbed fingers, rubbing behind his ears. Salaì's purring grew louder at his touch.

"I have watched you over this last year with Master da Vinci," he said, sympathy in his voice. "You worked sometimes in the library, but sometimes in the gardens. He was always teaching you something, always asking your opinions."

It was true. Leonardo had been an excellent mentor. Scolding her occasionally, but always with good humor. No one could have been a better guide. Anne had enjoyed three wonderful years with him, and each year was a gift. She realized that now.

"I am sorry for your loss," he said. "It must be lonely without him."

Matis's words fell, soft and gentle, on her damaged soul. She wasn't sure why, but she found herself drawn to this young man. He was so pure of heart, and so talented. She had not spoken to anyone for weeks, having made a point of keeping her distance. But the child was right, she realized. She was lonely. Achingly so.

"Aye," she said. "It has been difficult these last days."

Matis smiled sadly. "I have often wondered what it would be like to be apprenticed to Leonardo da Vinci."

"Would you like me to tell you about him?" she asked.

The boy nodded with an eagerness that almost broke her heart.

Anne dragged a chair from another study carrel and sat down beside him. And then she told him about Leonardo, about his genius, the endless fountain of ideas that poured from his mind. She explained a mechanical lion that could rear on its hind legs and present lilies to the king. She spoke of a flying apparatus that would set a man's destiny to the sky. But mostly she told him of their friendship, of their shared laughter, of their deep mutual respect.

Matis asked endless questions, wanting to know everything. It felt wonderful to talk to someone, to have a simple exchange of ideas.

As they spoke, the boy told her snippets of his own story. Matis had joined the priory as a route to be as close to the learned scholars as possible. He had no interest in the ways of Benedictine brewing. Instead, he sought training of the high holy writings and tutelage in science and math. But most of all, he yearned to be apprenticed in art.

He reminded Anne of what Leonardo would have been like as a young man. So talented, so thirsty for knowledge. This young monk's potential almost shimmered in the darkness.

"Why do you have blood on your fingers?" she asked, though she suspected she already knew the answer.

He showed her an ink horn, a pretty object crafted with great care.

"It was this," he said. "I made it myself."

"What happened?"

His mouth sagged. "Master gave me the strap. I spilled ink on the text I was copying yesterday."

Anne shook her head. It was common for the church to provide this type of training. All punishment but no reward. She was grateful that had not been Leonardo's approach.

"Master says he had to bloody my fingers to help me learn."

She frowned.

"Master says I should focus on my writing, and not waste my time on my useless drawings. He says if something is just pretty, then it has no value."

"And do you believe that?"

He hung his head again, his cowl sliding over his face. "It is Master's way. And so, I must accept it."

She put a hand on his shoulder. "It doesn't have to be like that, you know. A teacher can be patient. A teacher can be kind."

He played with the scapular at his chest, working it through his battered fingers.

"When you are the master scribe," she said, determined to make him understand, "with your many talents in illumination, you can teach your students differently. The way Leonardo did. With tolerance, encourage-ment, and trust."

He pulled back his cowl, his eyes wide. "I shall never become a master scribe. I could never reach that high."

Anne pulled Leonardo's false key from the pocket at her waist and it twinkled in the moonlight.

"Do you know what this is?" she asked, holding it aloft.

The boy blinked. "No, but it is beautiful."

"It is a key, crafted by Leonardo da Vinci himself. It does not open a single door nor lock. And yet it is a treasure like no other."

The monk stared.

"And now," she said gently. "It is yours. When others are cruel, let it remind you of your gift. And when you are the master, no longer the student, let it remind you to teach your pupils with patience and kindness."

"I couldn't accept it," he said. "It would not be proper."

"You need not tell anyone you have it," she insisted. "Keep it hidden, if you like, in your ink horn."

She put the key in his hand, closing his black-stained fingers around it. "May you always keep it near, Matis," she said. "It is *my* legacy for *your* legacy."

PRESENT DAY
CHÂTEAU DU CLOS LUCÉ, FRANCE

"Lil?" I called into the otherwise empty library.

I needed to be sure she wasn't hiding behind a study carrel or a row of shelving. Back home at Queen's university, Lily often blended in with the books and it was impossible to find her, even if I searched every nook and cranny. Instead, I had taken to belting out her name, letting her be the one to emerge from her librarian camouflage.

When she didn't reply, I made a mental note to peruse the vast array of books and scrolls after the wedding tomorrow. John and I had seen everything at the château except for the library. Oddly enough, I had planned to spend most of my time here in France in this book-filled space with Lily, but somehow it just hadn't happened. John and I were too busy on our own holiday, falling back into each other's arms in a pretend world of "everything is fine." But that had all been a lie. And I wasn't ready to deal with whatever was left between us.

"Lily?" I tried again.

When she didn't come, I headed through the arched doorway and turned left. Here, the walls were cast from a modest plaster, the rich red brick of the manse not part of the servants' wing. But the black-and-white marble flooring remained the same, and I followed the checkerboard pattern down the hall.

At the sound of my footsteps, my favorite librarian flung open her door. She wore a yellow rubber-ducky dressing gown and matching slippers. Her outfit didn't surprise me given her unusual fashion sense, but her hair was set in huge curlers that made her look like she could be receiving radio signals from outer space.

"Nice hair," I giggled.

Her eyes darted behind her frames. "I want to look my best at the wedding, but I've never used curlers before."

"You're going to be beautiful," I said, touching one of her plastic rollers. I always made a point of being encouraging about Lily's looks. It helped boost her confidence.

Lily's bedroom was sparse but large, just as Maurice had promised. A simple bed flanked the corner by the hearth, her suitcase tucked underneath. A wooden cupboard housed her clothes, Lily's wedding outfit spilling out the bottom. True to form, a narrow table along the far wall was piled with old texts. Obviously, she'd smuggled the books from the library despite the chains that fixed them there.

"I've been meaning to talk to you," I said. "Without the entire search party in tow."

"Me too," she returned in her usual librarian monotone.

Usually, Lily and I talked every day to put together the pieces of our research, but she had been so busy with Maurice, and me with John, we hadn't had the chance for our usual mind-meld.

"Something happened in my room yesterday," I said, "just before you arrived with that da Vinci notebook."

Lily perched on the edge of her bed and patted the spot beside her. But I couldn't sit. I was carrying around a jittery energy that needed some form of release, and I found myself pacing in front of the fireplace.

"You know that da Vinci portrait in Anne Boleyn's room," I said, "the one called Lady with an Ermine? Well, she talked to John and me. She told us she had an important message from Leonardo da Vinci."

Lily nodded slowly.

"I know that sounds bizarre, but I guess I'm a bit of a weirdo."

Lily raised a rubber ducky slipper off the ground. "That makes two of us."

Lily's lack of reaction to my news wasn't surprising. She, unlike John, was aware of all the witchy things in my life. I wasn't sure why, but I felt comfortable with her knowing everything about my strange family inheritance.

I thought back, trying to remember the Lady's exact wording. I knew it was important to get it right. "She said, *The key that winds the clock is the answer. Find it and protect it. That is your fate. It is the only way to keep the Goddess from your bloodline.*"

Lily stared down at the floor, processing this news. She went slower than most, but I relied on her careful thinking, and I needed it now.

"That is interesting," she finally said. "It fits with the message we found on the scroll."

"But there's more." I tented my fingers together as I walked. "Grapes remembered where she'd heard the word Garridan." I lowered my voice for dramatic effect. "It means spy."

One of Lily's eyebrows hitched up over her glasses. "Well, that works nicely with my hypothesis."

This got my attention. It took Lily a second to get going, but when she did, her words chugged along like a steam train gaining speed. "I reread the message we found in the desk yesterday," she said. "I've been over it a dozen times. The keeper of the key was supposed to hide the true key from the Garridan. Right?"

I nodded, chewing my thumbnail as I followed her logic.

"And we know that Anne Boleyn was the keeper of the key. It was her job to protect it," she continued, her gigantic curlers picking up their signals. "Anne Boleyn is long gone, but if the key remains in the castle, it still needs to be protected... So, who is the key's keeper today?"

She blinked at me, as though expecting an answer. But I wasn't following anymore.

"It's you, silly," she said. "The talking painting told you so herself. You are the keeper of the key. It's your turn to protect it from the Garridan now."

My eyebrows knitted together. The fact that I hadn't slept last night didn't help, and my temples were now softly throbbing. Frankly, I didn't want to be tied to the mystery like this. Our whole family game of find-the-key was supposed to be about Anne Boleyn. Not about me.

"It's obvious, isn't it?" she said. "You're Anne's great-great-great-granddaughter. So you inherit the responsibility."

Suddenly, my cheeks were burning.

"So?" she asked with a shrug. "Where is it?"

I stared at her, wondering if she was serious. It didn't seem possible she could go from surmising that I was the modern-day keeper of the key to assuming I would know where it was.

"I have no idea!"

Lily went quiet now, the steam fizzling from her choo-choo train. "Oh, I thought maybe you had known all along but didn't want to say anything. Grapes and the gang were having so much fun with the search and all."

"Honestly, if I knew, I would tell you, Lil. You know I would," I said, rubbing some of the tightness from my temples. "But I do have a hypothesis of my own about the Garridan."

It seemed like the right time to bring it up. We might have reached an impasse on Lily's theory, but maybe it wasn't a total dead end. "I think Maurice might be the Garridan."

I didn't want to hurt Lily's feelings, but I had to say it. Maurice had been overly friendly since we arrived, especially with her. He obviously knew she was a librarian and was probably using her to find the key. Lily was such a pushover, she would fall for any man who paid her the slightest attention.

"I couldn't agree more," she said dryly.

"Really? I thought you'd be heartbroken."

"Ellie, I'm no idiot. I know when a man is using me." She glanced at her bedroom door. "I've been trying to get rid of him all week."

I smirked, relieved she had wised up about men who came on too strong. She really had come a long way since she'd fallen for Landon Fishburn last year.

"Besides, Maurice is too disorganized to be a museum curator," she said with disgust. "There are boxes of misfiled texts written by da Vinci just sitting in the corner of the library. No true curator would ever allow it. And then there was the fact he didn't think of using a mirror to decode da Vinci's writing. Anyone who uses the internet knows that."

"So what do we do now?" I asked.

She got up from her spot beside me, padded to the fireplace, and threw me a Cheshire Cat grin. It was the kind Lily used only on special occasions. "We keep him the hell away from the secret passage, that's what," she said with a rare spark that made me laugh.

She put a finger to her lips. "I found it last night when I was trying to get the fire started. I thought it might take the chill from the air." Lily was whispering now, as though the walls had ears. "I got thinking about how my room was closest to the library. And I wondered if maybe there was a tunnel between them, like the passageway between the two castles."

I raised my fist. "Lily the librarian strikes again."

"At first, I tried the candelabra, and then the sconces. But nothing worked. Until I adjusted the damper. That's when the wall swung open."

She got down on her knees and fiddled with the mechanism inside the chimney. As she did, a mechanical thunk sounded from within. A square panel creaked open along the seam of the wooden framing at the right side of the mantelpiece.

Lily blinked owlishly. "Like I said, it goes to the library. I suspect this room belonged to the master scribe. It's way too big to be a maid's chamber. But I haven't checked it out yet. Maurice came snooping around last night, so I had to close it up."

I jumped off the bed and joined her at the shadowy entrance in the paneling, holding up my hand for a high five. And for once she slapped it. Hard.

* * *

The passage was dark and narrow, about twenty feet long. It smelled a bit funky after having been closed for so long, but it was relatively fresh compared to the stench of the underground tunnel. Besides, there were no rats, and that alone made it a lot more inviting.

We stepped inside, armed with the glow of our cell phones like a couple of detectives. Adrenaline coursed through my veins, giving me pins and needles along every inch of my skin. My headache had vanished, and my mind was clear.

Thin, gossamer spiderwebs draped the ceiling, and we brushed them away with an old broom to avoid getting them stuck in Lily's curlers. We had agreed we would walk the length of the cramped corridor, but because there wasn't much room, we were going to split up. Lily would start from the library access, and I would take the end closest to her chamber.

From the other end of the corridor, I could hear Lily sneezing. She had already roared three times.

"You okay down there?" I called.

On the hunt now, we traced every inch of the tunnel, looking for something, anything, that could be a place to hide a key. The passage was cracked with time, plaster splitting the walls in various places. Pine floorboards creaked occasionally as we felt along each beam, searching for a secret compartment or a trap door. It seemed to take forever as we combed the edges, working our way inward, scrutinizing each fissure and crevice.

I ran my right hand along the wall, hoping to receive a signal. The smoothness of the plaster was much more pleasant than the slimy rock of the underground passageway, but I was getting nothing.

At the tunnel's center, we stumbled upon a set of simple shelves. Lily found it on the other side at the same time I did, as we met together in the middle.

"Hold on," said Lily through the gloom. "What's this?"

It occurred to me, as we were searching, why Grapes's game of find-the-key had been so intriguing for the two of us. As historians, Lily and I usually made our discoveries in books. In the dusty library stacks, we lost our minds with the thrill of finding something, anything, that hadn't yet been written about by a hundred other academics. But here in this marvelous castle, we were on the hunt for something entirely new. Something never discovered by anyone else. This was our treasure hunt, and ours alone.

With our flashlights skimming every surface, we searched with our usual fastidiousness. I ran my hand along brass inkpots, silver penknives, writing quills, and even a pair of medieval reading glasses. Though I was getting no magical signals, the objects were still incredible.

"Look at these," I said with clipped excitement. "They were probably used by the scribes, don't you think?"

Lily hovered the light over the medieval glasses, blowing out a little breath before continuing her careful inspection of the many colanders and their accompanying pens.

Now the shadows around my phone gave way to a couple of hooks beside the shelf. A number of metal objects hung on strings, dull with age and grime. Lily held up some tiny inkpots attached to thin straps, studying them up close. She turned the small vessels over in her hand, the leather strings draping through her fingers. I could almost hear her searching the encyclopedia in her brain as she examined them.

"Most scribes and illuminators hung a quill and inkpot over a belt on their tunics," she said, "so they always had their writing tools handy."

On a roll now, we examined every item, taking our time with each one. The discovery of these simple objects pulled us in, and we were the dynamic duo once again, talking quietly over each find, considering how we might spin up a manuscript for every item in the passageway.

Lily picked up a larger ink horn about six inches long. This one seemed like something special, different from the other objects on the table. It was an exquisitely crafted object, two silver clasps securing it at both ends. She twisted the cork, but the stubborn plug would not come away.

"Here. You try," she said, handing it to me gingerly.

The smooth horn was a weighty little piece, and I ran my fingers over an inscription etched in the bone. *Legatum meum ad Legatum tuum.*

"My legacy for your legacy," I said, translating the Latin. "I wonder what that means?"

I scrutinized the vessel, running my hands over the words again. I got no signal from my scar for this item either, but even so, there was something about this particular object. It seemed to be examining me, rather than the other way around, and it clung to me like a magnet, not ready to let go.

I twisted the cork in the horn as hard as I could, but it wouldn't budge. It felt like it was daring me, tormenting me even. I bit my lip, pulling harder, but it refused to yield. With a little growl, I found myself manhandling it, pushing and twisting with all my strength.

"Come on," I said through gritted teeth. "Tell me your secrets."

"Be careful, Ellie!"

Ignoring the nervous librarian, I turned the petulant little inkpot over in my palms. As I did, the horn slipped from my fingers and hit the wooden floor with an awful crack. I winced, a wave of guilt rippling up the back of my neck.

Sweeping me out of the way, Lily bent to pick it up. Clearly, I had failed to follow her instructions and had lost my privileges. Treasure hunt be damned.

"Ellie, there's something inside," she squeaked.

A hint of self-satisfaction nudged the back of my brain. My instincts had been right. I shone the flashlight into the hollow of the horn and caught a glint of yellow.

As Lily emptied the vessel, a small golden key fell into her hand. It had a rounded circular bow, a long narrow shank, and a stubby square base with four notches in the bitting.

"Oh my God," she breathed. "We found the key."

I nodded. This was it. It had to be. We had found the key that had been lost for five hundred years. I took a sharp breath as she passed it to me, preparing for the searing pain I knew would come. But when the key landed in my palm, nothing happened. I frowned. Something wasn't right.

I tried switching it back and forth between both hands, but still there was nothing.

"What are you doing?" asked Lily.

Perplexed, I rubbed the golden object directly over my scar. But there was no pain. No heat. It might as well have been attached to a regular set of car keys.

"Two keys forged, one false, one true. Da Vinci's clock starts time anew..." I heard Lily reciting the verse from the scroll.

My eyes flicked to hers. The realization crashed through my mind like a jumbo jet full of screaming passengers.

"We found a da Vinci key, Lil," I said steadily. "But this one is the fake."

Anne peered into a looking glass the way her sister in England did, brushing her hair until it shone a deep auburn brown. She had ordered a bath, sweetened with rose oil, and selected her favorite dress. A split sleeve of yellow silk decorated her rich crimson gown, and the golden B pearl necklace hung in the delicate hollow of her neck.

Today she wanted to look her best. It had been the conversation with Matis that helped her finally see the way forward. The answer had been there all along, but her exchange with the youth had made it clear.

She hoped he would cherish Leonardo's key. Perhaps, if he understood her meaning, he might pass it on to one of his students. And like the Lady with an Ermine, another one of Leonardo's legacies could live on.

Checking her mirror one last time, she whisked an impudent hair under her hood and set out. She had chosen midday, as was her custom, because it would give her privacy. And to her relief, the great hall was empty.

Anne fiddled with the little B at her throat, trying to contain the jittering insects that were crawling up her neck. Back in her room, the plan had seemed solid, simple even, but now as she stood in front of the clock, she wasn't so sure. A five-hundred-year leap was no laughing matter. It had taken her hours to run and rerun the new numbers through the algorithm. It was only when she produced the same calculation three times that she felt confident enough to make her move. Now, as the task loomed large in front of her, she was more than a little nervous.

Anne withdrew the fishhook key and slid it in the winding mechanism, taking one last look over her shoulder.

We must have faith in ourselves, and in our students who will come after. Leonardo's advice echoed through her mind.

Anne turned the key counterclockwise.

A familiar indigo light burst through the gears, Leonardo's spring inside working its precision, splitting, arching, bending time. The chamber spun, Anne whirling along with it, as everything became spools of thread weaving and unweaving until there was nothing but the universe. Millions of stars shimmered in a resplendent streak across an inky-black sky. The sun boiled, popping and sputtering gases upon its red-hot surface. The moon, milky and cratered, orbited on its axis around the lush, blue earth.

When it ceased, Anne was ready. She did not suffer the same dizziness nor the nausea she had on her previous trips. And as she opened her eyes, she was pleased to see the great hall looked very different. Only Leonardo's mechanical lion was familiar.

Pieces of furniture she did not recognize were arranged in odd places. A polished mahogany table was so shiny, it could have been dipped in oil. Paper pamphlets splayed across its surface in the shape of a lady's fan, each one a perfect replica of the others. Even more odd, a candelabra shone from above with yellowy light, although it held no candles nor flame. The strangest object of all was a small flat notebook, with buttons marked with the letters of the alphabet and a screen that shimmered with an eerie pale backlight.

Anne pushed one of the buttons, and the screen blinked to life with a moving image of the château, large rolling letters sliding up the frame.

"Visit the Château du Clos Lucé and fall back in time," the device said in a disembodied voice. She snatched her hand away, wondering if the little machine was actually alive.

Anne backed up, reminding herself of her true purpose. She needed to find the girl.

She knew the way, of course. Anne had followed the same floor plan only moments ago, but now things in the castle were entirely unfamiliar. Tapestries hung on the walls, woven from fabrics in excessively rich hues. The dining room housed a long wooden table with ten studded leather chairs, and a cabinet that was too decorative and glasses too delicate to be real. The chapel was changed as well. Neat rows of benches faced the altar, all the kneelers removed. And an ornate brass cross was nothing like the simple iron crucifix she'd pretended to worship at just days ago.

At her bed chamber, she faltered, wondering if she should knock. Technically, it was no longer her room. Her stomach twisted, but there was no time for dawdling. She needed to be confident. It was the only way this was going to work.

When Anne opened the door, she saw the strangest thing she had ever seen.

A girl who could have been her twin was applying a deep shade of red to her lips. Her gown was a rich navy silk, and it fit her trim body like a glove, showing off every curve and following the sleek line of her buttocks. The dress was so immodest it didn't even have sleeves. To her horror, the skirt ended at the girl's knee. A set of sinewy bare legs and ankles gave way to a pair of high-heeled shoes. They were not the silk slippers of a lady, but men's shoes with a two-inch rise, much like the ones Domenico wore.

"Who are you?" asked the young woman in the improper dress when she saw Anne standing there.

Anne's eyes grew wide, and she stumbled for a second. But she could not allow herself to be distracted from her mission. She was going to be direct, just as she had been with Leonardo.

"I am Anne Boleyn," she announced with a false courage, before sinking into a deep curtsey.

The girl stared at her with a slack-jawed expression.

"What...the...fuck..."

Anne thought back to her conversation with the Lady with an Ermine. The painting had found the girl to be quite rude, and Anne couldn't help but agree.

Her twin advanced upon Anne now, stalking her like a lion. She was more muscular than any lady Anne had ever known, her wiry arms and shoulders flexing for balance as she wobbled on her heels. After circling a few times, the girl yanked up the strapless dress that was threatening to slip from her modest bosom.

Anne cleared her throat, attempting to quell a sour bubble of nausea that was edging into her mouth.

"I have come from the past with an important message."

Anne hoped this would catch her attention, but the young woman didn't appear to be listening. She kept circling, gawking, taking in Anne as though she were an object on display. The girl scrutinized Anne's French hood, her square-necked bodice, and the beadwork of her kirtle. Finally, her gaze settled upon the golden B pearl collar at Anne's neck.

"Wow," the young woman whispered. "It's really you."

"Yes," said Anne tightly. "It is."

This wasn't going the way she had hoped. This woman was rude, and she behaved in a most uncourtly way. Her lips were too red. Her hair was uncovered. Even her accent was all wrong, with harsh vowels and a sharp diction that grated on Anne's ears.

"Is this the day of the wedding between two men?" Anne asked with a new urgency.

The girl crossed her arms, her sinewy biceps flexing. "Yeah, why?"

Anne swallowed. She had the girl's attention now and she needed to keep it. "Please, my lady. May we sit? There is much to tell, and there is little time."

The young woman studied her, scrutinizing Anne under a suspicious gaze. Her expression was no longer doltish, but highly astute and calculating. She seemed to be considering Anne's request but was having trouble with this version of reality. This made sense, of course. Anne had felt similarly when she'd made her first trip through time.

Eventually, the girl extended a hand, palm up. It was a manly gesture, like that of a guild merchant eager to settle a business deal.

"I'm Ellie," she said. "Ellie Bowlan."

Anne shook in return, eager to get on with things. But when their hands touched, white sparks shot from between their palms. Fiery heat seared her fingers, and Anne's body flexed at the sensation. Her muscles and bones vibrated with an intense frequency. Still, they did not pull their hands apart. They stood staring at each other, connecting on a level that wasn't entirely within the realm of normal.

Despite the pain, there was something comforting about the girl's touch. In this precise instant, everything seemed to swing into balance, a yawing and stretching of time itself in a dance of transcendental harmony.

The girl had an energy to match her own. At her touch, Anne could sense the girl's intelligence, as sharp and keen as her own. Anne knew the girl's courage, a bravery that matched hers. She could even understand the girl's heart, complex and damaged, but loving all the same. While they were strangers, they might as well have known each other all their lives. And Anne knew unequivocally, that she could be trusted.

When they pulled apart, something unbreakable had been sewn between them. A kinship. A warmth. A partnership that required no words.

She smiled at her twin, and her twin smiled back—a perfect mirror image.

Anne reached into her pocket and presented the true key. "Leonardo da Vinci assigned this to me, but I now pass the role to you, Ellie Bowlan."

The girl's eyes fell upon the object with a look of surprise. She took a step back at first, her gaze still glued to the key, her body half-frozen with something that looked like fear. But as the minutes passed, she stepped toward it again.

Anne knew she couldn't force the girl to take the key. It had to be her own choice.

When Ellie finally reached out to take it, she did so without argument. As the golden piece touched her flesh, the girl winced, but she clasped her fingers around it all the same.

"By giving this to you," said Anne with a slight curtsey, "I protect it from the Garridan in my own time."

Ellie studied the key, running her fingers around the spiraling fishhook. "It is exquisite," she said softly, awe trailing through her awkward vowels.

"Aye, it is," Anne agreed. "But you must listen. There is much to tell. Leonardo devised a complex algorithm to determine the course of travel," she explained. "But you won't have time to do the calculations. Just know that one click counterclockwise will take you back one hour in time."

Ellie nodded, listening carefully now.

"You must maintain the key's protection," she explained. "Protect it above all else. If you are successful, you shall end the curse of our bloodline."

The girl frowned. "But my great grandmother ended the curse it last year. It's over."

Anne took Ellie's right hand and ran her finger along Ellie's scar. Someone had removed her sixth finger, but she knew in her heart the girl had been born with the extra digit. As her flesh made contact, Ellie blew out a deep breath.

"Ellie," Anne explained, threading her fingers through hers, "Leonardo saw you in his dreams. Now that the curse has ended in your time, you must end it in mine. I cannot do it myself. It is not my fate. Instead, you must end the scourge on both ends of the timeline. Fuse it shut, cauterize it like a rope. So that the threads cannot be rewoven to create new versions of our fates. It is the only way we can stop the Goddess from coming between us."

Ellie went pale. Anne thought she could finally see true understanding dawning across her face.

"Today at the wedding," said Anne, "something terrible is going to happen, but I have no insight into what will come to pass. I can only say it will be a matter of life and death."

Ellie seemed to sag under the weight of this responsibility. It was a substantial burden, Anne knew. But it had been Ellie's all along. She had to be the one to end the curse. That was what Leo had been trying to tell her. Anne's role was to pass the key to its true keeper and let her wield its power.

Feeling in her hidden pocket, Anne pulled out a small pair of scissors and passed them to the girl.

"What are these for?" Ellie asked.

"Leonardo da Vinci gave them to me. He only said they would be useful."

There was so much Anne still didn't know. She could only give Ellie the tools and then trust in her to know what to do. Just as Leo had done for her.

"You'll know when the time is right," said Anne reassuringly. "You must use your wit. Trust in your instincts."

Anne drew the girl into a hug, and they stayed like that for a time, holding each other tight. A pulsing energy coursed between them, but this time it did not hurt. Instead, it reminded Anne of their mutual strength, their mutual blood, their mutual gift.

"I must go," said Anne. "Time can only bend for so long before it springs back into place."

Ellie blinked. "I'll visit you," she said. "I'll use the key, and I'll find you."

Anne shook her head. "Do not come looking for me." It was the same advice Leonardo had given on his deathbed, but now it made sense. "The timeline must be severed completely."

Ellie reached for Anne just as the room began to spin, and the threads of time unraveled.

An indigo haze swallowed the physical objects around her, strings weaving and winding, twisting and fraying, until only the blackened void of space remained. The earth and the moon, the stars in the sky, the entire solar system collapsed on itself into a deep black hole.

The sensation was familiar now, but the return trip was always harder, and Anne closed her eyes to manage it. Her stomach surged. But when it stopped, she did not faint. As the physical world became solid around her, she reached for the clock to steady herself.

Suddenly, a hand clamped over her wrist, sour breath on her face. Bewildered, she opened her eyes to find Domenico so close, she could see the yellow of his teeth.

"Unhand me," she said weakly.

He laughed. "And why should I do that?"

She didn't reply. It was all she could do to stop herself from staggering in his grip. Her head was too thick, her thoughts too slow to put up a fight.

Domenico produced a cruel grin. "I have witnessed your witchcraft with my own eyes."

"You saw nothing," she insisted.

He narrowed a reptilian gaze upon her, ready to strike. "You materialized from nothing. I now have my proof."

A chill slithered up her spine, threatening to unravel her.

"Give me the key," he said steadily. "Or I shall have you arrested."

Ice settled in Anne's veins. Domenico's look was menacing, but they had an agreement based on their mutual interests for self-preservation. He would not go back on it.

"I have given the key to someone I trust," she said, pretending once again at a confidence she did not feel. "Someone you can never find. Search my pockets if you like."

Domenico's nostrils flared, anger turning his neck blotchy. For a moment, it seemed like she might have put him back in his place, but he raised his voice to the rafters.

"Guards!" he shouted. "Call the magistrate. Place this woman under arrest."

PRESENT DAY
CHÂTEAU DU CLOS LUCÉ, FRANCE

"Wait," I called. "Please don't go."

I watched, grasping at the air, as Anne Boleyn faded into nothing. One moment she was there and the next she was not. And what she left behind was an emptiness that gnawed at the edges of my soul. She was being cut from my own flesh, and I didn't know how to say goodbye. In a bewildered heap, I crumpled back onto the bed.

When I first saw her standing in my room, in her deep ruby medieval gown with the little golden B at her neck, she had startled me. In fact, she had almost scared me to death. Until I understood she had used Leonardo's clock to find me.

It took me a while to get used to her stiff mannerisms, her dramatic airs. At first, she seemed lofty, a princess with an imperious edge. But we were strangers then. It was only when our hands touched that something was forever changed between us. To feel her palm against my own had been painful, but it filled me with a celestial calm that descended over me, blanketing me like a soft cotton quilt, warm and familiar and strong.

I stared down at da Vinci's true key. It was a magnificent design, shaped like a fishhook, a double helix forged in gold. Anne had made me its keeper, and somehow, that had felt right too. The cells in my body

vibrated with a knowledge, resonating in a way I didn't entirely understand, but something connected Anne and me in an impossible umbilical
cord across time.

Anne's message jarred through my brain. Something was going to go
very wrong today, and I was the only one who could fix it. And now,
there was only one thing to do.

I had to find Grapes.

I tossed the true key along with the false one into a pocket in my
dress. Then I slipped in the little pair of scissors. Despite the dress's
tight fit, I had chosen the gown because of the hidden pocket at the
waist.

Stepping out of my heels, I broke into a run.

Today the castle could have been the setting for a fairytale. Clarisse
had left no detail untouched. She had decorated every part of the
château for the wedding, even the upper floors. Fine white silk ribbons
trailed through the corridors, understated and elegant. They were
nothing like the hot pink crêpe-paper streamers and tacky balloons my
family used for parties back home.

I almost collided with Maurice, who was standing at the top of the
stairs, fiddling with a basket of flower petals.

"Sorry, Maurice," I called as I flew by. "Best man duty."

I raced at top speed past the great hall, around the library, and
through the dining room until I reached Grapes's chamber. The door
was ajar, and I heard a male voice inside. For a moment, I paused. The
Titanium Trio were always squabbling and loud whenever I went to their
room, but there was never a man among them.

"Your mom and dad will come around," Grapes was saying. "When
they get to know Lucien, they're going to love him. You'll see."

"Thank you for walking me down the aisle today," said Dez, his voice
oddly scratchy. "It means a lot."

"It's an honor," she said with motherly pride. "You know, I thought
Ellie would tie the knot first. But it turned out to be you. My wonderful,
handsome boy."

I opened the door to find my great-grandmother fixing the knot in
Dez's bowtie.

To my surprise. my best friend looked nervous, more vulnerable than

I'd ever seen him. His eyes were even a little wet, and I realized I had barged in on a private moment.

"Sorry, guys," I said breathlessly.

I had never seen Dez cry, but here he was, letting Grapes see the deepest hurt in his heart. I knew it was hard for Dez that his parents refused to accept him for who he was, but he had never been able to talk about it with me. And here was Grapes, helping him face that pain the way she had helped me so many times before.

"Damn it, Ellie," said Dez. "What are you doing here? You're supposed to be at the altar. Remember?"

It was true. I was out of position. We had practiced the ceremony three times yesterday. Clarisse had insisted she wanted everything to be perfect. Our wedding party was small, and I didn't see why we needed three run-throughs, but I had gone along with it so Dez wouldn't get more mad than he already was.

"I had to come," I said, trying to find the right words. Dez was not going to be happy about what I had to say. "We have to stop the wedding."

Grapes's lips formed a perfect O, but Dez just rolled his eyes.

"Honestly, Ellie," he said, "I can't believe you."

My mind spun. I had to find a way to make him understand.

"Dez, listen," I said, slowing my ramble, and trying for a more rational tone. "It's important."

He straightened his tie in the mirror, making a show of getting it just right. I waited for him to look at me, to listen to what I had to say, but he continued to preen, combing and recombing his hair.

I understood Dez's frustration with me, I suppose. But this wasn't about our disagreement over his horrible boyfriend. And right now, he was being stubborn. My cheeks flushed as I stood there, an angry flame igniting in my belly. Not for the first time, I found myself wondering what had happened to my snarky, rumpled scientist best friend.

Normally, Dez would at least have been willing to hear me out. But he was becoming a carbon copy of Lucien. He was disappearing and being remade as a high-fashion, love-sick replica of his fiancé. Dez was even wearing Lucien's spiced musk cologne, and it was strong enough to make my eyes water.

"I met Anne Boleyn!" I shouted.

Dez stopped fussing with his hair and swept a slow gaze my way.

"I realize it sounds crazy, but it's true," I pressed. "She gave me da Vinci's key. The clock in the great hall can really bend time." I searched my pocket. "She also gave me these."

I showed them the medieval scissors. An intricate scrollwork pattern on the handles graduated into shiny blades.

Dez looked at them with a haughty snort. "What the hell are those?"

"They're scissors—obviously," I said sarcastically. I couldn't help myself.

He scowled, his freckles twitching.

"Listen," I said with mounting impatience. "Anne Boleyn told me something bad was supposed to happen today. A matter of life and death. She came to give me these things on the day of a wedding between two men."

Grapes's eyebrows were quirking a mile a minute. "What is supposed to happen?"

I winced. This is where my story got a bit shaky. "Well...she didn't tell me exactly. She told me I had to figure it out."

Dez was incredulous now. His pre-wedding jitters were not making it any easier to handle this weird, magical situation. Dez was a scientist like me. He liked things to be predictable, and he was as stubborn as they came.

"Give me a break, Ellie," he spat. "You've been trying to stop this wedding since I told you about it. And here you are, minutes before I'm supposed to walk down the aisle, with all this weird stuff you've collected from the castle." He gestured to the scissors in my hand. "And all you've got is some crazy story that doesn't make any sense about why I shouldn't get married? I mean, come on. Do I look like I was born yesterday?"

My lips formed a thin line. "You think I'm making this whole thing up?"

He laughed bitterly. "The lengths you are going to ruin this wedding are getting ridiculous. I thought you would be a lot more supportive."

Dez's words stung, far sharper than I had expected. After all our years together, I had never lied to him once.

"Anne Boleyn said it had to do with the Goddess," I blurted.

Grapes gasped.

Dez, however, was unimpressed. "I should have asked John to be my best man," he said under his breath before storming from the room.

I turned to Grapes, throwing my arms in the air. Surely, she would see how unreasonable he was being. How unfairly Dez had treated me.

My great grandmother was fiddling with the white rosebud corsage on her gown.

"You believe me, don't you, Grapes?" I demanded.

"Of course, I do, dear," she said softly. "Bernice saw it too—last night."

"You see?" I said with satisfaction.

But Grapes could only shake her head, her shoulders sagging. "Bernice said everything was covered in a thick blue haze, so she couldn't actually see anything. She could only say it was going to be bad."

Grapes took her walker and began pacing. My great-grandmother always did this when she was thinking, and she always came up with something good. So I waited, my heart revving like a race car, as I listened to the *schlump bum bum...schlump bum bum* on the marble floors.

"Did Anne Boleyn say anything else?" she asked. "Think, Ellie. This is important."

I sat on the bed, reflecting on our visit. My scar still ached from where she had touched it.

"Anne said I was the keeper of the key. That it had always been my destiny. She told me I had to protect it, no matter what. And if I did, it would end the Boleyn curse."

Grapes stopped. "But we ended the curse last year."

"I told her that too. But Anne Boleyn explained it differently. She said I have to end the curse on both ends of the timeline. It's like a rope that has to be fused shut so the line can't be harmed on either side. So that the Goddess can't reweave the threads of time."

"I've never heard of such a thing." Grapes started pacing again. "And what about the scissors?"

Dread crawled up my spine on a hundred hairy legs. "I don't know why she gave them to me. And I realize it makes me seem like a lunatic.

But it doesn't matter what they're for. The point is we need to stop the ceremony."

Grapes's walker was edging forward and back. "Dez will never allow it," she said firmly. "It's too important to him."

"But Grapes!"

She wagged a finger. "Look, I know it sounds irrational. But he's in love. And all of us need to be supportive. Especially you, Ellie. He doesn't have anyone else."

"I do support him, but..."

Grapes shot me a funny look. "Dez told me you don't like Lucien. Is that true?"

Now it was my turn to scoff. No, I didn't like Lucien, but I was nice enough to him. Besides, he was the obnoxious one. Certainly not me.

"This has nothing to do with Dez's choice of partner," I insisted.

"It's hard to see a loved one find their match," she said gently. "It can feel like someone else has come between you. But it is normal, dear."

I didn't want this to turn into a discussion about my friendship with Dez. "Listen, I admit I'm not crazy about Lucien. But that is irrelevant right now. Something bad is going to happen today, and we have to stop it."

Grapes gazed out the window, the sound of her pacing a steady thrum in the room.

"I don't think so," she said. "Something tells me we have to let this wedding happen. And you are going to have to act like you're happy about it." She gave me an imploring look. "You're going to do that for Dez because he's your best friend."

"But what about Anne Boleyn's message?"

Grapes's ancient hands flexed around her walker as though it was the only thing anchoring her to the real world. "I'm afraid things have already been set in motion, fated in the cosmos," she said in a faraway voice. "And they need to play out the way they're meant to."

Bile rose in my throat, and I swallowed it back down.

She stopped walking now, her blue eyes piercing mine. "Whatever happens today, Ellie, you must protect that key."

SEPTEMBER 1519
CHÂTEAU D'AMBOISE, FRANCE

Anne stared out her bedroom window, her guts roiling with worry. She always loved this view of the poppies blowing in the fields, and she wanted to have it engrained in her memory. She had been locked in her chamber for two days, and no one was allowed entry save for a servant who brought her meals. The king's sentries stood at her door, so she had no news of the outside world.

Still, she could watch the castle's comings and goings from her window, and she was glad of at least that. The lawns bustled with clergymen hurrying from chapel to chancellery. Each morning, the larderer directed new livestock to the flesh kitchens, and every afternoon, the cook left the butchery covered in blood. Anne even thought she had seen Marguerite crossing through the garden with her familiar determined stride.

"It is time," a deep voice bellowed.

Anne turned, her legs suddenly growing weak. She gripped the back of a chair to steady herself.

Two large men seized her by the shoulders and tied her hands with thick, rough twine. The guards did not wear chainmail, but the king's blue and yellow livery was imposing enough. They flanked her, hands on swords, as they escorted her through the Clos Lucé.

"Where are you taking me?" she asked.

One of them gave her a light shove, and she stumbled to catch herself. The other pointed to the stairs leading to the underground passage. They descended the steps, and Anne focused on her walking. She had eaten little in these last days, her stomach refusing to accept anything heavier than broth, and she wanted to make sure she didn't fall into one of the slick, black puddles.

As they marched, her hands bound tight, she thought of Leonardo. How she had trailed after him in the same passageway the day they met Domenico. How he had told her he did not trust the Italian architect. And now that she knew why, it did not matter. She was back in the same tunnel, imprisoned by the king's guard, and Domenico had won.

She had let Leonardo down in so many ways. He had asked her to find the girl in the future. And she had managed to. But everything after that had been her own guesswork, and something told her she'd gotten the whole thing terribly wrong.

Anne thought about Ellie Bowlan, her energy, her mind, her spirit. It had been the only thing that kept her going these last few days. She had found her soulmate, someone who understood her so well, no words were required. But even that gift was tainted.

Anne had tried to follow her instincts, as Leonardo asked, and give the key to its rightful owner. But now that the key was gone, she was helpless without it. Even if she could find a way to escape the sentries, she could no longer use the clock to change the course of things. If she hadn't given it away, maybe, just maybe, she could have found her way out of this mess. But now, all she could do was be dragged down the dripping underpass on her way to her fate—whatever that was going to be.

Torches flickered against the wet walls, an oily light cutting through the dank air. The heavy steps of the guards echoed ominously through the passageway. When they arrived, the guards pointed the way through a maze of underground corridors. Archways hewn from rough stone gave way to the smoother, more polished walls of the Château d'Amboise.

For a minute, she wondered if perhaps she was to be held in one of the castle's rooms. At least she would be treated with civility. But as they ascended the steps, she realized her mistake. They were heading to the prison tower of the Château d'Amboise. She had thought little of it when she and Leo were here on business. It was something courtly people did not speak of, but everyone knew it was a horrible place.

The stone stairs spiraled upward, and as she climbed, weakness threatened to have her trip again. But the guards forced her up, jostling her roughly.

At the top of the steps, a man emerged from a barred oak door, a set of iron keys jangling at his waist. Anne's stomach twisted at the sight of him. He wore a filthy brown tunic with rough leather boots. A felt bonnet covered his head, and under it, a linen coif was stained with something dark. He did not carry a sword like the king's sentries, but a wooden bat with several nails buttressing the barrel flexed in his fist.

The guard thrust Anne toward him.

"This lady is to be held as she awaits the Inquiry of the Magistrate," said the other.

The warder took Anne by the arm and pushed her through the doorway. She swallowed back the sour bubble of nausea that wanted to come.

"Please, sir. What is the Inquiry of the Magistrate?" she asked.

The warder's wet tongue darted as he inspected her. He jostled Anne's pockets, felt along her bustline, and ran his fingers through her neatly coiffed hair. Anne coughed at the smell of him as he put his hands all over her, but she did not fight back. The bat with the nails was too real, too threatening, as it swung at his hip.

When he was satisfied, he led her through a darkened maze, his grip tight on her arm. At the final holding cell, he shoved her through the iron grate and released her hands from their bonds. The jangle of his keys rattled as he locked her inside, and her legs finally gave way. She collapsed into a pile of rancid straw.

Anne shuddered as she took in her new squalid surroundings. Though she had not thought it possible, the smell here was worse than in the underground passage. A filth bucket sat in the corner in her own cell, unemptied of the refuse from its previous tenant. She curled her legs underneath her gown and wrapped her arms around her knees.

For a long time, she sat staring down at the straw pallet that had turned slick and green with some unknown fluid. In the silence, the shadows edged in on her. She was afraid to move, afraid to even lift her eyes. For a while, it was all she could do to breathe.

From somewhere in the darkness, Anne detected a light moaning, something far worse than her own despair. As she squinted, she thought she could make out a young woman, her shaved scalp reflecting in the dull torchlight. Anne scrambled to her feet and gripped the iron bars, peering into the inky shadows.

"Hello?" called Anne.

The woman lay in a mound on the floor, unmoving, a rough woolen blanket draped over her naked body. Her face was bloodied and swollen, and pus oozed from a large split in her lip.

"Hello?" Anne tried again.

This time the girl stirred, a single eye opening, the other too purple to follow suit. She

drew herself up and wrapped the blanket around her bony shoulders.

"Please, lady," the young woman said weakly, "have you anything to drink?"

Something pinched at Anne's heart, sharp and hard. The girl was so thin, so frail, so dirty.

"I have had no water for two days," said the young woman, her mouth crackling with dryness. "I cannot afford it."

Disgust scuttled under Anne's skin like a cockroach, its legs clacking. It was one thing to be convicted of a crime, but everyone needed water. No matter their offense. Besides, the girl reminded her of her sister. Her voice was sweet and pure, and she moved with the same gentle grace. It was hard to imagine what she could possibly have done to deserve such treatment.

"Warder," called Anne with some of her usual backbone, "bring this woman a draft of ale. I shall pay its price."

The thin girl grasped her hands together in a grateful gesture. Soon, the jailer shuffled toward them, thrusting a grubby hand between the bars of Anne's prison cell. Clearly, he would not do her bidding without payment.

Anne punched a coin into his hand.

"There now," she said. "I have been generous. See to it this girl has food and drink for as long as she is here."

The jailer gave her a toothless smile, his pink tongue darting. "Whatever you say, lady prisoner. If you have coin, I have drink."

He returned with a wooden goblet and a pitcher of ale and slid them through a squared section of the iron bars. The girl hurdled toward it, her blanket falling to the ground. She gripped the pitcher to her mouth and drank in earnest, unconcerned with her nakedness. Anne watched the woman's strained effort; it was all she could do to hold the ewer aloft. The crack in her lip was bleeding, but the girl did not seem to care. She drank, sucking in the liquid until the vessel was empty.

When the girl noticed Anne watching, she shrank back into the darkness. She stayed there cowering for a while, but Anne didn't press her. She could only imagine what this young woman had suffered, what kind of terrors she had known.

"Thank you for your kindness," the young woman said eventually from the shadows. This time she spoke in English. "It is the first generosity I have had in weeks."

"You are not French?" asked Anne, switching to English too.

Anne could hear the girl shuffling in the darkness, retrieving her blanket to cover herself. Then, ever so slowly, she edged forward, settling tentatively at the edge of her iron cage. She lowered her head, the angry grooves of flesh in her almost hairless scalp catching the light.

"I come from London," she said shyly. "My name is Margaret, but you can call me Mags."

Anne's lips curled upward despite herself. It was a small but familiar comfort to hear her mother tongue.

"I am Anne," she said. "Anne Boleyn."

"I know who you are. You are Leonardo da Vinci's apprentice."

Anne nodded. It made sense. The young monk had known her too.

"I have admired your courage for several years now," said Mags. "That you would play the role of apprentice despite your sex. I often wondered what would come of you after Leonardo's passing. The rumors have been so unkind."

The sourness found its way back into Anne's throat. So it was true. Domenico had told her of the rumors, but she thought he had only been trying to frighten her. Perhaps it was worse than she thought. If the townsfolk were talking about Leonardo da Vinci's strange female apprentice, Domenico would have little work to do to see his threats through.

"What do they say about me?" asked Anne.

Mags was the first person she had spoken to in days. If she could tell Anne what wagged the tongues of the people, perhaps she could think of a way to defend herself.

The girl's shoulders sagged. "They say that you bewitched Leonardo da Vinci. But they say far worse things too. That you fornicate with the devil. That you practice Lucifer's magic."

An icy brume crept over Anne's skin and settled there, unwanted.

"I don't believe any of it if that helps at all," Mags said kindly. "I was accused of witchcraft too. And I am no more a witch than you. But I do pity what is to come."

Anne glanced up. "And what is that?" She needed to know what she was facing. Now that the key was gone, this knowledge was the only thing that might help her.

The girl's fingers traced the split in her lip. "Pray don't ask me to speak of it. It's better that you don't know."

"Please, Mags," asked Anne. "I must know."

Mags hesitated, the kindness in her heart as plain as the black eye on her face. Clearly, she was struggling with how much to say.

Anne wrapped her hands around the iron bars, her sixth finger fully exposed. As the girl's gaze settled upon it, her face fell. When Mags finally spoke, her words were hollow.

"The Inquiry of the Magistrate is the first step. The guards will bring you before the king's magistrate and the men of the Balliages so your accusers can give their evidence against you. It is said that three separate accusations, by three separate people, must be levied. But that is often overlooked. Only two people made the claim of witchcraft against me, but the magistrate approved the Hammer of Witches."

"So you were found guilty?"

"No," said Mags. "The inquiry is only the first step. Once the magistrate is satisfied, he grants permission to the king's inquisitor to draw a confession. That is why I look the way I do. The inquisitor is a vile man, and he lusts for blood."

"But if you are not guilty, what confession can he draw?" asked Anne. The icy sensation was sinking into her bones now.

The girl blinked her good eye. "My innocence matters not. The *Malleus Maleficarum* guides the inquisitor, and he follows it to the letter.

On the first day, he stripped me naked and stood me upon a table, looking for witches' marks. And when he found none, he beat me and cut off all my hair." Her lips trembled. "It has been weeks now and the inquisitor tries some new torture every day to draw my confession."

Anne wanted to reach through the cage and touch the young girl's cheek, but she could not. Her own limbs were useless.

"And what happens if they cannot break your will?" Anne asked softly.

The girl shuddered. "Then I will be taken for a public trial by the Parlement de Paris."

"And if you confess?"

"I would never confess," Mags insisted. "I am innocent."

"But if they break you?" Anne asked. "If they force you to confess against your will?"

The girl's voice came out as a rasping whisper. "Then I will be burned alive."

PRESENT DAY

CHÂTEAU DU CLOS LUCÉ, FRANCE

A cloudless blue sky formed a dome over our little wedding party, the light breeze scented with wildflowers from the fields beyond. We had assembled in the parterre garden on the east side of the estate, the hedgerows draped in the same fine ribbon that decorated the castle. Ice sculptures flanked the edges of the terrace, chubby Cupids with their arrows melting in the midday sun. Lively bouquets of crimson roses dusted the lawns, a burst of color adorning the otherwise elegant black-and-white affair.

The ceremony had gone off without a hitch, thanks to Clarisse's dress rehearsal, and I dragged myself through every one of the carefully chore-ographed steps.

Grapes and Dez had shuffled arm in arm down the aisle with such steadiness, she didn't even need her walker. Clarisse had escorted Lucien, her eyes filling with tears as her son met his new husband under a leafy green altar. When Dez and Lucien had sealed their vows with a kiss, my best friend had never looked happier. And I thought I was going to vomit.

Grapes had asked me to be supportive, and I was doing my best, but it was all I could do to pretend to look cheerful about the whole sicken-ingly sweet affair.

"You did well, Ellie," said Grapes quietly. "You were exactly the best man Dez asked you to be."

I sipped my Chardonnay with a stiff nod, glancing at the new couple. "They do look happy," I admitted with a mild chuff.

Grapes gave my arm an extra-long squeeze. "Keep it up, dear. It'll be over soon."

Dez and Lucien were holding hands now as they jested with the group in the shade of the poplars. The wedding party was happily munching on plates of hors d'oeuvres, and Bernice was entertaining everyone with stories of her own wedding years ago. Maurice lingered at Lily's side, her lovely loose curls bobbing at her shoulders. Her hair experiment had worked out well, so at least there was something to be happy about. Although her canary-yellow princess dress was a bit of an eyesore, and I was secretly grateful that Lily's sunshiny brightness would mess up the adoring couple's wedding photos.

I stood back from the group, trying not to look sulky. My stomach was twisted tight, and I didn't want any of the treats that accompanied the wine. I couldn't have eaten anyway, because my teeth clenched every time my eyes landed on the newly married couple. Actually, it happened whenever I looked at John too. We had made of point of being polite through the whole ceremony, but it couldn't help but feel awkward.

John popped a hot pepper jelly cracker in his mouth and closed his eyes.

"Mmmm...that one was delicious," he said in his usual good-natured way.

Normally, his huge appetite would have made me laugh, but this time, I could only pretend to focus on fixing one of the white bows that had gotten tangled in a tree.

Clarisse emerged from the château, floating across the lawns in an elegant black chiffon gown. "Dinner is served."

* * *

Clarisse's elegant wedding theme continued into the dining room. A linen tablecloth and covered chairs were a perfect crisp white. Center-pieces ran the length of the table, towering glass candelabras filled with rose bouquets and pale vanilla-scented candles. In each corner, tall crystal sconces spilled with carnations, a dizzying arrangement of florals draping the floor. At each place setting, a single red rose lay across an elegant bone china plate.

If the table wasn't magnificent enough, the gastronomic feast set upon it certainly was. Platefuls of scallops and monkfish, platters of lobster, roast pheasant, and saumon en papillote, piping hot and heady-scented, were ready to be eaten. Every dish was paired with a corresponding wine, and I couldn't help think about how gluttonous it all was. My stomach remained a fisherman's knot, tighter than any sailor could make, and I couldn't eat a bite.

"Mother, you have outdone yourself," said Lucien, blotting his mouth with a linen napkin.

I forced down a piece of bread, the thick crust scraping my esophagus.

"A meal worthy of kings," agreed Dez.

Clarisse smiled, the dimple in her cheek flashing. "Thank you, my darlings. I wanted everything to be exactly right for my two boys."

She put her hands over Dez and Lucien's, and they both kissed her on the cheek. I pinched my leg underneath the table.

"Not only is this meal perfect, Clarisse," said Gerty as she took a swig of wine, "our whole holiday has been wonderful."

It was true that Clarisse had tended to our every need, and every day of this vacation had been a decadent luxury. But there was something odd about it. It had been almost too perfect. I mean, nothing in real life ever went as smoothly as this, did it?

"I think we can all agree that our burst water pipe was most fortunate after all," said Maurice with a wink. "I got to spend the week with the lovely Lily. And just look at her now. She is a beauty to behold."

Lily's yellow gown was so puffy it stuck out from beneath the table, as though it was fighting back. She produced a weak grimace, but her darting eyes suggested she didn't welcome the compliment, and I had to stifle a guffaw.

"I have only one regret," Maurice continued, lowering his voice for dramatic effect. "I thought for certain we would find the da Vinci key. But alas, there shall be no victor in our little competition."

Dez shot me a dirty look, and I returned a warning glance. Thankfully, he said nothing. But I wasn't sure if it was because Dez understood my meaning or because he didn't want to think about my crazy charade this morning.

Heat burned my cheeks as I thought about how I had barged in on Dez and Grapes. How I had demanded that we stop the wedding because something terrible was going to happen. But we had been through the whole ceremony, the entire reception, and now the wedding meal and nothing had gone wrong. No one had broken a nail or even stubbed a toe.

"I think we need to have a speech," said Clarisse with a light chuckle. "How about we hear from the best man?"

All eyes settled on me as I gave the group a tight smile. I had prepared something last night before everything had gone sideways, and I was determined to give it my best. Like Grapes said, I owed it to Dez.

Clearing my throat, I rose from my seat and held my glass aloft. I wasn't much of a speech maker, but I didn't want to read my notes. It had to sound like it was coming from the heart.

"It is my privilege and honor to stand here as Dez's best man today," I began. "Dez and I found each other as first-year students, two nerds who loved academia. Over the last ten years, we have become more than best friends, we have become family. Sometimes we argue, sometimes we fight, but we always forgive each other in the end. And I think that's because we are so similar—a little crazy, a little cranky, and a lot stubborn."

A reluctant smile broke across Dez's face and it gave me the courage to continue.

"I will admit it," I said, addressing Dez directly now. "At first, I was jealous of your relationship with Lucien. From the day you met, you were so happy together. You and Lucien are different from each other. And maybe that's why you make such a good couple. You fit together like pieces of a puzzle. And that is a beautiful thing."

I swallowed, forcing myself to finish. The next bit was the part I was dreading.

"Lucien, we haven't really gotten to know each other over the last few months. And that is my fault. I let my envy prevent a friendship from growing between us. But you are family now. And that means you and I can start again. I am truly looking forward to getting to know you. Because if Dez loves you, then I do too."

Dez and Lucien exchanged loving glances and the group cooed with appreciation. We toasted the groom and the groom, and I scuttled back to my seat, relieved to have completed my mission without making a total mess of it.

Grapes rose to her feet, holding the edge of her chair to steady herself. "And now...it's time for the cake," she announced.

The Titanium Trio made their strange line formation and filed from the hall in search of their masterpiece. The group mixed and mingled while we waited, everyone helping themselves to the fresh coffee on the sideboard.

Dez approached me as I fixed my lipstick in a hand mirror. "Thanks, El," he said softly. "That meant a lot."

I smiled, wiping a blob of pink from my teeth. "If you're happy, I'm happy. I'm sorry I've been a bit of a shit."

He hugged me and laughed. "You're always a bit of a shit."

I gave him a light punch. "That's what you love about me, isn't it?"

When the Trio returned, they were pushing a massive wedding cake on wheels. I stared, wondering how we had gone from a fifty-pound bag of flour on the kitchen floor to this seven-layer masterpiece.

Delicate pale piping covered the white fondant tiers, each layer decorated in a unique design. The top layer spilled with white edible flowers, paper-thin petals that poured from the cake's apex like a fountain. A refined lattice on the second tier was so delicate it could have been made from the finest lace in France. The third and fourth layers boasted variations of scalloping, accented with dusty, opulent sugar pearls. The fifth and six tiers shone like alabaster marble, tiny pale fleurs-de-lis piped in a pattern to mimic the ceilings of the Clos Lucé. And finally, the bottom layer burst with deep orange and red roses the color of dancing flames, each sugar petal so blazing and luscious, the cake could have been engulfed in real fire.

"I want an extra-big piece," called John, and the group laughed.

"None for me," said Clarisse. "Lucien and I are allergic to fruit cake."

"Then I'll take an extra-big piece too," said Lily, carried away with the fun.

The Trio made sure everyone got an enormous helping. The cake was huge, far too big for such a small gathering, so there was no reason to scrimp on portion size.

I did my best to contain the scowl that was trying to inch across my face as everyone dug into their dessert. I couldn't help but thinking of my meeting with Anne Boleyn. How had we gotten all the way through the wedding and nothing had gone wrong?

John moaned as he inhaled his piece and then went back for a second.

"Oh my God," he moaned, a bit of white icing at the corner of his mouth. "It's delicious."

He plunged in as he always did, groaning with pleasure. Until he made a gurgling noise. It happened fast. His hands flew to his throat, his face turning a deep, angry purple.

"Are you okay?" I asked with alarm.

John clutched his neck, gasping and sputtering, desperate to draw a breath. He began to shake, his muscles convulsing with a violent seizure. Gripped by apoplexy, he tried to speak, but no words would come. He could only gag, before his body stiffened completely and he fell to the ground like a block of wood. My heart almost stopped as his head hit the ground with a loud thud.

There was commotion among the wedding party as I threw myself down at his side.

"Grapes, hurry!" I screamed. "Something's wrong with John!"

My vision was suddenly blurry, and I tried to hold back tears as I wrapped my arms around him. He looked so helpless. So frightened. And there was nothing I could do but plead with him to be okay. Any resentment I was still harboring from our fight was wiped away like chalk on a blackboard, and I was left with only raw, gritty fear.

Grapes was almost at his side when she coughed too, a low gurgling that sent chills down my spine.

My eyes darted to my great grandmother as she fell now, collapsing on the floor, her walker clattering with a sickening crash. I couldn't believe what was happening. Dread sloshed like raw sewage through my intestines, my heart thrashing in my chest.

Now, to my horror, everybody began to fall in a frenzied moment of madness. Lily clutched her throat, and Maurice sputtered into a napkin. Gerty and Bernice collapsed too, their frail bodies gripped with convulsions. It was a monstrous calamity, worse than any nightmare I had ever had. And all I could do was sit, watching it all happen around me, unable to drag myself from John's side. My fingers were wrapped around his collar so tight, I couldn't have removed them if I tried.

"Oh mon Dieu!" exclaimed Clarisse through the chaos. "What is happening?"

"Clarisse, call an ambulance," I cried. "Hurry!"

I was kicking myself for having left my cell phone upstairs. We had all agreed to leave them in our bedrooms. It was a promise we had made to Clarisse at the rehearsal yesterday, so we could focus on the wedding without distraction. And I silently cursed her request.

Clarisse's dark eyes flashed as she set off in search of a telephone.

The wedding party was like the scene of a doomsday massacre, bodies strewn on the black-and-white floors, some rigid and stiff, others still gasping for breath. Suddenly I was so dizzy I thought I might pass out. It was impossible. This couldn't be happening.

I turned back to John, panic sending shockwaves through my body. What would I do if I couldn't talk to him, to apologize for everything? We couldn't leave it like this. There was too much left unsaid.

John's amber eyes burned almost green with distress. His brawny arms were useless and frozen, his shoulders raised high around his neck and I buried my face in his hair.

"Please be okay," I whispered in his ear. "Please, John."

He lay in my arms, helpless and stiff, and I found myself stroking his cheek, as if my own fingers could wake him from this horror. If only the paramedics would come, there could still be a chance to save him. To save everyone. A low moan registered from somewhere far away and I realized it was the sound of my own voice.

"You don't like fruit cake either?" asked Lucien from across the table. He smiled at me lazily, rolling a toothpick along the linen tablecloth.

My eyes snapped to his. "What the hell is wrong with you? Do something to help!"

Lucien looked down at Dez, petrified on the floor beside him. He chuckled, slow and menacing.

"Aphalloides. It's the most incredible mushroom. When they are dried and ground, they blend into cake icing quite nicely." He smacked his lips. "The sweetness covers up the bitter. Works like a charm."

My heart fell through the floor and kept on going. The bastard had poisoned the wedding cake? The world felt like it was going to open up and swallow us all.

"They're quite a nasty little fungus though. The paralysis will lead to death in about half an hour."

Something about this last statement nudged at the back of my panicked brain. I narrowed my eyes. My great-grandmother had an incredible gift for all things herbal. She would have noticed if he had messed with her wedding cake. She would have known something was wrong.

"How... how did you get the mushrooms past Grapes?" I sputtered.

He cocked an eyebrow. "It might surprise you how the right scent can overwhelm the mind. Perfumes and colognes can be marvelous tools."

I wanted to run at Lucien, strangle him, punch him. But I did not. I could only hold John in my lap and check his breathing again. He had wolfed back two slices, twice as much as the others.

"I always knew you were a bastard," I spat. "You never deserved Dez."

Lucien snapped the toothpick in half, his lip curling into a snarl. "You still haven't figured this out, have you, Ellie?"

I didn't reply.

"I'm willing to make you a deal," he said. "I have a vial of antidote in my pocket, but in exchange, you have to give me the key."

Finally, my grey matter kicked into gear. This was the matter of life and death Leonardo da Vinci had told Anne about. Except that the horror hadn't befallen one person in my family, but all of them. My mouth went dry. This was my fault. I hadn't insisted on stopping the wedding. I hadn't trusted my gut despite Anne's warnings.

"You're the Garridan," I said, the hairs on the back of my neck standing on end.

He tipped an invisible cap with his fingers. "Guilty as charged."

I tried to think fast, my eyes darting, but it was no use. "We've all been searching the castle for that stupid key," I fumbled. "You heard Maurice. No one found it."

He chuckled, low and throaty. "Come now, Ellie. Don't play me for a fool. You are Anne Boleyn's granddaughter. And you are a witch. Of course, you have the key. And now you're going to give it to me."

My mind was a frazzled mess of wires, but I had to think of something. Did I hand over the key and fail my twin across time? Or did I watch my entire family die?

"I'm going to call the police," I said, trying my best to sound threatening.

He smiled, slowly adjusting the cufflinks on his perfectly pressed white shirt. "Call whoever you want. They won't get here soon enough. Not if you want to save your friends. So, I suggest you give me the key."

My brain was short-circuiting again, the edges of my vision closing in. I could only think about losing every last one of them, and I took a breath to steady my nerves. I had to calm down or I would be no good to anyone. This wasn't the time for a meltdown.

"I'll give it to you," I said, "but you show me the antidote first."

"You're not in an excellent position to bargain, Ellie. Time is ticking..." He arched an eyebrow. "And John is looking particularly bad."

Exasperated, I dug into my pocket and pulled out the key, the one that Lily and I found in the ink horn. I threw it at Lucien with a desperate sob. I needed him to believe I was giving him the true one.

"You are an asshole," I cried. "Now hand over the antidote."

Lucien snatched the key as it flew mid-air, a victorious grin slithering across his jaw. He pushed his chair back from the table and stretched like a cat. "There is no antidote, you fool," he called over his shoulder.

I sat watching helplessly as he sauntered from the dining room, real tears streaming down my cheeks now. I had been so stupid. So naïve. And I was drowning in self-loathing.

When the true key twitched in my pocket, the idea emerged from my jumbled thoughts like a phoenix rising from the ashes. And without hesitation, I threw off my heels and flew into a sprint.

NOVEMBER 1519
CHÂTEAU D'AMBOISE, FRANCE

The days turned to weeks in the tower's darkness, with only the comings and goings of poor Mags. Every day the warder dragged the girl from her cell, only to return her, even more bloodied than before. When the inquisitor smashed her kneecap, Anne ordered extra ale to comfort her. When the inquisitor kept her awake for days on end, Anne sang songs to help her through her delirium. When the inquisitor broke all her fingers, Anne paid for the girl to be moved to her own jail cell so she could feed Mags herself.

Every day her friend grew weaker, her life force draining, but she remained resolute in denying her accusation. Mags was innocent, she told Anne every day. And even at the worst of the inquisitor's brutality, this defiant young woman would not confess.

Anne had heard nothing more of her own Inquiry of the Magistrate. It was all she could do to care for the girl who had the heart of a lion. And she provided friendship as best she could. Still, her own spirit weakened in the gloom of the prison, her soul turning to shadow.

Anne spent many hours thinking back to the day she had been taken to the tower. How her earliest worries were that she might never see the poppies in the fields again. But it was so much worse than that. One day

Anne, too, would be called to the magistrate. And once that was done, she would meet the inquisitor and follow in Mags's footsteps.

If she had only fully understood the danger she was in when Domenico first threatened her, she might have taken a different course of action. But she had given Ellie Bowlan the key, and she would have to live with that decision. If there had been any hope that perhaps the girl from the future could use the key to change the course of their fates, that had faded too.

Now, Anne spent most of her time, thinking of her home back in England. Had word reached them that she had been imprisoned for witchcraft? She prayed not. It would put such shame on her family. It was the reason she had been sent to France in the first place, to learn to control her powers so she would not be discovered. And now that she was imprisoned, not only had she failed Leonardo, she had failed her family too.

The warder approached with a leering smile. Anne didn't notice the smell of him anymore. She had been wearing the same dress for months and was just as dirty as he. Anne held Mags in her lap, the pus from the girl's eye smearing on the fabric of Anne's skirts.

The jailer leaned between the bars, a look of sick delight in his eyes.

"My lady prisoner. Finalement, c'est à toi."

Anne had spoken only English for months, but she understood him well enough.

Finally, it is your turn...

* * *

The Chambre de Justice was an imposing space. Wood-paneled walls were decorated with formidable tapestries with forest scenes of dancing white stags holding the king's official coat of arms. The ceiling was painted in gold with a daunting message from the heavens: *As above—so below.*

Anne pushed out a ragged breath as she struggled to contain her nerves.

Men of the clergy and the judiciary filled the house, dozens of them lining the perimeter of the hall, and the room buzzed with anticipation.

The lesser magistrates, with their red felt robes and fur-lined hoods, were seated on a raised platform. The chief magistrate, in darker crimson with matching cap and coif, stood at the center of it all, like the pit of a cherry.

Anne stumbled through the crowd with hands bound, escorted by the king's guard. Her legs were so weak, she almost fell to her knees. The dark eyes of the inquisitor flashed with something bordering on hunger when he saw her.

One member held a hand over his nose as she passed. Anne was repulsive now, her dress soiled with unmentionable things. She had lost so much weight, her face had become gaunt, and dark shadows circled her eyes. The men gawked at the sight of her. The stink of the tower on her person, the greasy mat of her hair, the dirt on her face.

As she was seated on the platform, she heard the whispers of the members of the Balliages.

Whore. Filth. Witch.

Anne now understood there would be no such thing as a fair Inquiry of the Magistrate. Not for a crime of witchcraft. A woman like Anne could only threaten these men. She could read and write in French and English. In Greek and Latin too. She was schooled in science and math in a tenure far beyond the education of these jurors. And she had been apprenticed to the greatest scholar, designer, and artist in France. These were the basic facts, and they would be used against her. It was that simple.

The chief magistrate brought his stave of office down upon the raised platform, and it sounded through the legislature with three resounding clacks.

Anne couldn't breathe.

"We come together today as the Parlement de Balliages for the Inquiry of the Magistrate, to fulfill the king's manifold of duty as judge, legislator, and protector of the realm." His voice boomed, loud and sanctimonious. "This woman, Anne Boleyn, is accused of witchcraft, and today we shall hear first testimony to determine if there is sufficient evidence to enact the Hammer of Witches."

This drew a lusty murmuring from the crowd, the inquisitor twisting the *Malleus Maleficarum* in his grip.

The chief turned to Anne, and she clasped her hands to keep them from trembling within their bonds.

"Do you understand you are being tried, not of a lesser crime, but of the Cas Enorme? A crime so severe it is among the ranks of heresy, blasphemy, and murder."

Anne's mouth had gone dry, and she found she couldn't speak.

When she did not reply, the chief raised his hand. "Bring in the first accuser."

The heavy chamber doors swung open, and Domenico da Cortona's heeled shoes made an ominous clack on the marble. She allowed herself a quick glance as her nemesis produced a low bow. The sight of him made her stomach lurch.

The chief magistrate greeted him, and Anne forced back the tears that wanted to come.

"Let us begin, da Cortona," announced the chief magistrate. "Tell us of your accusation. It is a grave one, and I am sure you have good reason to make it."

Anne winced, anticipating the damaging words that would bind her to her fate. It was inevitable. Her pulse thrummed through her body with a heavy pounding beat.

A commotion at the door disturbed the proceedings, and the royal herald burst into the room.

"All hail for the king!"

The clergymen scrambled to their feet and bowed low as King Francis sailed through the chamber, accompanied by his chancellor and the men of his Privy Council. Francis mounted the steps with pompous ceremony as a group of page boys darted in with rich silk cushions. Hastily, they assembled a royal seat, and the king took it, his chancellor at his side.

Anne stared openly. She could not help herself.

"You may begin," said Francis. "I shall partake in this hearing by royal séance."

The magistrate frowned. "But, Sire, are you certain you wish to enact the Lit de Justice for a simple accusation of witchcraft?"

Francis leveled an impudent gaze upon the chief. "It is my divine right to oversee any trial of my interest. This girl was apprenticed to my dearest friend, Leonardo da Vinci. And it is for that reason that I preside today as the judicial authority."

Anne studied the king in his cushioned seat. His fingers were covered with rings, his robes a fine velvet. He was the very vision of grace and power. And she could feel his disgust at the sight of her.

The magistrate's lip twitched peevishly, but he bowed all the same. "Fine then, your Grace. The first witness is ready. Domenico da Cortona, what say you?"

The king frowned. "You have only the one witness?"

The chief tutted. "There is a second accuser, sire. He is being sought by the royal guard." He shook his head, a deep scowl running lines across his brow. "I can assure you, this case is dire. We must protect the public from this...ungodly woman."

The king nodded. "Very well then. Let the case proceed."

Anne's guts coiled like a snake inside her. It was all too obvious King Francis had already decided her guilt. She was a danger to the royal family. Marguerite had told her as much. Thanks to the Goddess, Anne threatened the welfare of the King's wife and children. Francis would only wish to be relieved of her as quickly as possible.

The chief cleared his throat. "Now then. Monsieur da Cortona, do you accuse this woman of witchcraft?"

Domenico nodded. "I do, your honor. Anne Boleyn is a witch and I have the evidence to prove it."

Anne knew she should drop her gaze and sit as demurely as possible, to pretend at feminine humility, but she had to see it. She had to bear witness.

Domenico paced the length of the platform, preparing a damning speech upon his tongue. "This woman keeps with the devil in the moonlight. She is his muse," he said steadily. "She has six fingers on her hand. It is a monstrous deformity and an abomination to God."

To her horror, the chief magistrate grabbed Anne's arm and held it aloft. She tried to ball it into a fist, but everyone could see there were six fingers there. There was a raucous reaction from the men as they studied her hand. Anne's cheeks burned, but there was nothing she could do but be subjected to their jeering.

"There is more," continued Domenico with fervor. "There are

rumors all over the kingdom that she bewitched the great Leonardo da Vinci. It is the only reason he kept her as his apprentice instead of taking on a male, as would be appropriate. A good, godly woman would never do a man's work. It is not only evidence of her masculine ambition, but also a sign she is a witch."

The crowd buzzed with this new evidence, with appreciative nods from the jurors around the edge of the platform.

The snake in Anne's guts sunk in its fangs, and the pain ripped through her. Leonardo always told her that her sex mattered not, only her mind. There was a time that she had dared believe him, but obviously, Leo had been wrong.

"I saw her myself, Sire, several months ago," said Domenico. "I was admiring da Vinci's clock one late morning, having completed my business that day. And there was Anne Boleyn, conducting magic in the great hall of the Château du Clos Lucé. She appeared before my eyes as if from thin air. One moment I was alone, and the next she was standing before the clock, as though the devil himself had delivered her there."

The jurors grew impassioned with this evidence, and the magistrate clacked his stave to silence them. "We have located the second witness, your Majesty," he announced. "The guards are escorting him now."

The doors of the Chambre de Justice burst open, and the king's guard brought in a young, lanky boy, his face covered in spots. He stumbled under the guards' heavy-handed escort. It was the young lad who had driven her and Leonardo through the snowstorm. She sensed his fear under the scrutiny of the clergy, and her neck grew blotchy at the sight of him.

Domenico produced a vicious grin. "This boy was witness to the greatest of evil doings," he bellowed. "He saw Anne Boleyn set fire to two men using only her mind."

"Is this true, boy?" asked the magistrate.

The child doffed his cap and held it over his chest, his voice cracking as he spoke. "They were wicked men, your honor. They sought to harm Leonardo da Vinci. I tried to defend him, but they knocked me out. When I awoke, Anne was standing in front of Master da Vinci, and the two men were running off, howling at the fires set in their furs."

Anne's whole body was trembling now. The boy had spoken the

truth, and everyone had heard it. The room exploded with excitement, hushed whispers turning to open contempt.

The magistrate clacked his stave of office. "Now then. Let us hear from the accused. What do you have to say for yourself, Mistress Boleyn?"

Anne dropped her eyes in shame, but she said nothing.

She'd had months to think it over, and she knew she could not use what Leonardo had told her of Domenico's secrets. By doing so, she would implicate her master, and she simply could not do that. She could not tarnish his reputation. And besides, no matter what she said in her defense, nothing would help her. The evidence against her was too great.

The magistrate's eyes bulged with satisfaction. "Clearly, this woman is a danger to us all. This witch is so powerful, even the brilliant Master da Vinci suffered at her hands. Monsieur da Cortona, you deserve high praise for ferreting her out."

Domenico sank into a chivalrous bow, his hand over his heart.

The magistrate turned to Francis. "What say you, my king? Surely, you see there is sufficient evidence to proceed with the inquisition."

All eyes were on Francis now as the room fell silent. There was no shuffling of feet, no rustling of cloaks. No one dared even breathe.

Anne prepared herself for what was to come.

For the first time since the hearing began, the king leveled a hateful gaze upon her, his mouth twisted with contempt. He waved a heavily bejewelled hand ceremoniously.

"Have the prisoner returned to the tower as she awaits my decision."

PRESENT DAY
CHÂTEAU DU CLOS LUCÉ, FRANCE

I bolted through the castle, desperate to get to the clock before Lucien. He had a head start on me, but I was a runner and I could be faster.

My tight dress was slowing me down, and I ripped the hem of my skirt so I could make a full stride. The balls of my feet tracked like a cheetah as I forced my muscles into a sprint. I took a shortcut through the library, and I could only pray Lucien hadn't thought to take the same route. I knew now that getting to the clock was the only thing that could set things right. It was just as Anne Boleyn had said. If I could go back by one hour, I could stop this whole thing from happening.

Flying through the servants' wing and across the staircase to the kitchens, I skittered past the front entrance and into the great hall. When I reached the clock, Lucien was nowhere to be seen. I couldn't understand where he might be, but there was so little time, I didn't stop to check.

Flinging open the frontispiece, I stabbed the true key into the clock. I took a second to catch my breath, my heart thundering in my chest. Carefully, I turned the key back just one click.

As I did, a thin hand touched my shoulder. It was not Lucien's, but a set of soft, feminine fingers.

"Ellie?" said Clarisse. "Are you alright?"

"Don't!" I shouted. But it was too late.

Without warning, we were swallowed by a milky blue haze, circling inside a vortex. We spun with a dizzying force, and I gripped Clarisse's hands, desperate to steady the two of us. Somehow, all the cells in my body were pulling outward, then coiling around like a gigantic spring, no longer obeying the laws of physics.

"Hold on, Clarisse," I called as my mouth, my nose, my whole face was pulled into the funnel.

I could barely make sense of what was happening. The world was a whirling eddy, everything in it a terrible blur.

"Don't let me go, Ellie," Clarisse pleaded.

We clung to each other like woodland burrs as the room unraveled. Tiny strings in thousands of colors wound and unwound into oblivion and I blinked to be sure I wasn't hallucinating. Everything in the great hall, the clock, the table with the museum brochures, Leonardo da Vinci's replica inventions, all disintegrated into frayed threads, disentangling themselves into nothing.

The force of it sucked the air from my lungs with such an intensity, I couldn't even scream. My mouth was hitched open in a frozen mask, and I was helpless to do anything but watch.

The threads looped around in a dizzying array of color, bright red strands for the poppies in the fields, mossy sages and hunter greens for the gardens, deep blue shades for the perfect summer sky. They twisted and turned, growing like vines and then disappearing again until they wound into oblivion.

When every last filament was gone, Clarisse and I found ourselves floating somewhere out in space. The spinning sensation melted away as our bodies hovered in the blackness, a million stars flickering above. The milky white moon spun around the earth, the sun at the center of the orbiting planets. I tried to clear my vision, to attempt to anchor myself to reality. But it was no use. We floated, suspended in the ether, not part of the real world anymore, but hanging above it in a strange kind of purgatory.

"Stop!" Clarisse commanded with a voice that was ancient and old.

I stared at her. And then back to the bizarre emptiness around me.

The universe had screeched to a halt like a blood clot in the arteries of time. A spewing storm on the sun froze, the earth failed to rotate on its axis, the moon useless in its orbit. Time itself had been thwarted, and the silence of its void was deafening.

My guts went slick.

Clarisse's hands were still entwined with mine, but now her shape was morphing. I watched with dawning horror as the dark-haired woman mutated into something not quite human. She was as vaporous as smoke, a shimmering miasma. The black of her hair grew into a new fiery red, long curling tendrils covering a voluptuous torso. Her legs dissolved into the mirrorlike tail of a fish, wispy and swishing.

"What the hell are you?" I cried.

Clarisse's forked tongue slid over full, luscious lips. She licked the air, her serpentine body wriggling through the nothingness. A set of piercing emerald eyes collided with mine, her gaze impossibly beautiful, yet equally vile. Something dark burrowed inside me as our eyes locked, and instantly I felt her evil trying to attach itself to my soul.

"Ellie Bowlan," she hissed, "we finally meet."

I recoiled at the sight of her, my skin wriggling as though it was covered with grub worms. She was an abomination of flesh, and yet she was not flesh at all.

"Surely, you know me. I am the Goddess," she said, her tone almost motherly now. "You are the one I have been waiting for."

I twisted from her grip. It was an instinctive reaction, one I didn't quite understand. But something told me I had to hold her gaze. And so, I endured the discomfort, determined to keep her in check.

Drawing her mouth into a pucker, the Goddess blew a light gale across the expanse, and it thrust her upward until her sinewy form was far above me. She grew larger now, more beastly, and I had to twist my neck to look up at her.

Without warning, finger-like threads grew from the ends of her red hair and snaked toward me. I skittered back to avoid them, but my own locks began to grow too. Betraying me, my hair sprouted auburn coils that inched toward hers, braiding together until we were tethered in this strange, darkened void. As our tresses became fastened, I could feel the Goddess sinking further into me like a hungry parasite.

"You see?" she said. "We are connected. It has always been that way."

Sickened by the sensation of her maggoty energy, I pulled at the strands of hair, but they were as strong as silk, and I could not break them. My pulse was barbwiring through my veins, threatening to tear away every ounce of my remaining sanity.

"Get away from me!" I shouted.

She laughed wildly. "You cannot deny it. You are my fire child. I am yours and you are mine."

New strands of the Goddess's hair grew in another direction. Suspended in the frozen universe, high above the atmosphere, the threads wove earthbound, down, down, down, until they found a young woman sitting in a castle tower. The Goddess's red tresses reached into the girl's matted chestnut locks, braiding meticulously until a new bond was formed.

I gasped. A set of cymbals crashed in my ears at the sight of her. Anne Boleyn sat in a darkened jail cell, dirty and thin, tears spilling down her cheeks. I could feel the hollow in her chest, the desperation that permeated every fiber of her being. The acuity of her pain quieted something inside me. I remembered our fundamental bond now. I needed to be strong for her.

"You come from Anne Boleyn," said the Goddess. "Do you see it now, Ellie? I am connected to you, just as I am connected to Anne."

The hairs that linked the Goddess to Anne Boleyn rippled in the obscurity, fine gossamer strings just as strong as the ones that bound the Goddess and me. But there was one more coupling. Light silvery threads joined Anne and myself, but this linkage shimmered with something different, an incandescence that was honest and true.

We were, each of us connected, in a strange, unknowable triangle.

Instinctively I despised this creature. She smelled of evil, and I wanted no part of her bondage. In my heart, I knew Anne Boleyn wanted no part of her either.

"What do you want from me? From us?" I spat.

"We are tethered, through the cosmos," said the creature, seductive and low. "And now the Trifecta is complete."

My connection with Anne Boleyn was helping to quell the wriggling sensation in my chest, and it allowed me to think.

"The Garridan's Trifecta?" I asked.

The Godess nodded with pleasure, the scales of her fishtail reflecting in the light of the stars. "Indeed, my child. You are a smart one."

"But I am no spy," I said with disgust.

She laughed. "Of course not. I have an army of Garridans to do my bidding. But you are not among them." She pointed a sinewy finger at me. "Don't you see? You, Anne, and I. We are the Trifecta. The three most powerful witches in the world. It was always meant to be this way, fated in the cosmos."

The ribbons that connected our threesome danced and cajoled. I found myself shaking my head, refusing to accept her words. I didn't want this. I couldn't be part of it. I pinched my lips, fighting the urge to vomit. The Chardonnay I had drunk at the reception roiled in my stomach, and I wasn't sure it was going to stay down.

"You come from a talented bloodline, with an incredible gift and an incredible mind. It seemed logical that I would choose you and Anne Boleyn to help me accomplish the greatest feat in a thousand years," she said with a joyful slither. "Now that we are three, our power is vast. I needed that strength to achieve it."

"To achieve what?"

The Goddess looked upon me, jubilation in her eyes. "To conquer time, of course."

I blinked. "But that is not possible."

She twirled a strand of copper hair in her fingers. "Oh, but it is. It has already happened. And we each had our part to play. But I needed *you* most of all. As the true keeper of the key, I couldn't have done it without you."

Without thinking, my hand went to the pocket in my dress, and the true key flinched against my hip.

The Goddess's gaze followed my hand, but she did not make a move for it. "That key is what I have been waiting for. It took Anne's curse to give Leonardo da Vinci reason enough to build the clock. It was a feat of science. A labor of love, to protect a girl he loved like his own daughter. He never would have gone to the trouble if she were not in such grave danger."

The creature flicked her reptilian tongue. "And then it was another five hundred years of waiting for you to be born so the Trifecta could be completed."

The Goddess twisted, attempting to mesmerize me, but I wouldn't let her lure me into a trance. Though I could feel the pull of her desire, attempting to beguile me.

"It was Anne's job to set the Boleyn Curse in motion," she continued, "but it was never hers to end. That was always your fate, Ellie."

Understanding splashed my face like cold water and startled me from my panic. That's why Anne and I shared such a strong bond. We both had a role to play in the cosmos. That's why the filaments that connected us shimmered, untarnished, and unsullied. We were the two ends of the bloodline, where the curse began and ended.

As the realization hit me, something inside me hardened, like the pit of a peach. I had promised to protect the key at all costs, and that's what I intended to do.

"I'll never give it to you," I seethed.

The Goddess smiled. "Perhaps not, but you have done something better. You brought me inside the void of time, to a place I could not travel. And now that I am here, time is mine to conquer and reconquer as it pleases me. I am the puppet master. And as long as that key exists, that lovely little portal to time itself, I am the most powerful creature in the universe."

Gritting my teeth, I slid my hand into the pocket of my dress, wrapping my fingers around the little gold fishhook. The Goddess would never take it from me. I had made a promise to Anne. To Grapes.

I glared, laying bare my repulsion at the site of her.

"Do not look at me like that, child," she simpered. "You must see why I wished to have it. Time is the one constant in the universe. The ability to change it, to make it my own, is the greatest power that exists."

Loathing scraped the back of my throat and made my voice raw. "You only want to wield it for your own pleasure."

She pouted, the lines of her mouth becoming ugly. "That may be true, Ellie. But were you not planning to use the key only moments ago to change the course of things? Events that did not suit your preferences?"

The Goddess pointed down again, but now the lens focused on the tragedy in the dining room of the Clos Lucé. It was the scene of the wedding massacre. The Titanium Trio were sprawled on the marble floor, grasping for one another. Lily and Maurice lay side by side, clutching their throats. Dez's hands were furled into claws trying to fight the poison's terrible wrath. But it was my beautiful John, his eyes bloodshot, that stopped my heart.

I covered my mouth, my resolve weakening. I tried to keep the pain from my eyes, to hide the tears that lingered there. All the jealousy, all the guilt, all the fear collided on my face in a perfect display of humanity. Intrigued by my reaction, she touched my cheek, and it burned hot and cold at the same time.

"Let me show you, dear Ellie. I can do anything. I can make the flowers yellow if I like."

She pointed at the scene, and the white flowers that decorated the wedding table became a bright lemon yellow. The single crimson rose at each place setting was now a pale gold.

My eyes grew wide.

She licked her lips with pleasure. "Impressed? Well, that was nothing. As the puppet master, it is all up to me." She scanned the scene, her gaze settling on the bodies scattered on the floor. "Let me give the Titanium Trio back to you," she said. "It is a shame to think they were poisoned. There was so much talent between them."

The Goddess snapped her fingers, and the Trio now sat at the dining room table, no cake plates in front of them. Grapes, Bernice and Gerty held their glasses aloft, toasting their boy Dezzie.

I gasped, a thousand-pound weight lifting from my body. Without warning, my heart was pulling in two directions. I knew it wasn't right. But my need for my great grandmother was too strong. And despite this creature's evil, I wanted her to continue with her magic.

The Goddess frowned, as though she was not sure how to read my silence. "That wasn't enough for you? Well how about I return Desmond, and Lily too? I like them both. Smart, those two."

Now Dez was in his seat, laughing at a joke someone had just told. Lily was fiddling with her skirts, working the stiff fabric back under the table. A tear ran down my cheek and I swiped it away before she could see it.

The Goddess was moving people around like dolls at a tea party. It was reprehensible, but there was something about her power, her ability to change things on a whim. Its vastness was inconceivable. But with each swipe of her hand, she was setting my family back in place, safe and sound. And like a greedy child, I wanted more. There was one more person I needed her to restore. I needed it badly.

"What about John?" I asked, trying to keep my voice calm.

She put her hands over her heart with a mocking gesture. "Oh, how sweet. Does Ellie Bowlan finally understand her love for John? After all these months."

"Please give him back to me," I heard myself pleading.

"John cannot live, I'm afraid," she said with a nonchalant shrug. "He was to be the father of your child. And that child cannot be born. You must be the last of your bloodline. We are the Trifecta. A fourth would upset the order of things."

A door slammed shut around my heart. I drew my lip into a snarl. It was obvious there would be no negotiating with this creature. She did not care about me. And I would not be her puppet. No matter what.

The answer came to me then, as clear and true as my contempt for her.

For the Goddess, the threads between us formed her Trifecta, a way to bind us to her. But for Anne and myself, they would always be our curse. Unless the threads of time were severed, we would never be free. It was Anne's job to set the curse in motion, and it was my job to end it.

"What about Maurice?" I asked, my voice steadying. "Don't you want to spare him too?"

The creature frowned as she considered the question. Maurice lay petrified on the floor, grabbing at his collar. She tilted her head, toying with the idea, acting like a spoiled girl at her birthday party.

I slipped the silver scissors from my pocket, confident now that I knew what to do. It wasn't exactly as Anne had counseled, but it was close. It wasn't so much a disconnecting of a single bundle of threads, but the severing of the entire triangle. And it had to be done.

"I don't think so, " she said, still enjoying her tea party game. "I have no use for him."

I took hold of the threads tethering the Goddess and me and snipped as quietly as I could. Leonardo da Vinci's scissors cut through the gossamer strings with ease, the silver tines firm against the ethereal strands. I winced as they sliced, thinking the Goddess might notice. But she did not.

For me, the writhing inside me retreated a little, so I knew I was on the right track.

"Well, what about Lucien?" I asked. "He was useful, wasn't he?"

As the Goddess searched the castle for her Garridan, I sought Anne in the tower. She existed on a different plane than the one playing out in the Clos Lucé dining room, but she was still visible from my aerial position. My heart went out to her. My twin across time sat on a heap of rotting straw, staring empty-eyed at the iron bars of her prison.

"You must sever the link between our timelines," she had said. "It is the only way."

Fortified by the memory, I knew I had to do it. I grabbed the shimmering threads that connected Anne and me. With a determined snip, the link between us was dismantled. For a second, my heart spasmed, pain radiating along my bones. But Anne had been right. Severing our connection was the only way.

"Lucien was good, I suppose," said the Goddess, looking for her favorite doll. "But there will be other spies in the future."

Watching her carefully, I pushed through the darkness, blowing myself across the expanse the way she had done earlier. When I reached the threads that tied Anne to the Goddess, my hands trembled. I was almost there. If I could just sever this last bundle, we would be free of the Goddess forever.

"If Lucien was a good soldier," I continued, playing her game for a bit longer, "don't you want to reward him?"

Clutching the last braid of threads in my fist, a lone filament danced just beyond my reach. The Goddess turned toward me as I snipped, the single strand escaping the wrath of my scissors.

The creature looked upon my handiwork, her eyes darting to the blades. "What are you doing?"

We were a floating, tangled mess of strings undulating through the darkened vacuum, a solitary remaining thread connecting her to Anne Boleyn. Tiny strands, every color of the rainbow, dangled and frayed, twisted haphazardly without form or function. The triangle that once bound us neatly together was a jumble of chaos.

Desperate now, I reached for the remaining strand, trying to sever it once and for all. But the Goddess jerked it away.

"You ungrateful little witch!" she howled.

I tried again, grappling to reach it with my scissors. But the Goddess was mutating, fury rippling off her in waves. Her fishtail coiled in on itself, winding like a top into her naked torso. Her arms spiraled, even her face twisted into nothing, until the only thing left was her fiery red hair.

Long, luscious ringlets became an irascible vortex of fire. She was no longer a figure, but a tornado of blazing malevolence. The Goddess roared, raising a boiling claw and hurled a fiery maelstrom at me.

I crouched into a ball to withstand her wrath. Thick lava slammed against my body, flames licking at my flesh, heaps of ash clogging my lungs. Her fireball should have killed me instantly, but somehow it did not. The heat of the flame was hot on my skin, but it did not burn. The smoke collected in my throat, but it did not choke me.

It was terrifying, but I finally understood. I was the Goddess's fire child, after all. I was a part of her, and she of me. I could not be damaged by the power that connected us.

Her assault continued, orange magma spewing, but still, I did not burn. I hadn't used my gift in months. I had always refused to acknowledge the witchy part of myself. It seemed so abnormal, so frightening. And yet, at this moment, it was the most natural thing in the world.

From my crouched position, my scar flared, a strength building from a ruthless loathing of this creature. It came from my gut, a deep, unrelenting umbrage. This demon was going to try to take John away from me. And I was going to fight, no matter what.

An angry energy traveled through my limbs, prickling my veins, and irritating my flesh. This time, I didn't worry about controlling it. I wanted the Goddess to know my full vengeance. To hurt her, to maim her, to destroy her. I raised my hand to the twisting whirlwind of fire and released my wrath. It shot from my fingertips in a hostile wall of flames.

The Goddess was temporarily repelled by my inferno, but she did not back away. Nor was she surprised at what I could do. She seemed to know I would be her equal adversary.

Releasing the flames felt so good, I let it radiate through me. Our standoff raged, two fiery streams battling, a red-hot conflagration bashing and slamming, unleashing a torrent a white smoke that billowed upward.

"You can't hurt me," I shouted over the roar.

As the intensity of her storm grew stronger, mine increased in equal measure. We were a perfect match, our fire power ratcheting up and down in unison.

"Perhaps not, but I have still won," she shouted maniacally. "Thanks to you, I now control time."

As the flames wrestled between us, the true key in my pocket twitched. I was so focused on fighting the Goddess, I almost didn't notice. But when I did, an idea took hold. I wasn't sure if it would work, but I had to try. For myself. For John. And for Anne Boleyn.

I pulled the little fishhook from my pocket and held it aloft for the creature to see.

"You forget, Goddess. I am the true keeper of the key."

Her green eyes flashed. "Don't do it, Ellie! Don't you dare."

The fire raged between us as I forced the key into the blaze. It was stubborn at first, refusing to cede to the heat. But it must have been the magic of the torrent, born from our mutual malevolence, that finally caused the little thing to yield. It melted in my grasp, softening, mollifying, bending, until it was nothing but a lump of charred gold. With a victorious grin, I showed her the blackened hunk of metal, ruined and useless.

"Nooooo!" the Goddess howled.

The sound of her cries went on and on, touching the very edges of time itself. As her moans reverberated through the inky blackness, the universe undulated, expanding and contracting on itself. And when it was ready, it vomited the Goddess from its clutches. It knew what she was, and it did not want her any more than I did.

She wailed furiously as it flung her from the darkened void of space, expelling her like an unwanted piece of trash.

"I told you I would never give you the key," I shouted.

I could almost hear the cosmos rejoicing as the Goddess's flaming form dwindled to ash, and then into nothing at all.

I sucked in a breath.

But there was no time to rest, because the threads of time were reweaving into the objects in the great room at the Château du Clos Lucé. Leonardo da Vinci's mechanical lion formed first, followed by the heavy oak doors of the great hall. A rainbow of strings were thrashing on a great cosmic loom of time until the clock itself came into view. The strands twisted and turned as the black and white of the floors and red brick of the walls knitted into place, followed by the tapestries, the fountains, and the gardens beyond.

When it stopped, it was violent, like someone had just slammed their foot on the brakes. It threw me to the floor, gasping. My eyes were filled with soot, and I heaved a deep breath.

Slowly, the room cleared, and the ash fell away.

Da Vinci's clock stood as it always had, and I grabbed its edge to pull myself up. My arms and legs were jelly. My vision was blurred, and my head pounded. But there was no time for any of that, because I had to get to John.

NOVEMBER 1519

CHÂTEAU D'AMBOISE, FRANCE

The warder greeted Anne with a treacherous grin. He peppered her with questions as he escorted her through the prison's gloom, but she was too devastated to reply. Anne had spent months preparing for this day, but that hadn't made things any easier. The evidence against her was so insurmountable, she hadn't been able to utter a single word in her defense.

"Things didn't go well then?" the jailer chided.

She ignored him, refusing to take the bait.

"It's fine if you don't want to talk, lady prisoner. It has been an exciting day anyway." A giggle bubbled from his throat. "While you were at your inquiry, your companion was introduced to the rack."

Anne's eyes grew wide. "What did you say?"

Ghoulish shadows danced along the man's pale face, his wet tongue darting over yellow teeth. "The inquisitor's rack is a nasty device. It'll take the fight out of the feistiest of prisoners. I'm afraid your Mags isn't so stubborn anymore."

Anne ran toward her cell, stumbling through the darkness.

"Slow down, lady," he called. "You'll get there soon enough."

Mags was a mangled heap in the straw, her bald head reflecting in the torch's light. The girl whimpered, a piteous mewling that set Anne's nerves on fire.

She was so crippled, Mags had not even drawn the blanket around herself. Her wrists and ankles were bloodied from where they were tied to the rack, but that was just the beginning. Her arms hung at awkward angles, no longer attached to their sockets. Her legs too had come unhinged, and they lay like a marionette on broken strings.

"Oh, Mags," said Anne, sinking to her knees. "What have they done to you?"

For a time, Mags did not stir. She lay barely moving, with only the rise and fall of her chest to signal she was still alive. Anne lay the blanket over her nakedness and stroked the girl's cheek, hoping her touch would provide the smallest of comforts.

"Anne?" Mags whispered through her delirium. "Is that you?"

"Yes, it's me. I'm here now. I'll take care of you."

Mags's eyes fluttered. Blood pooled in the corner of her mouth from where they had pulled out three of her teeth. "I wasn't strong enough..."

Anne wiped the reddish drool from Mags's lips. "What do you mean?" she asked. "Mags, you are the bravest woman I know."

The girl shook her head feebly. "I did it. I confessed."

Anne stopped, her hands trembling so hard now, she was afraid to touch her friend anymore. This girl had withstood the beatings of the inquisitor. She had even endured the Choke Pear. But today she had been completely and utterly broken.

Mags shook her head. "Soon, they will take me to the pyre."

"No, please," begged Anne. "That can't be true."

The girl gave her the most fragile of smiles. "At least, it will be over soon...and then it won't hurt anymore."

Anne wanted to wrap her arms around her friend, but she could not. Mags was so brutally damaged, she didn't want to hurt her. She could understand why Mags had finally given in. The rack had destroyed her so completely, her body could never heal. Even if she lived, she would have spent the rest of her life in agony.

Mags gazed at her tenderly. "Thank you for being my friend, Anne Boleyn," she whispered. "I don't know what I would have done without you."

A fat tear slipped down Anne's cheek, tracing a line through the filth on her face. It was so terribly unfair. Mags was so kind, so gentle, so innocent. But none of that mattered. The inquisitor had decided her fate, regardless of the truth.

In that instant, a dam broke inside Anne, and she couldn't hold back the tears any longer. She buried her face in her friend's neck. Rasping sobs shook her whole body.

"When I am gone," said the girl, "you must try to be strong. It will be lonely with only the warder for company. But you mustn't let yourself sink into despair."

Anne clung to her friend, furious with what the inquisitor had done to her. Faced with Mags's suffering, she could see her own future. She knew she would have to go through the same ordeal alone. And perhaps that was the most frightening thing of all.

She was crying so hard, she barely noticed the king's sentries standing above them in their blue and yellow livery. They yanked Mags ruthlessly from Anne's grip, and the girl groaned in their arms.

"No!" Anne howled, spittle flying from her mouth. She scrambled on her hands and knees like a dog, grabbing at their feet.

The men heaved up the girl's ruined body, and Mags cried out, her eyes rolling back in her head.

"Please don't hurt her!" she pleaded.

But the men shoved Anne into the straw and dragged Mags away. She could do nothing but watch them go, her friend's limp form swinging over the guard's shoulder, her arms and legs dangling like they had never been part of her at all.

* * *

When the day of Anne's inquiry came, she was a filthy, sodden mess, and her state of disarray titillated the representatives of the Parlement de Balliages. Her hair was caked with excrement, and she smelled of it too. Her body was so thin, she might have been a skeleton inside her dress. She truly looked like a witch, and judgment was written on the faces of every juror in the room.

Anne sat in the defendant's seat awaiting the verdict, staring vacantly into nothing. The rope that bound her hands ached, but she didn't care. Her mind was an empty void. She only wondered when the trial might begin so she could make her confession. As Mags had pointed out, at least being burned alive meant it would be over soon.

Alone in the tower, Anne had given in to the hopelessness that gnawed at her skin like the prison's resident rats. The last part of her heart, the tiny piece that the loss of Leonardo had not crushed, had been destroyed when they had taken Mags away. And after that, time had seemed to circle around her, the threads warping and weaving, strangling her into despair.

"All hail for the king," announced the herald.

The page boys assembled the king's Lit de Justice as Francis sailed through the hall, his furred robes trailing behind him. Members of the king's Privy Council took their respective places, but the magistrate did not have to silence the chamber. This time, all eyes were on the monarch.

"Is the king ready to make his pronouncement?" the chief asked ceremoniously.

Francis was grave as he leaned back in his seat with an air of divine judgment. "I have heard the indictment of Domenico da Cortona and have made my decision."

Anne felt her chest tighten with a force that threatened to crush her ribs.

There was a low murmuring in the hall, and the magistrate clacked his stave.

The king passed a scroll to the doughy man at his side. "My chancellor shall read my answer to the members of the Parlement."

Anne lowered her gaze, her heart railing against its cage.

"By the grace of God," the chancellor read with imposing authority, "King Francis the First of France and Navarre has reviewed the evidence for the Inquiry of the Magistrate against this woman, Anne Boleyn, apprentice to the late Leonardo da Vinci. The king has made his decision on the basis of the four pieces of evidence presented. They are as follows."

There was an audible pause as the chancellor unwound the scroll, and a familiar bubble of nausea burned away at Anne's insides.

"First, upon the accusation that Anne has six fingers on her right hand and that this deformity is an abomination by God. The king acknowledges Anne's six fingers. He has seen them with his own eyes. But such a deformity, he determines, is not grounds enough to levy a valid accusation. The king's own wife, Claude d'Angoulême, suffers a deformity of the spine. And yet, she reigns over France with a dignity and grace divined by the angels. And so, upon this first claim, the king finds it insufficient evidence of witchcraft."

The court filled with an excited buzz. Clearly, the members of the judiciary were surprised by the king's logic. Although Anne did understand it. To accuse a woman of witchcraft, based solely on her deformity, would be difficult when the queen herself suffered such a thing.

Anne thought about Claude now, how her father had hated her because of the curve in her spine. But it was that imperfection that had given the queen such immense compassion, such kindness. It was that infirmity that had made Anne love Claude best.

The chancellor cleared his throat, and the room hushed again.

"Second, upon the accusation that Anne Boleyn performed duties not befitting a woman by being apprenticed to Leonardo da Vinci. The king accepts this young woman has been trained in science and mathematics. That she can read and write, translate and transcribe like that of a cleric. And this knowledge is thanks to Leonardo da Vinci's tutelage. But while her skills were his gift to her, they do not make her a witch. The king's own sister is a writer, a translator and transcriber. Marguerite de Navarre is educated like a man and is highly respected for this virtue. Anne Boleyn's education is no more evidence of witchcraft than his sister Marguerite's. And so, upon this second claim, the king finds it insufficient evidence of witchcraft."

The judiciary reacted with silent outrage this time. Only the sounds of bodies shuffling filled the room. For a second, Anne allowed herself a glance at King Francis, who sat somber in his chair. His verdict on this account was more surprising. Although perhaps on this accusation, Francis merely sought to protect his sister in the same way he protected the Queen.

Anne resigned herself that the worst was coming. It was inevitable. She took a ragged breath and waited.

"Third, upon the accusation that Anne Boleyn set fire to a group of thieves in the woods of Chambord. The witness admitted that he was unconscious at the time of the attack. He did not see Anne do anything other than stand over Leonardo da Vinci as the men fled into the woods with their furs alight. In this respect, the king believes Anne showed only courage in defending her master. She is no more someone who can start fires with her mind than the boy who gave witness. And so, on this third claim, the king finds it insufficient evidence of witchcraft."

At this finding, the jurors exploded with indignity. It was one thing to dismiss the charges that would have disgraced Queen Claude and the king's sister, but here the monarch was dismissing valid testimony.

Anne's stomach tightened. She wondered if she had had misunderstood. Or perhaps she was simply losing her mind. She checked the room to be sure. The members of the clergy were mumbling their dissent, an indistinct grumbling at this last judgement. But it was the young boy who caught Anne's eye. He squirmed in his seat, picking at the spots on his face. She couldn't be sure, but she thought he looked relieved.

A strange buoyancy was starting to build in her chest, something she hadn't felt in months. But she dared not allow herself to hope. There was the matter of her time traveling, and that would be evidence enough of her craft.

The magistrate banged his stave, calling the court to order, his nostrils flexing with disdain.

The chamberlain held his head high with the authority of the monarch at his back.

"Fourth, and final, upon the accusation that Anne Boleyn materialized in front of the clock at the Clos Lucé, having been seen by one man, and one man alone. The witness in this case, Domenico da Cortona, has complained to the king of an excess of work put upon him by the building of the new hunting lodge at Chambord. With the passing of Master da Vinci, all efforts of oversight have fallen to his shoulders, and he has made repeated complaints of weariness. It is the king's opinion that the magnitude of this man's fatigue has led to hallucinations and misremembering of events. And so, upon this claim, the king finds it insufficient evidence of witchcraft."

Now, the court erupted with egregious outrage, but this time the

magistrate did not flex his stave to settle them. The muscle in Domenico's jaw clenched as the men's voices intensified, but he maintained his
courtly decorum.

Anne's breath caught in her throat. She stared at Francis with brazen
confusion. The king could not have just dismissed this last claim. It
would have been impossible to question Domenico's credibility in a
witchcraft trial. And yet, that was what had happened. At least she
thought so. The whole thing was like being part of one of Leonardo's
missives, with his secret handwriting that turned everything on its head.
It was all backward and confusing and impossible to understand.

Now, she thought she saw a faint blue light shimmering from the
white collar of Francis's robes, and she blinked, trying to clear her vision.
Perhaps she was simply so drained, her mind was playing tricks on her.

The chancellor's voice boomed over the din. "It is the divine right of
Francis d'Angoulême, king of France and Navarre, to preside over this
Inquiry of the Magistrate, through the edict of the Lit de Justice. And
the king makes his final judgment." He took a long breath before
concluding. "The accuser, Domenico da Cortona, has provided insufficient evidence for the Hammer of Witches. Anne Boleyn is innocent."

The chancellor grabbed the twine that bound Anne's wrists and cut it
loose with a knife. He thew her bonds to the floor as the room prickled
with injustice.

Anne gasped as her hands fell into her lap, freed from the bloodied
twine. She stared straight ahead, unblinking, barely able to breathe.

The chief magistrate flushed the color of his four-pointed crimson
hat. "But, Sire, surely you shall want to reconsider?"

The king rose officiously from his chair. "My word is final," he
commanded, his voice breaking through the chaos. "You are all men of
the court, and you understand the law. There shall be no further opposi-
tion on this case."

The men of the judiciary and the clergy muttered their discontent,
but the rumbling petered out quickly enough. They filed from the room,
the chief magistrate first among them. The clergy followed, then the
men of the Balliage. Domenico shuffled along with the others, shooting a
hateful glare at Anne as he passed. The king and his Privy Council exited
last, a potent sign that King Francis would have the final word.

Alone in the room now, Anne found she couldn't move. Her heart had become so thickened over these last months, her spirit so black, she couldn't process any of it. And so, she sat for a long time, her shoulders frozen high at her neck, her back as straight as one of the iron bars of her prison.

She waited for the guards who would rush in and drag her back to the tower. Back to the foul breath of the warder, who would delight in telling her the inquisitor wished to begin with his Hammer of Witches. And then to the flames that would lick at her feet, roasting her flesh as she was burned at the stake.

But no one came to fetch her. No twine bound her wrist. And now the silence in the room served as her proof. Slowly, painfully, the realization dawned. It was like waking from a dream.

She was free.

Anne reached down to pick up the twine from the floor, the chair creaking beneath her. Somehow, she wanted to keep it as a token of her suffering. As a reminder of Mags. And as she did, she heard the clunk of the heavy doors. When she looked up, she set eyes upon someone she thought she would never see again.

Queen Claude stood quietly, the stoop in her back setting one shoulder higher than the other. She hovered by the door, her hands gathered demurely at her waist.

"Hello, Anne," she said.

The queen's gaze swept along the oily trim of Anne's skirts, to the patches of Mags's blood that stained the silk. She eyed the yellowed fluid on the edges of Anne's sleeves, and the refuse that caked in her long dark hair and the hollows of her cheekbones.

Claude faltered for a moment. "I'm... I'm sorry for your ordeal."

Anne shrank back into her chair, unable to acknowledge her. Perhaps it was shame. Perhaps it was resentment. Her best friend was standing before her now, after all that had happened, and Anne was frozen.

Claude edged a little closer. "The king had no choice but to follow the law, Anne. You must understand," she said a bit more steadily now. "A king may reign as sovereign, but he is not exempt from the politics of court."

Anne still couldn't look at this woman. She had once loved Claude like a sister, but Claude had abandoned her. It was as simple as that.

"When you were accused of witchcraft, there was no alternative but to have it taken to the Inquiry of the Magistrate," said Claude. "It had to be litigated by the Balliages. They are the judiciary of the land. The king could not overstep them."

Anne realized she was holding her breath, her chest refusing to expand and contract. It was making her so dizzy, she almost couldn't focus on Claude's words.

"Marguerite has been working for months to find a legal means by which the king could take action," Claude explained. "A king can make the edict, but he cannot control the tongues of his people. Domenico has seen to it that your reputation is ruined here in France. If you stay for too long, they shall hunt you until they find better evidence against you. And we both know that evidence exists. Evidence that would put us all in the tower."

Bile made a bitter taste in Anne's mouth. It was true. Anne was a danger to them all. She always had been. Self-loathing climbed up her throat. She was probably to blame for poor Mags too.

"Now that Leonardo is gone, there is nothing left for you here," Claude said with contrition. "The winter winds blow too hard for travel right now, so I have arranged for you to stay on over the next few months, under my protection, as my personal translator."

Finally, Anne's gaze flicked to Claude's, her eyes betraying her.

"But you shall not join my court. It would be too dangerous," Claude said with a melancholy ache. "You will stay on at the Clos Lucé until the spring. And while you wait, you shall see that any writings of the Inquiry of the Magistrate for a person by the name of Anne Boleyn are stricken from the public record."

The queen knelt before Anne now. Claude did not speak, but her body language was clear enough. It was just as Marguerite had said. They could no longer be friends—the Goddess had made sure of that. And yet, as Anne looked upon her old companion, the queen's head bowed in deference, there was regret in the hunch of her back, a silent apology in the sag of her shoulders.

"Thank you," Anne whispered through cracked lips.

Claude rose to her feet and handed Anne a letter.

"Francis has been negotiating with King Henry," she said. "They shall gather early next year in Calais in a meeting of the state that will be called the Field of Cloth of Gold."

Anne's hands shook as she took the fine paper, the red wax set with the king of England's seal. She could not take her eyes off it. It could not be real. Not after all that she had been through. Still, as she touched the letter, something warm bloomed in the winter of Anne's bewildered heart.

"You shall accompany me to Calais, and then you will return home to England with King Henry's entourage." Claude retreated to the door. "But I, too, have been conferring with him in secret."

Anne closed her eyes and held the paper to her nose. She inhaled its sweet perfume. It smelled like him, her beloved Henry.

"We have been speaking..." Claude paused, checking over her shoulder, "about the English king's desire for divorce. This note indicates that matters are well in hand, and he is ready for your return."

The queen nodded slowly, as if to make sure Anne understood her meaning.

Anne's world expanded and contracted all at once. It was almost as though she was back inside Leonardo's clock, her mind twisting and spiraling in on itself. She had just been freed from the bonds of the tower, and that had almost been too much to believe. But was it also possible Claude had given her the one thing she wanted more than anything else? That her marriage to Henry could come to pass?

The hard shell around Anne's heart dissolved into a bitter pool of acid. Her breathing became ragged as a torrent of tears spilled down her cheeks. She put her face in her hands and sobbed, the horrors of the last few months fully confronting her.

Anne thought of Mags. The girl whose life was taken at the whim of the inquisitor, the suffering and cruelty he had inflicted. It wasn't fair that Anne could be spared and allowed to return to her beloved, when Mags would never feel the comfort of another kindness.

Claude hesitated at the door, but when she saw Anne crumble, the queen flew across the room to her.

"Just this once," said Claude, pulling Anne into an embrace. "I must hold you in my arms and beg you for your forgiveness. Please know that I love you. You are my dearest heart."

Anne clung to her best friend, so hard she thought she might break. The softness of Claude's cheek had not changed. Even the lilac scent of her hair was marvelously familiar. And as they held one another, Anne was filled with something she couldn't quite name, but it restored her just a little. Just enough to find the strength that Mags had asked her to hold onto. It was damaged, battered and bruised, but to Anne's surprise, it was still there.

She could never forget these last few months in the tower. She could never forget what had happened to Mags. But her friend had the heart of a lion, and Anne did too. And maybe, with Henry at her side in England, time would help heal her broken heart.

PRESENT DAY
CHÂTEAU DU CLOS LUCÉ, FRANCE

White wedding tulle, ribbons, and bows streaked an alabaster blur as I raced through the castle corridor, my feet slapping against the marble. The ripped hem of my dress flapped against my legs as I took the shortcut through the library and past the servants' quarters.

The dining room was in the same state of post-dinner disarray as when I left only minutes ago, and yet it felt like a lifetime had passed.

Plates were stacked on a sideboard, and silver cutlery soaked in a bucket of water. Soiled napkins littered the table, along with half-empty glasses of wine and flutes of champagne. But the Goddess had changed things too. The candelabras dripped with canary-yellow roses, the color of Lily's dress. The nine-foot crystal sconces flowed with carnations, their petals now the color of gold. The wedding cake at the room's center was still a masterpiece, but only two slices were cut.

My breath hitched to see my family seated at the table, wearing dazed expressions. They all moved with an uncanny slowness, as though molasses was running through their veins. Lily fussed with her fluffy skirt, fiddling with the petticoat. Grapes and the rest of the Trio rubbed their eyes like little girls waking from a dream. Dez stared at the ring on his hand, blinking sluggishly. But they were upright, and for now, that was enough.

The Goddess, however, had not restored everyone in her tea party game. Maurice lay on the floor, hands on his collar, frozen fingers clutching his neck. On the other side of the table, John was a slab of cement, his face a contorted mask.

I threw myself at John's side and gripped the lapels of his tuxedo. My knees screamed as they hit the marble floor, but I didn't care.

"Oh God, John," I whispered. "Please be okay."

I lowered my lips to his, desperate to know if he was still alive, and felt a faint intake of breath. It was dangerously shallow, but it was there all the same, and something light exploded in my chest. My heart swelled so full, so fast, it actually hurt.

"Ellie, what the hell happened?" asked Dez with a groggy voice.

I looked up at my disoriented family, trying my best to remain calm, but my hands were shaking uncontrollably.

"They were poisoned," I said, shifting John's rigid shoulders into my lap. Even if he was still a block of wood, I needed to feel the warmth of him against me. "Lucien laced the icing of the wedding cake."

"What?" ask Dez, bewildered.

I pushed the heels of my hands into my eyes and growled, trying to find my patience. Every neuron in my brain was firing. Every inch of my skin prickling with urgency. I didn't have time to explain what had happened. I wasn't even sure how I could.

I took a deep breath. I needed them all to pay attention.

"Grapes, you have to listen to me," I said gravely. "Lucien told me he made the poison from aphalloides. You mentioned them the other day at the wedding brunch. Do you remember?"

She nodded with glacial slowness, still staring with those odd, empty eyes.

"Good," I said, slipping the bowtie from John's neck to make his breathing a little easier. "Do you know if there's something else in the forest we could use to counter it?"

Grapes's cheeks were ghostly pale. She gripped her walker with a wobble and set her feet apart for balance. In this moment, she looked very much her age—a frail ninety-year-old—and my stomach twisted with doubt.

"Grapes, please, you need to focus. Do you know if there is an antidote?"

She frowned, shaking her head with growing effort, the way a dog might shake water from its scruff. Her hands went to her brow, and she massaged her temples. It felt like forever as I watched her lips moving, but she made no noise. Only her dangling diamond earrings made a clicking sound as they swung at the nape of her neck.

When one of her white eyebrows hitched, my heart almost jumped out of my chest. I knew what it meant. She was combing through that magnificent mind of hers. Grapes had a vast knowledge of herbal medicines, a gift she had inherited from her own granny. She never used a grimoire, she kept it all in her head. And if there was something, anything, we could do, Grapes would know it.

"There may be something," she said with a mild slur. "There is another kind of mushroom with a purplish hue. It grows by the duck pond. If we could make it into a tea, it might counter the aphalloides."

The hairs on my arms, my legs, the back of my neck, all stood on end. This was it. The team plan was a go.

"Okay," I said steadily, calling the next play like the quarterback of a football team. "Everyone is going to search for it. Look for a purple mushroom by the duck pond. Go now."

But none of them moved. The group stood looking around, unabashedly stunned. Gerty was staring at the back of her hand, and Bernice was playing with the little needlepoint hearts she had sewn on her bridesmaid's dress. Lily was fiddling with a napkin that had a smear of her bright pink lipstick on it.

I felt myself come unhinged, just for a second. "Go now!" I screamed at the top of my lungs. "Or John is going to die!"

Now all eyes were on me.

Lily's mouth fell open when she noticed John lying in my lap. She blinked, baffled and befuddled, still as foggy as the rest of them. But my beloved librarian made a beeline for the door, her lemon-yellow skirts puffing behind her. The Trio seemed to come alive now too, making their line formation as they marched from the hall like white-haired robots.

Dez was still staring at his ring, twisting it on his finger like it didn't quite fit.

"Please go, Dez," I breathed. "You're the fastest one. And there isn't much time."

"Okay," he said reluctantly as he took off through the château, the leather soles of his wedding shoes clacking against the polished floors.

As the room fell silent, I looked down at John in my lap and kissed his forehead. He was heavy against my legs and as stiff as a plank, but he was breathing, and for now that was enough.

"Please don't leave me," I whispered. "You've got to keep fighting."

I ran my fingers through his sun-kissed hair, pleading with him plaintively. His beautiful amber irises, green against the bloodshot arteries, seemed to track me now.

When our eyes locked, a jolt of electricity coursed through my body. Could he understand me?

The walls I had so carefully built around myself were broken and disheveled. There was no protective layer to hide behind. The Goddess had ripped it all away. But I was glad of it. I didn't want the barricade any longer. I no longer needed to hide behind it.

"I've treated you so badly, John," I said with a trembling voice, my commanding tenor completely gone. "I'm truly sorry. You're the best thing that has ever happened to me. You've been so patient, so forgiving, and I took that for granted. I held you at a distance, refusing to let you into my heart, and now all I want to do is keep you there."

John stared up at me, tracking my face. He was listening. I was almost sure of it.

"I've never been in love before," I said, tears filling my eyes. "I always thought there had to be something logical about it. But I see how stupid that was. Love isn't a formula. It's something you just know."

I threaded my fingers into his frozen hands, hoping he could feel the warmth of them, the reassurance of my touch.

"The truth is…I was afraid to get hurt," I admitted. "But that was stupid too. Because I know you would never hurt me. You have stayed by my side, no matter how terribly I treated you. No matter how hard I pushed you away."

I ran my thumb along the palm of his hand, like I had done so many times before. It was one of our little signs, our little affections, and I hoped it meant something to him now.

"I'm sorry it took me so long to figure it out. But I know how I feel," I said, choking on my words. "I am in love with you, John Chelsea. I love you more than anything else in the world."

One of John's eyelids twitched, and I stared at it with disbelief. It ignited a warmth in my belly that fluttered gingerly, quaking and fragile, daring to hope.

"I think I found them," called Lily as she flew into the room, clasping half a dozen purple mushrooms in her palm.

My eyes darted to Grapes, who was straggling behind Lily with her three-step shuffle, along with Dez and the rest of the Trio. I held my breath as my great-grandmother inspected the fleshy little polyps, their tiny lilac caps speckled with raised white blotches.

"Good work, Lily," Grapes said with approval. Her voice was stronger now, more like the confident witch I had always known, and the soft fluttering in my belly grew a bit stronger.

The Titanium Trio worked in silence, a noiseless three-part harmony. They bickered about everything else, but in witchcraft, their cooperation was seamless. They had done it for years, and they understood each other perfectly. Gerty cut the mushrooms into thin slices and Grapes prepared the hot water. Bernice muttered the healing spell over the tincture as it steeped, a violet hue slowly coloring the liquid.

I checked and rechecked John's breathing as we waited, willing the brewing process to hurry. My foot jiggled with nerves and it rapped against the floor with a light rhythm. When it was done, Grapes handed me a cup.

"Pour it in his mouth, but only give him tiny sips," she advised. "He'll have difficulty swallowing."

She turned to Lily now, taking over the command like the family matriarch she was. "Help Maurice. We have to try to save him too."

So much adrenaline was coursing through my blood, I had to concentrate hard to keep the my hands steady. I raised the tea to John's lips.

"Please," I said, "you've got to try."

I poured some into his mouth, careful not to spill the precious liquid. John took the first sip, and I thought I saw a faint swallow.

"That's good," I said tenderly. "Now a little more."

I poured the violet liquid again, administering small doses just as Grapes had instructed. John's mouth was still rigid, but after the third sip, I thought I saw the cleft in his chin move. I ran my finger over it, the way I used to.

"I think it's working!"

Tears spilled openly down my cheeks as I held him, slowly administering Grapes's medicine. The flutter in my belly was now a butterfly flapping its wings. My tears were coming too hard for me to speak, but I kept my eyes focused on his, willing him to grow stronger.

John's body began to tremble in my lap, his muscles quaking, nerves fighting against the poison that held him prisoner. His breaths grew more determined as the paralysis reversed itself.

Grapes stood over us like a sentinel. Monitoring. Watching. Making sure.

When John finally blinked, relief cracked through my skull like a thunderclap, and I found myself sputtering out a disbelieving laugh.

"You're doing it, John! You're actually doing it!"

Now he was drinking steadily, pulling the tea into his mouth and swallowing it down. The red of his bloodshot eyes was retreating. The throbbing vein in his neck was shrinking away. And I could feel his muscles relaxing into mine.

He reached for my hand, and we threaded our fingers together again, staring into each other's eyes, locked in our own little world like we were the only two people in the universe. Nothing else mattered in that moment but him and me, and I wanted to stay lost in his gaze forever.

"I love you, John Chelsea."

His lips parted, his tongue finding its strength again. I leaned down to hear him, in an angel's breath whisper.

"I...love...you...too..."

EPILOGUE

PRESENT DAY
KINGSTON, CANADA

ONE YEAR LATER

I stood in line at the dry cleaners, tapping my foot with a hint of impatience. It was a busy day, and I needed to get to the library to work with Lily on our latest publication. After almost an entire year, I was finally picking up our dresses from Dez's wedding. Somehow, I hadn't been able to face them before this. The memories were still a little too real.

The store wasn't much, but they specialized in fine clothing. And between the Trio's outfits and my own, it seemed like the right dry cleaner for the job. Besides, it was the one closest to our house.

"Nice gowns you got here," said the lady behind the desk. She plopped the big bag on the pickup hook. "Must have been quite a wedding."

I smiled, thinking back to that crazy day. "It really was."

The wedding between two men, that's what Anne Boleyn had called it. And it was what Dez had wanted more than anything in the world. I still felt terrible for him whenever I thought about it.

Lucien had simply vanished after the wedding. There was no trace of him whatsoever. Dez had been heartbroken, and he still didn't like to talk about it, so I didn't push him. But if anything positive had come of his failed marriage, it was that he had found a way to reconcile with his parents. Somehow, his mom and dad could see the hurt in his heart, the pain that still lurked there. It had helped his parents to understand. They were working through their issues now, and most weekends he went home to visit, slowly rebuilding the relationship he had lost almost ten years ago.

Maurice had been baffled by the whole experience, still not the sharpest knife in the drawer. He was never sure of what happened to his cousin, Clarisse. He and Lily stayed in touch for a while. The last I checked, Lily said he didn't remember ever having a cousin by that name at all. Nonetheless, he got the museum's water pipes fixed and reopened the Château du Clos Lucé to tourists in the fall.

"Oh say," said the lady at the counter, "I found this inside the pocket of the navy blue dress. You know the strapless one with the hem that needed fixing?"

She dropped a charred piece of metal in my hand. It was melted and black, an unrecognizable blob, but when the gold touched my hand, my scar seared with pain.

"You found it in the dress pocket?" I asked.

"Yeah," she replied. "But I don't know what it is."

"Thanks," I said. I tossed it in the air and caught it with a cheeky grin. "I think I do."

* * *

John looked into my eyes, his gaze full of longing. We were enjoying our first-year anniversary at Chez Piggy, a fine dining restaurant with the best French cuisine in Kingston. I dragged my thumb along the inside of his palm, loving the feeling of his fingers woven between mine.

"Cat got your tongue?" he gave me a lazy smile.

I flushed. Even after a year together, he could still give me butterflies.

Once I had finally let John into my heart and allowed myself to trust him, our relationship had flourished. We fit together like the puzzle pieces from my wedding speech. John and I were not the same. In fact, we were incredibly different. But we were a perfect complement to one another. He was calm, I was edgy. He was easygoing, I was neurotic. He was a jock, and I was a witch. We couldn't have been more opposite, but it worked.

"I'm grateful you've been so patient with me." I smiled.

"I told you I'd wait for you forever."

When John and I returned home, we'd had work to do. There were a lot of honest conversations in the days following our holiday. And some of them weren't easy. We needed to work on avoiding the tough stuff and practice telling each other the truth. But it was work we were prepared to do, and our bond had grown strong.

I realized that day, as he lay there on the marble floor, his body stiff with poison, I had no other choice. I loved John Chelsea, and I couldn't live without him.

"I have something for you," I said shyly.

I had been waiting for the right moment all evening, and now it seemed like a good time. We had finished our meal and a bottle of wine, and there was nothing to do but enjoy each other's company. I picked up my purse and dug out a little black box.

I bit my lip and handed it to him.

When he pried it open, his eyes grew wide. "What is this?"

I laughed. "It's a ring, silly. I had it made from Leonardo's true key. When I put it in the firestorm between the Goddess and me, it got melted down. But somehow it ended up back in my pocket. I guess I really was the true keeper of the key."

John's muscular shoulders flexed under his linen shirt. His amber eyes, flecked with green, danced in the candlelight.

"And now I'm giving it to you." I blushed. "If you'll marry me, that is."

John gave me that goofy grin, the one I loved best of all. He picked me up and spun me around in front of everyone at the restaurant, but I didn't care who was watching. The warmth of his body, the pressure of his muscles, stirred a longing in me.

"Of course I'll marry you, Ellie Bowlan."

He lowered his mouth to mine, the scruff of his five o'clock shadow tickling my chin. The wetness of his kiss set my heart on fire. It was that same fire I had inherited from Anne Boleyn, and it whirred in my belly with a knowing that John and I were meant to be together.

I closed my eyes and sank into his embrace as the colors of the flames danced in my heart, anchoring me to the here and now. To the soft pink of John's tongue as it explored my own. To the rich golden-yellow of the band he now wore on his finger. And to the red rosebud of the child that was already growing inside me.

* * *

Thank you for reading! Did you enjoy? Please add your review because nothing helps an author more and encourages readers to take a chance on a book than a review.

And don't miss more of *The Boleyn Bloodline,* coming soon. Until then read THE MEDIEVALIST by City Owl Author, Anne-Marie Lacy. Turn the page for a sneak peek!

You can also sign up for the City Owl Press newsletter to receive notice of all book releases!

SNEAK PEEK OF THE MEDIEVALIST

* * *

Don't stop now. Keep reading with your copy of <u>THE MEDIEVALIST</u> by City Owl Author, Anne-Marie Lacy.

Don't miss more of *The Boleyn Bloodline* coming soon, and find more from Deborah Cohen at www.deborahcohen.ca

Until then, discover THE MEDIEVALIST by City Owl Author, Anne-Marie Lacy.

* * *

A modern woman in the court of King Richard III is torn between saving the man she loves and stopping a historic wrong in this time-travel romance.

English historian Jayne Lyons has pinned her career hopes on proving that her ancestor, King Richard III, was not the nefarious villain of Shakespeare's tragedy. In fact, she believes he is innocent of the infamous murder of the Princes in the Tower. But while volunteering with the search for his missing grave, Jayne gets a much closer look at Richard than she expected. Cast back into the brutal 15th century, she suddenly finds herself in the middle of Richard's army camp.

Realizing that she may not be able to return home, Jayne begins to adjust to her new life. And the more she gets to know the true Richard, the more she is drawn to him.   She even starts entertaining the hope of saving him.

But the Princes are missing, and all evidence points to Richard. When he asks her to spy for him against his enemy, Henry Tudor, she must decide whether to help the man she loves, even though he may be one of history's greatest villains.

* * *

Please sign up for the City Owl Press newsletter for chances to win special subscriber-only contests and giveaways as well as receiving information on upcoming releases and special excerpts.

All reviews are **welcome** and **appreciated**. Please consider leaving one on your favorite social media and book buying sites.

For books in the world of romance and speculative fiction that embody Innovation, Creativity, and Affordability, check out City Owl Press at www.cityowlpress.com.

ACKNOWLEDGMENTS

I would like to thank my publisher, City Owl Press, and the executive editor, Yelena Casale, for all her guidance and advice. I would also like to thank my beta readers, Judy Cohen, Cheryl Evans, Laura Guilbeault, Kirby Lighthouse, and Drema Deoraich. Their insights and suggestions helped take an early draft into a polished novel. Finally, and most especially, I would like to thank my husband for his unwavering support as I wrote, rewrote, edited and re-edited this story. You are the reason I got this one across the finish line.

ABOUT THE AUTHOR

DEBORAH COHEN is an author of historical fantasy and mystery. She is an adjunct Professor with the University of Ottawa and an epidemiologist for a National Health Research Institute in Canada. She lives in Ottawa with her hubby, son and daughter, and two large crazy dogs – a Bulldog and a Great Dane – that love to be spoiled rotten.

www.deborahcohen.ca

ABOUT THE PUBLISHER

City Owl Press is a cutting edge indie publishing company, bringing the world of romance and speculative fiction to discerning readers.

Escape Your World. Get Lost in Ours!

www.cityowlpress.com

 facebook.com/YourCityOwlPress

 twitter.com/cityowlpress

 instagram.com/cityowlbooks

 pinterest.com/cityowlpress